Retreads

Retreads

Steve Hobbs

www.hobbspond.com

ISBN-13: 9780999317709
ISBN-10: 0999317709
Library of Congress Control Number: 2017912786
Hatchet Mountain Press
Manchester, NH

For Judy and Elston,

who had great courage. . .

Contents

Ten Rules for Retreads

1) *Retread* must have historical value.
2) *Retread* must have an offer of employment.
3) *Retread* must live with a host for at least two years.
4) *Retread* host must have sole claim of genealogical lineage.
5) *Retread* must renounce all financial ties to family estate.
6) *Retread* minors are not allowed to engage in school sporting events (exceptions made for intramural and non-school events).
7) *Retreads* are prohibited from joining any branch of the military unless called upon to do so.
8) *Retreads* do not have the right to vote in state, local, or federal elections.
9) *Retreads* are not allowed to testify in a court of law.
10) *Retreads* are unable to conceive or bear children (nature, not law).

From the Diary of Margaret Dearborn:

July 10, 1813, Saturday

    Micajer visited for a short time. We stayed outside, near the big tree, and held hands. His uniform gave him the appearance of a much older man. He promised to return soon and will again ask my father for my hand. I did not tell him that Father will not change his mind and that I fear all of this is just an attempt to gain the favor of a man who cannot change. Though I know that John Dearborn is a great man, my heart still burns with anger and sadness…

Part I
(Living in the Past)

1

The Desert

The car cautiously cruised past the dusty caravan of delivery vehicles, moving trucks, and company cars that led to the unmarked warehouse at the center of a small collection of structures. A sign posted at the gate read "Ahearn Industries," and another smaller sign warned "No Trespassing." Sam Ahearn eyed the procession from the back seat of the tinted rental with little interest and continued tapping the keyboard of his new laptop. He was shivering from the air conditioning and considered turning it down. Sam knew things would heat up soon enough and instead went back to work.

Sam's driver, Oscar, pulled up near the entrance to the warehouse and put the car in park. He stepped out from the vehicle, circled it, and opened Sam's door. Sam put down his computer and got out of the car. The bright sun practically blinded him, and angry heat steamrolled over him like a runaway truck. *I hate the desert,* he thought.

Sam was in his forties now but looked much younger. He wasn't tall, but he was built like an aging athlete, and he was often listed as a "most eligible bachelor." His dark hair was still thick, but he knew it was beginning to thin out, and that nipped a little at his vanity. He wasn't generally self-conscious about such things, but middle age was an untested obstacle.

He said, "Thanks, Oscar."

Oscar Larsen was a tall and lean man with salt-and-pepper hair and a somewhat crooked nose. Sam knew that the deviated septum was a result of a brief career fighting as a light heavyweight back in the nineties. Oscar was not skilled enough to challenge for championships, so he retired and moved into the field of professional thuggery. A chance encounter with Sam set the wheels in motion, and he was now Ahearn's head of security. He followed his boss into the warehouse.

Sam thought the building was more like an airplane hangar than a warehouse. The roof was wide and triangular, and the warehouse itself was open and deep. There were dozens of his people moving about the place, most of them wearing company uniforms. The room was loud, and voices carried, but there was no feeling of chaos or disorder; instead, there was an atmosphere of controlled enthusiasm. Several oversize fans redirected the hot air in inconvenient directions but failed to cool the room in any positive manner. The far end of the hangar was covered by an enormous purple curtain.

"Mr. Ahearn," someone yelled. "Sam, over here."

Sam and Oscar approached a small group of men standing apart from the happy madness. He recognized one of the guys from Homeland Security and nodded at him, then turned his attention to Mike Standish, the operational leader and a long-time employee. He was fiftyish and balding but still looked like an accomplished bench presser. Mike was admired for his calmness and his quiet strength. In many ways, this was his show.

Sam shook Mike's hand and said, "How's the extraction going?"

"We're just about ready, Sam," Standish said. "We've got the Hole cordoned off over here."

The men walked away from the crowd toward the large drape at the end of the hall. Mike lifted the curtain and said, "This way."

Sam climbed through, followed by Oscar and then Mike. The curtain blocked out a lot of the light, but they could see well enough to move about. There were no men in the area, as Sam wanted to get the first look. The cordoned-off section was roughly a twenty-foot-by-twenty-foot fragment of the building. There was a back door, but it was chained shut, and all of the windows were painted black. Sam wondered if this was what Area 51 looked like on the inside.

There were some boxes on the floor and a few power tools lying off to the side. At the center of the room, there was a large wooden scaffold. Sam nodded his approval. He had waited a long time for this.

"Anyone been inside yet?" Sam asked.

Standish shook his head. "No. We're waiting for you."

Oscar was standing close to his employer, uncharacteristically distracted by the assembly in front of them. He said, "Where is it? I don't see anything."

Mike said, "Kind of turn your head—don't look at it straight on. Do you see a sort of glow?"

Oscar and Sam turned and squinted. After a few seconds, they could see a vague line floating behind the scaffold. It was thin and long, and there was a slight spark of white light emanating from it. Sam knew that Oscar was dreading the next few hours.

"What exactly is that thing?" asked Oscar.

"We're not sure. A rupture, I guess—a dimensional crack, maybe," said Mike. "We don't know how long it's been here."

Oscar said, "How many men can go in at a time?"

"Three or four. Then the Hole sort of shuts down and recalibrates."

"What do you mean it recalibrates?"

"The crack contracts briefly and then reopens. To us, it'll be just a few minutes, but it might be half an hour or more on the other side."

Sam smiled and said, "Second thoughts about going in, Oscar?"

"I go where you go, Boss."

"Good," said Sam. "Let's get to work. The Hole's open for business."

2

The Hole

Sam and the others were in gray jumpsuits with breast insignia bearing the words *Ahearn Industries.* They wore durable hiking boots, and each was armed with a rifle, a holstered handgun, and a long knife. He knew the first team should be on the other side, waiting for their ride home, but the Hole was a funny place. Nothing ever went as planned on the other side.

James Wallace stood at the front of their small line atop the scaffold. Wallace was a tall man with red hair and a pockmarked face, and Sam liked his résumé. The kid had seen action as a marine in Iraq and Afghanistan and had almost stayed in the marines until a friend directed him to Sam. Men like Jimmy Wallace were good candidates for projects like this; they liked the idea of going away for a few months of adventure and coming back to a small fortune.

Wallace was the point leader for the initial extraction, and Sam was supposed to defer to him. He would interview and replace the current site leader and oversee the timely removal of existing team members while hastily replacing them with new players. Sam and Oscar would follow Wallace into the rift and make a quick inspection of the complex. Sam planned to be in the Hole for no more than an hour, which would be closer to a day Earthside.

The screened-off area of the hangar was mainly empty. Twenty or so volunteers were waiting in the main part of the building while the lead men took off. Ten years ago, team members had been allowed to watch the entries and exits that took most of the day, and this had led to four resignations from the squad. Apparently, Sam learned, the men were better off not viewing the specifics of what their bodies were about to go through.

Mike Standish was on the floor beneath them. He said, "I can't talk you out of this, Sam?"

Sam shook his head, "I haven't seen this place in more than ten years, Mike. Our partners are going to want to know how things are going."

"Our men can't just send them a postcard?"

"No." Sam smiled. "They want a firsthand evaluation."

Oscar stood familiarly beside his employer. Sam knew that Oscar did not care to step into the fissure that glowed dimly in front of him, but his protector followed him everywhere. There had been two attempts on Sam's life during Oscar Larsen's tenure at Ahearn Industries, and both had led to life-threatening injuries—not to Sam but to the fools that had gotten close to him. Oscar dispatched them with an ease that scared even Sam.

"Are you ready to go, sir?" asked Wallace.

Sam nodded, though he wasn't sure at all that he was ready, and turned again to Standish. "Hold down the fort while I'm gone, Mike."

"Grab hands," said Wallace. "Let's get ready."

Oscar said, "Why do we have to hold hands?"

"You have to remain connected while in the rift, or things could get confusing on the other side. Now grab Sam's hand, and let's get going."

The men clasped hands as Wallace took a tentative step into the Hole. With that, they melted into the chasm's increasing glow. Mike Standish watched as the radiant fracture closed behind them. He wondered if he would ever consider allowing himself to be sucked into the Hole and decided that he would avoid that opportunity at every cost.

"Send the next crew in," he said to an assistant.

Four men soon entered the waiting room and approached him. He knew all of them and had personally approved each man for the squad. They were all young and able men who knew exactly what they were getting themselves into. He gestured at some folding chairs located near the scaffold.

Standish said, "You guys have a seat. The door's going to reopen in about forty-five minutes, and then we'll be sending you in."

But the door never opened.

From the Diary of Margaret Dearborn:

September 4, 1813, Saturday

It has been nearly two months since Micajer went missing. His friend, Joshua Martel, has returned from Fort Stephenson and promises to tell me all that he knows. Though I still hold out hope for his safe return, I cannot help but fear the worst has happened. Without Micajer, I worry that I shall never again experience true joy and happiness...

3

Family Reunion

Carrie Heath sat uncomfortably on the grass near the front steps of the old farmhouse that she knew as home. The white house was really too big for just her and her dad, as it was built more than a century ago to house multiple generations of the Heath family. Now, there was no need for such a large home, but her dad grew up here, and he had no desire to move. He was not a farmer, though, and the acres of land that had been home to crops of corn and sometimes potatoes were now just weedy fields where Carrie and her friends played hide-and-seek or kick the can. It was one of the largest lots in Bainbridge, New Hampshire, and had an inspiring view of the town from its vantage point atop Big Berry Hill.

It was early summer, and the teenager was wearing denim shorts and a green T-shirt that displayed an image of an evil-looking bird flying below the words *Bainbridge Buzzards*. Carrie played point guard on the girl's high school basketball team and enjoyed the sport very much. Although she was not a starter, she was an elected co-captain of the team. She wished she was good enough to be first string, but she knew her physical talent was limited. It would be great if her cousin could join the team, but she knew Meg was prohibited from playing any sports at Bainbridge High School. Maybe she could be an assistant or a manager.

Her father's green Jeep Cherokee turned onto the long paved driveway, and her heart jumped. What would her new family think of the house or the town? Would Meg be as wonderful as Carrie imagined, or would there be a letdown like the time that she had wanted a unicycle, and her father had finally given her one for her birthday? That didn't work out the way she planned.

Would she and Meg come to see each other as family or as unicycles?

Her father parked beside Carrie's Toyota in front of the old barn, which he used as a garage, and stepped out of his vehicle. Tom Heath was a large man and still looked like the linebacker who had dominated southern New Hampshire high school football for much of the late 1980s. He was smiling, and he waved his nervous daughter over to him.

She ran over and hugged him. She said, "Daddy! I can't believe it…"

Tom Heath grinned at his only child, and Carrie smiled back. One day, he would look at her as an adult, an equal, and she would no longer be his strawberry-blond baby girl. Oddly, she was in no hurry for that day of discovery. She liked her current role.

He said, "Sorry we're late, honey. I had to sign a few papers in triplicate when I picked these guys up."

A man in the passenger seat was fumbling with his seat belt. While her father headed over to help him, Carrie peered into the back and saw two women patiently waiting for assistance. She opened the rear driver-side door and saw a girl who she just knew had to be Meg Dearborn.

"Meg, I'm Carrie," she said excitedly while helping the girl from her seat. "I'm so glad you're here."

Meg was wearing ill-fitting slacks and a man's rugby shirt. She looked thin and a little frumpy in her borrowed garments, and her hair was shockingly short, but her beauty was clear, and Carrie felt almost mesmerized by the sight of her new friend. Meg said, "Your father has told us a lot about you during our journey to this home. He says wonderful things about you."

Carrie's father helped his passenger out of the front, and together, the men assisted another young lady unaccustomed to climbing in and out of motorized vehicles. He guided them over toward Carrie and said, "Honey, this is John and Sally—I'm sure that you'll have a lot to say to them over the next few days."

Meg's mother looked more like her slightly older sister, and Carrie thought that Sally Dearborn might be even more stunning than Meg. Her short hair was blond and wavy, and her features were almost without imperfections. She stood and walked with the kind of grace and balance that, Carrie supposed, had to be learned over a great period of time. Sally smiled at her and said, "I look forward to getting to know you, my dear."

Carrie turned her gaze to John Dearborn and said, "I have heard so many things about you, sir."

John Dearborn stood a little less than six feet tall and was not as physically imposing as Tom Heath, but he looked like the kind of guy who was always in charge. His hair was dark, and his face matched the paintings and sketches that Carrie had seen online and in books. Only, he looked more handsome and so much younger now; he seemed to be no more than twenty-five years old. Carrie wondered how Meg was dealing with her parents looking so young now.

"Would you show our guests into the house, Carrie?" her father said.

"Oh, sure," she said. "Shouldn't we get their bags first?"

Carrie's dad shook his head. "They have no bags right now, honey. We'll take them to the mall later and get them some clothes."

Carrie turned to Meg and said, "Have you ever been to a mall?"

Meg smiled. "I have no idea what such a place will look like. I look forward to the adventure, though."

Carrie said, "I'll take the girls, and you can take Uncle John. Is it OK for me to call you that, sir?"

John replied, "I understand that you and Tom are our only relatives, my dear, and I am honored to have such a title."

Carrie sort of squealed as she grabbed the man and hugged him. She looked over at Aunt Sally and pulled her into the embrace. She said, "I'm so happy that you guys are here."

Her father pulled her away from their visitors. He said, "Come on, team. Let's go get situated."

4

A Visit to the Mall

Shopping at the Mall of New Hampshire took a lot out of the new family. John Dearborn was a formal man, and he had difficulty finding clothes that matched his demeanor. Tom was able to find a few suits and ties at Men's Wearhouse and a nice pair of shoes at Macy's. The real trouble came when he tried to explain to John the importance of informal clothing. Tom had pulled a lot of strings to get the school board to hire an inexperienced assistant coach for the football team, and coaches did not show up for practice in seersucker suits. Not since the fifties.

"You'll need sneakers, John," Tom said as they made their way to Foot Locker. "You'll be running the kids through some sprints and drills while you figure out the game. You'll need some shorts or at least some sweat pants—the school doesn't pay for any of that stuff."

Dearborn nodded. He was listening to his new friend but was disoriented by the sheer number of people walking past him. He said, "How do you get around in such crowds, Tom?"

Tom smiled. "This is hardly a large crowd, John. Wednesday's a pretty slow night even in the summer."

They found the store Tom wanted and headed over to the sneaker section. A helpful kid had Dearborn sit down and then measured his feet. He said, "Size nine for a taller guy is kinda rare."

Tom said, "We'll try those Nikes over there, son."

John said, "How will you pay for all of these clothes?"

"With my credit card. You'll pay me back when you have a chance."

The sneakers fit, and Tom wanted to get out of the store. He said, "Why don't you keep the sneakers on and ditch those old shoes you're wearing?"

Tom's cell phone rang. He recognized Carrie's number and said, "Hey, honey."

"We have seats at Ruby's if you guys want to meet us here," Carrie said. "The girls seem to be having some trouble with the menu."

"We're on our way, Carrie," Tom said. "Tell the ladies that it's all good there."

He hung up and said, "The ladies are waiting for us."

Ruby Tuesday's was a little bit of a walk, but it wouldn't take very long to get there. John said, "I suppose it is quite convenient for all of these establishments to be in such proximity to one another."

Tom said, "Sure, but I thought things were fine before they brought in all the malls and such. Kids walked around town more, and going out to eat was a much bigger deal."

"Yes, things certainly have changed for you, Tom," said John.

Tom smiled and said, "I guess it's a bigger change for you."

Ruby's was always fairly dim, but Tom spotted the ladies in a far corner near the window. Carrie was drinking a diet soda with a lemon in it, and the others were sipping from glasses filled with water. Sally and Meg were watching people entering and leaving the mall and whispering familiarly. All three were giggling.

They were seated at a medium table, and a pile of bags was stacked between the table and a wall behind them. Sally and Meg were both wearing summer dresses borrowed from Carrie's closet. Tom noted that they both looked stunning in the loaner outfits. He looked at Carrie's overflowing bags and wondered if he shouldn't have loaned his daughter the other credit card. She caught his eye and smiled happily, and he forgot about the expense. He tried to remember the last time that he had seen his little girl look as happy.

All of this is worth it, he thought.

He sat across from Carrie, and John sat beside him. John reached across the table and held his wife's hand. He said, "Did you have an exciting time, my dear?"

Sally gently pulled her hand away from his. "This place is quite stirring, John. The people are so...different."

Tom said, "Did you have a chance to look at the menu?"

Carrie ordered a burger, and Meg reluctantly followed suit. Sally asked for country fried chicken with potatoes, and the two men ordered steaks. Tom had a beer and was surprised that John was willing to give that a try.

"You're used to warm ales, I think," Tom said. "This will be a little different."

"Daddy," Carrie said. "Sally and Meg had a lot of trouble finding clothes that they were, um, comfortable in."

Sally said, "Some of the clothes that your daughter recommended may have been received negatively by my husband."

Meg snickered.

John pointed at a young girl wearing particularly form-fitting short pants and said, "Did any of the clothes look like that?"

"Oh my gosh, no," said Carrie. "Those clothes aren't looked on too favorably by most people."

"Then why do these young ladies dress like that?"

Tom said, "It's still a free country, John. It's up to that girl and her parents, I guess, to decide what she can wear."

The food came, and Tom found it very enjoyable. John ate his steak without complaint, grunting as he chewed. Sally and Meg seemed to enjoy their meals, but both looked slightly embarrassed. Meg wiped her face constantly and only bit into her sandwich when she felt she wasn't being watched. Tom made a point of looking away as they chewed.

Sally said, "Tom, your daughter has described something that she calls a *supermarket* to me. Would it be possible to shop for some supplies at one of these establishments?"

Tom said, "Sure, we can get some *supplies* anytime you like. How about Carrie drives you down there tomorrow?"

"That would be fine," Sally said. "After which I would like to prepare a meal to thank you two for taking us in under such conditions."

"I'm not turning down a big meal, Sally," Tom replied. "But I want you to remember that we're family, and Carrie and I are quite happy to have you here."

"As are we, Tom," John said. "When were you approached about sponsoring our family?"

Tom said, "We got a call from a company called Ahearn Industries a little more than a year ago. They told us about a pilot program they're running in association with the feds. Apparently, there is a Department of Historical Archives, which is in charge of locating candidates for the program. They wanted subjects who had some historic value, but they didn't want any complicated family problems."

Carrie explained, "They didn't want big family disputes over whether or not to agree to the program. But I guess we're the only ones with any claim to you."

Sally Dearborn said sadly, "We never had any more children after..."

Meg looked uncomfortable enough for Carrie to say, "But you're all here now, and we're wicked glad to have you."

Sally perked up. "What is *wicked* glad? Does *wicked* now mean *very* glad?"

"Only in New England," said Tom. "The rest of the country doesn't get that phrase either."

The conversation turned to brighter topics, but Tom sensed coldness at the table when the conversation turned to Meg's tragic death. He decided that he would never speak of it unless the Dearborns brought the subject up. He and Carrie had already decided not to mention the book in Carrie's dresser. Meg didn't need to know that Carrie had read Meg's diary many times and that the book never failed to bring her to tears.

5

The Lodge

"So," Jimmy Wallace began. "Where is everybody?"

Sam's head was still spinning from the jump, but he was beginning to gather himself. He realized that he was lying sideways in a field of weeds and bushes. He rose to his feet and offered a hand to Oscar, who lay in a similar position beside him. His bodyguard shook his head and got up slowly without help. Oscar was always stubborn like that.

Wallace was standing a few feet away, his rifle pointing toward the ground, calmly appraising the landscape. The field was a jumble of four-foot weeds and bushes that seemed to stretch a few hundred yards in every direction before being absorbed into a forest of towering trees. It had taken the first crew several days to clear the area and begin work on the lodge that would serve as base camp for the company.

Sam said, "The lodge should be over that way."

It was difficult for Sam to see his hands in front of his face. The perpetual cloud cover and the heavy shadows falling from the enormous trees darkened the sky to an early dusk. Sam said, "I'm sure it's this way—we should head over."

Wallace said, "We should wait for the next wave, sir. They should be here any minute, and we don't want them getting lost."

"You wait for them, Mr. Wallace. We'll head over and inspect the site—we're just here for a quick visit."

Jimmy Wallace looked concerned. He said, "I'm not sure that I should let you two just wander off, sir."

Sam smiled. "I've got Oscar, Mr. Wallace."

"I know about Mr. Larsen," said Jimmy. "I guess you guys'll be OK."

Sam nodded and started toward the lodge, or at least to where he thought the lodge was located. It had been more than a decade since his last visit to this strange place, and he had never been very good at directions. After a few minutes of marching, the frame of a large structure became quite visible, and he felt himself breathing a sigh of relief. He'd have felt damn silly if he had had to turn around and look somewhere else.

Oscar said, "What are those things?"

Oscar was pointing at several piles of debris circling the house. The mounds were evenly distributed around the building and looked to be the remains of burned furniture and large branches. Sam thought that one of the pits had a part of a wooden door spilling over its side.

Sam said, "Looks like ashes from bonfires. Maybe they cook out a lot?"

"Most people don't roast weenies over a love seat," said Oscar.

Oscar had his pistol out and was letting it dangle ominously by his side. Sam remembered his rifle and held it clumsily in front of him. He said, "I don't like what I'm seeing, buddy."

They passed the fire pits and approached the cabin, which was quite large and expensive-looking. It was prefabricated and had been modeled after an old-time hunting lodge. Although the house looked to be made from wood, the material was actually a thick metal-based alloy designed to keep intruders out. There was an intruder alarm system, but curiously, it was not yet installed. The lower level had no windows, and the top floor only allowed for a few small ones at the corners of the house. The prefabricated sections had been painstakingly moved from the desert to this spot over the course of several days, and the actual construction of the lodge took several weeks. Sam had only overseen the early stages of construction, as the Hole did not stay open long enough for him to see its assembly through to completion.

"Seems to be some damage to the wall," said Oscar. "Like some wild animal came calling."

Dents and long, deep scratches scarred portions of the house; some of the marks stretched from the second floor down to the ground level, while others were smaller and more concise in their design. The cabin was sturdy and had apparently withstood the punishment, but Sam wondered what kinds of beasts could have left such marks on the cabin.

"The door's open," said Oscar. "You stay here."

"We go in together, Oscar."

Oscar sighed. "Stay behind me, then, and don't shoot me. Shoot anything else, but don't shoot me."

"You know I won't shoot you, Oscar."

Oscar nodded and walked in, both hands on his weapon, and carefully looked around the huge hallway that greeted them. The lodge was damp and musty; the entrance smelled like a crypt. The foyer had no furniture, and part of the wall that separated the hallway from the next room was knocked out. Sam remembered a switch near the entrance and tried to turn on the overhead light.

"Power's out, Oscar," he said. "Not a good sign."

"Where's the fancy generator?" asked Oscar.

"In the basement. Let's look there first."

The basement entrance was in the kitchen. A cellar door was missing, and there was no furniture, although there was a large Maytag refrigerator propped against a side door and a dishwasher was still hooked up near the sink. The cupboard doors and the drawers around them were missing, presumably burned in the bonfires that were so popular with the residents of the house. There were a few dishes and pots on the counters, and there was a pile of silverware at the side of a large stainless-steel sink. Sam twisted the cold water tap to the on position, but no water came out.

He said, "We drilled a well before I left. The men had running water."

Oscar stood at the top of the steps and looked down into the darkness. He brushed something that might have been a cobweb out of the way and said, "Maybe we should wait for the rest of the team before we go down there."

Sam, relieved that it was Oscar who said it, nodded. "You're probably right, Oscar. I'm sure the rest of the guys will want to do some exploring when they get here…"

The bottom floor was as bare as the kitchen. Most of the space had been designed for interaction among the workers; there were two rooms with wide-screen television hookups and another with several pool tables and other games. All of that was missing now. Sam wondered if the men had actually tried to burn the TVs.

"Where are all the decorations?" asked Oscar. "I remember you told me that the house resembled an old hunting lodge. You said it looked sort of like Bugaboo Creek."

"They burned everything, Oscar. We'll probably find some interesting bits and pieces in the pits."

Oscar pointed to the wide brick fireplace mounted on the far wall. He said, "Why didn't they just use that instead of all of those fire pits outside?"

"They weren't burning those fire pits for warmth, Oscar," said Sam. "They were scaring off the locals."

An inspection of the top story found almost the same results. There were two upstairs bathrooms, but both were bereft of running water. Sam found a closet with some blue and gray Ahearn Industries uniforms inside as well as some weight-lifting plates and bars. Ahearn could recall a couple of weight benches and assumed that they had been deemed flammable and were tossed into the fires. He realized that the men must have been running the fire pits around the clock.

What were they so afraid of? he wondered.

Oscar said, "Do we have an idea of the time? I'd like to get back before the sun goes down and whatever comes out at night decides to visit."

Sam said, "I'd sure like to know where my men went off to."

"Sam, they've probably been digested by whatever wild animals are roaming this area. We should get you out of here."

The two men started down the staircase that led to the first floor. The cabin was still, but Sam's nerves were a mess. They stepped outside onto the front lawn and looked around. He suddenly realized he was still gripping the cumbersome rifle in his hands and decided to strap it back on. He'd probably just shoot Oscar by mistake if he fired the thing.

Oscar said, "Where's Wallace?"

"Forget that, Oscar—where's the rest of the team?"

All around them was silence. The two men trudged briskly across the weed-infested field to the spot that they knew to be the location of the Hole. There was nothing there.

"Do you think he went back Earthside?" asked Sam.

"He wouldn't have left without us," answered Oscar. "Where's the Hole?"

Sam tilted his head back and forth and half closed his eyes in an effort to spot the entrance to the rift. He could find no trace of the Hole, and there was no sign of Jimmy Wallace, either. Sam Ahearn could feel his heart beating a little more hastily than usual.

He said, "I think we should get back to the cabin and barricade the doors. It gets dark fast around here."

6

A Map

Night was worse than day in their new world.

Sunlight seemed unable to penetrate the cloudy sky of the pocket universe the men were trapped in. This meant that nighttime was as dark and dismal as Sam and Oscar had ever seen. Sam was suddenly afraid of the dark, and rightly so. The monsters came out at night.

After much discussion, the two men decided that the top floor was a tactically superior position. If a giant predator was able to enter the house, Sam wanted to hear it coming and have a clear shot at it. Sam and Oscar spent the first night with their backs to the wall of a small room at the far end of the upper level with their rifles pointed wearily toward the doorway.

At sunrise, which came early, Sam said, "We need to check out the basement."

Oscar said, "You think there's something down there?"

"Our generator, for one thing," Sam answered. "Anyway, there has to be more here. They couldn't have burned everything, but we've found nothing up here."

"Might as well do it now, then," said Oscar. "Maybe they have some food or water stored down there."

They worked their way past the many rooms built for the twenty men who had lived in the place. Sam remembered that each room held three workers, while the team leader had a room to himself. Sam and his planners had done everything possible to prevent fighting among the men, and no expense had been spared. He had seen the lodge as the first of many across this little world and had envisioned an orderly expansion across this new frontier. Now he felt trapped in an empty monolith.

They reached the kitchen and once again stopped at the top of the stairway. Oscar said, "You wait here, and I'll look around."

Sam looked into the darkness and said, "How, exactly, are you going to look around?"

"I'll feel around, then, Sam," Oscar said. "I'll call you if it's all clear."

Sam shook his head. "I'm going with you—I think it's absolutely crazy for us to split up right now."

Oscar said, "You're probably right. It didn't work out too well when we left Mr. Wallace out in the field."

Oscar pointed his pistol into the darkness and quickly reached the bottom of the creaky wooden steps. Sam, one hand on his friend's shoulder, followed close behind. The basement was mustier than any room in the house and was colder than the men expected. Cobwebs, or something like cobwebs, brushed across Sam's face, and he fanned wildly in the dark. Oscar stumbled over something and swore quietly.

"Oscar…" Sam said.

"I'm OK. I just tripped over a box or something."

Sam felt around and found a wooden crate. The two men tried to lift it but decided that it was too heavy. The cover was not bolted, and they were able to slide it off easily. Sam felt around the box until he pulled out a large plastic object that felt like an industrial flashlight.

He flicked the switch, but nothing happened. He shook it, with no positive result, then tapped it gently against the crate. A significant stream of light gleamed from the gadget and lit up much of the room. Sam noted that the brightness of the flashlight was more potent than what passed for daylight in the Hole.

There were three or four musty mattresses leaning against the far wall, a stack of blankets piled beside one of them, and several crates scattered around the room. A large device that looked sort of like a giant lawn-mower engine sat at the center of the room; it appeared to be covered with dust. Sam looked at Oscar, and both men grinned.

"If we can get this generator working, then we'll stand a chance," said Sam. "A fair chance."

"Our trained specialists couldn't get that thing going, Sam," said Oscar. "I doubt we'll have any better luck."

"I have some skills, Oscar," said Sam. "I bet I can fix it."

"Maybe you can, Sam, but somebody damaged this equipment on purpose, and we should probably figure out why."

Sam put that thought aside and said, "We should look through the rest of the boxes."

They slid open the nearest crate, and Oscar was ecstatic to see a large cache of sturdy-looking rifles. The box beside the rifles held a significant supply of ammunition. Oscar said, "This makes me feel better."

Most of the crates contained weapons made by the Remington Company. In addition to the high-caliber rifles, they found a crate of shotguns and another with several pistols. It seemed that the pistols had been the most popular with the men, as there were only a few left in the box. Still, Sam felt that they had enough firepower to ward off any predators.

"All Remington models, Oscar," he said. "We had a pretty good contract with them a few years back."

Sam stumbled over something and shined his light on a dust-covered CD player. Sam looked at a disc lying on the floor beside the stereo and said, "Van Halen—*Diver Down*."

"Wonderful," replied Oscar. "Let's check out the crates and see if there's anything a little more useful."

One box was filled with tools of varying applications. There was an unopened all-purpose hammer, whatever that was, packed near a soldering iron. Replacement nails, screws, nuts, bolts, switches, and wires were placed beside an assortment of screwdrivers, wrenches, and some high-tech gadgets that looked like magic wands. Sam found an assortment of batteries layered beneath the tools. There were several manuals, which would help in repairing the generator and anything else that might be broken around the house.

Sam refocused on the first crate, the one that Oscar had tripped over, and found another flashlight and a battery-powered lantern. He pounded the side of the lantern, and it flooded the room with neon light. Nearly blinded, Sam turned off his flashlight and sifted through the box. He discovered a hunting knife, a baseball cap, two more hammers, a notepad, and a box of ballpoint pens.

He opened the notepad. "We've got something here, Oscar."

Oscar was sitting on a crate disassembling one of the Remingtons. "What does it say?"

"There's no note or anything, but it appears to be a map of the area."

Oscar, his weapon reassembled, walked over and looked at the book. He said, "Does it point us to a nice hotel or a restaurant?"

Sam smiled. "No, but these round spots are marked with the word *Mud*. This leads me to believe that they found what they were looking for."

"Good for them."

"We have to go check it out. If they found HRC here, then we have to know. We drained the other well twenty years ago."

"You know my feelings on that stuff, Sam."

"Yeah, well you know my feelings about staying alive. We need some of that stuff in case of injury. You're not against using the mud for normal medical needs, right?"

Sam knew that Oscar wasn't against using the compound for medical use but was disturbed by what he viewed as ethical lapses at Ahearn Industries' Clinical Studies division. Sam was uncomfortable with the partnership, too, but his father had made the deal with the feds, and it was ironclad.

Oscar said, "Just as long as you respect my feelings on this subject, Sam."

Sam nodded. "You know I respect you, Oscar."

He scanned the map again and said, "Look at this—it seems they found something else worth marking."

Oscar looked at the map. A spot on the map was a suitable drawing of a log cabin, presumably their cabin; three spots to the south of the house were marked as mudholes, and another spot just south of one of the mudholes was marked with a cross. Oscar looked at Sam and shrugged his shoulders.

Sam said, "I don't know what it is either, but I think that we should look."

"You're right, Sam, but I think that we should first collect some wood and build up one of those fire pits."

Sam said, "I don't have any matches. Do you know how to start a fire?"

"I used to be a Boy Scout, Sam."

Sam said, "Me too, but I don't remember all of my badge requirements."

7

Short Face

"How much further?"

"I don't know, Oscar—these guys weren't exactly cartographers," said Sam. "They were here to clear some brush and build a base camp for the next team."

Branches were snapping across Sam's face and body as he followed his friend through the thick brush of the outer forest. Oscar had his pistol drawn, safety on, and insisted on leading their little expedition. Sam pointed out that an attack would just as likely take place from the rear as from the front, but his bodyguard was insistent.

"Where's all the machinery? I don't think any giant squirrel or whatever is going to take the riding lawn mowers and the tree shredders."

Sam said, "Maybe they weren't just hiding from the animals. Maybe something else took all the equipment."

A branch from a small sapling managed to swat Oscar in the eye. He said, "Why are the leaves upside down?"

"I don't think it rains much here," replied Sam. "I think condensation builds up in the little cup-shaped leaves, and that's how the trees and plants get watered."

The thick shrubs and tall weeds began to thin out as they fell under the shadows of giant trees. The forest was noticeably darker now, but Sam's eyes were growing accustomed to the gloomy light of this little world. He stared at the map and said, "I think we need to go in that direction."

I wish I had a compass, he thought. *One that works.*

Oscar agreed, and the two men headed generally east. If Sam had read the map correctly, then the first of three mudholes would be coming up soon. The men had found a small temperature-resistant lunch box in one of the crates, and Sam planned to scoop up some of the goo and store it. He wondered how many days had passed Earthside since yesterday. Mike Standish must be going nuts trying to figure this one out, he thought.

The map was rudimentary but accurate; within minutes, they found a small clearing that contained what they were looking for. Weeds covered most of the area, but the shadows from the trees kept the plants from overgrowth. Almost exactly centered in the greenery was a six-foot-by-six-foot pool of slimy brown and red mud. Sam was elated as he approached the small chasm in the ground. This was what his partners wanted to see.

"This is it?" asked Oscar. "This is what we're trucking back home with us?"

Sam nodded. "This stuff is unquestionably the greatest scientific discovery of all time."

"Found by a drunk," added Oscar. "Out on a bender."

"That's right. One of our construction guys wandered in while tying one on and came out with some *mud* all over his shoes. He'd cut himself somehow and wiped this stuff over the wound, healing almost immediately. Human Regenerative Compound."

Oscar asked, "How much did the company pay him for his discovery, Sam?"

Sam said, "He got to keep his job."

"Generous. Very generous, Mr. Ahearn."

"Oscar, that was my father's decision. I..." Sam stopped talking and took a step back. Something was staring at them from just beyond the line of the forest. It was at least six feet tall, probably more, and had a frighteningly wide skull. Its fur was thick and dark, and Sam was sure that he could see long jagged teeth smiling cruelly back at him. Under the silhouette of the tree, the beast appeared to have the head of a bull-dog, but Sam knew that this was no canine. The beast began to stand, and Sam was horrified to see that the monster had been on all fours and was now more than ten feet tall.

Sam reached for his rifle, struggling to pull it off of his shoulder. Oscar turned and saw what had startled his employer and immediately started firing his pistol. The creature roared but did not move.

Sam said, "Let's get out of here."

The pair scampered deeper into the forest, firing occasionally, stopping only briefly to see if the beast was upon them. After a while, they tired and stopped to catch their breath. Sam was bent over and breathing hard, but Oscar, always supremely conditioned, leaned against a tree and breathed slowly and purposefully. He stared back into the gloomy woods and said, "I don't think we exactly covered ourselves in glory with our retreat."

Sam half chuckled. "Daniel Boone, I'm not."

"That thing must weigh more than a thousand pounds," said Oscar. "It's enormous…"

The jungle behind them began to move, and the men were stunned to see the beast tearing straight at them. Branches were flying, and the forest floor was actually shaking under the beast's assault. It was growling and barking odd noises at them and the two men, even Oscar, froze briefly in place.

"Jesus, run!" cried Sam. "Run!"

Oscar fired his pistol at the beast, and the men again ran from the monster. They sprinted through the jungle as the beast followed them. They dashed between trees that slowed the creature, forcing it to knock over or bend foliage in its way. After a few moments of this, the men stopped and fired their rifles at the monster. Sam didn't know if he was striking the thing with any of his shots, but he had no doubt that Oscar was making contact. The animal slowed and turned away.

"Let's keep going," said Sam. "Until we can't go any farther."

"I think it's gone, Boss. I think we scared it off."

Sam realized that Oscar was right; the creature had backed away and wasn't within eyesight. He said, "The sound of the guns probably hurt it more than the bullets."

"Especially the bullets fired from your gun," grunted Oscar.

"You're saying that my bullets didn't hit that thing?"

Oscar said, "I'm saying that your bullets almost hit me, but they came nowhere near the thing that was trying to have us for lunch."

"I'm the brains of this operation, Oscar. You're the gunner."

"Yeah, Mr. Brains?" Oscar replied. "Then where are we? Did you happen to notice what direction we went in?"

Sam said angrily, "We went in the direction opposite the giant carnivore."

Oscar paused. "I guess that was the right direction, then."

Both men smiled. Sam said, "I think it was a bear."

"No way, Sam. Its face was all wrong."

Sam shook his head, "There was an extinct mammal called the *short-faced bear* that I remember from high school science class. It was supposedly one of the largest mammalian carnivores ever known."

"You think it crawled into the Hole a thousand years ago?"

"More like twenty thousand years ago Earthside. Who knows how long ago it was Holeside."

"So, what else is here?" asked Oscar. "If we have giant bears walking around, then there's gonna be something else, right? Maybe a giant rabbit named Harvey?"

Sam wasn't listening. He pointed toward a lighted area to his right and said, "Look over there."

"What?"

"Another clearing, I think."

They marched toward the light, this time with their rifles out, and stepped into the clearing. Oscar kept his weapon ready as Sam moved out into the open. The spot was similar to the other clearing, but there was no sign of mud. But there was an interesting pile of stones located at the far edge of the area. The two men approached the stones, and Sam saw a piece of wood standing at the head of the stone pile.

"Oscar," he said. "Is that a cross?"

Oscar Larsen nodded slowly. He said, "Someone must be buried here."

"It must be one of our men, Oscar. He'll know what happened to the team."

Anger flashed across the bodyguard's face. "You can't possibly be thinking…"

"Of course I'm thinking that, Oscar. Why else would this be on the map?"

"No, no, no," said Oscar. "You know my feelings about this."

"It's got to be one of our men, and he can help us. All of the men signed an AFR—an Affidavit for Regeneration. You're the only team member who won't sign."

"Sam, we are not digging that poor soul out of the ground. I won't do it."

"I'll do it, Oscar. But first, let's find the nearest mudhole. We're going to need to know where we're moving the body to."

From the Diary of Margaret Dearborn:

November 14, 1813, Sunday

 Father is furious with me for shirking church duties today, but I just could not bear the pain that I would feel. Mother told me that he informed Reverend Duncan that I was very ill. I feel that this was a true statement.

 I have not spoken at length with Father since Micajer was reported to be missing. Mother barely speaks to him either, although I think that she has different motivations. I still hold out hope for Micajer's safe return, as my heart still beats in rhythm with his. Perhaps one day, all will be well…

8

Retreads

"Where is she?" asked Marissa. The teen was standing in the doorway, bobbing her head every which way, and smiling as though she had won the lottery. She was a girl on a mission.

Carrie giggled. "She's upstairs right now."

Marissa Robinson was Carrie's closest friend and the starting forward for the Lady Buzzards. They shared a babysitter when they were young and had remained close. Marissa was taller than most girls and was quite gangly, but she was always regarded as one of the cuter girls in town. Her funky haircuts were often the talk of the school, and her old-school metal braces enhanced her well-deserved image as the least self-conscious kid around. Guys often asked her out, but she rarely dated.

"What is that smell?" demanded Marissa. "It's wonderful."

"Aunt Sally's making dinner," said Carrie. "She can't understand why we have it so late."

"What's she cooking?" Marissa asked, following the aroma down the main hall.

They made their way into the kitchen located at the east end of the farmhouse and across from the long dining room. Sally Dearborn was standing over a network of old-style cooking pots, somehow managing to look wonderful and in charge while fretting over which spice to add to which soup. She was wearing a long dress and an apron and seemed oblivious to the heat generated by the many foods she was preparing.

There was a giant loaf of bread sitting on the table and a bowl of something that looked like pudding.

"Hello, Carrie," she said. "Won't you introduce me to your friend?"

"This is Marissa, Aunt Sally; we've known each other forever."

Aunt Sally smiled brilliantly and said, "I am so happy to meet you, Marissa. Are you able to stay for dinner today?"

"I would love to, Mrs. Dearborn," said Marissa as she eyed the pots and pans that covered the long metal stove. "What are you making?"

"Oh, you'll find out soon enough, Marissa. Have you met my daughter yet? I believe she's upstairs."

Carrie said, "We're headed up there now, but we'll be down in a while to help you set the table in the common room."

The girls retraced their steps toward the main entrance and then raced up the stairs and down the hall to Carrie's room. They were elbowing and pushing each other as they slammed into the hard oak door, and both managed to fall clumsily to the floor as the door opened.

Meg stood at the entrance, smiling quizzically at them, politely waiting to be introduced to Carrie's guest. She was wearing one of her light summer dresses, a yellow one with a floral print. She was holding a brush in her hand, though her hair already looked perfect to Carrie.

Carrie was the first to stand. She said, "Meg, this is Marissa."

"I recognize you from the portraits of you that Carrie has on her desk," Meg said. "She speaks very highly of you."

Marissa said, "I'm so happy to meet you. Carrie's been looking forward to your arrival for a long time."

Carrie's room had actually been two smaller rooms before Tom Heath made the decision that his daughter deserved more space and tore out the wall that separated the rooms. Now the bedroom was the size of a small trailer and, Carrie thought, was too big for just her. But now she was sharing the room with her cousin, and it was just right.

Meg's bed was in the far corner of the room underneath an oversize window that opened onto the side of the roof. She sat formally atop the mattress, and her two friends took a seat on Carrie's bed, which was a few feet away from hers. She said, "Listen to this."

The girls stopped speaking briefly and listened to the sound of pots and pans clinking, water running, and feet stomping. Carrie said, "I never realized that we could hear the kitchen so clearly beneath us."

Meg said, "Shh—listen."

They listened some more, Carrie and Marissa exchanging a look, and then they heard muffled words that sounded slightly foul. Carrie said, "Is your mother swearing?"

Meg grinned. "She's been doing that for most of the afternoon. I don't even know what some of those words mean."

"What's she so mad about?" asked Marissa. "Is she upset about having an extra plate at the dinner table?"

"No, I think it has something to do with my father," said Meg.

Marissa looked at Meg and said, "Your mother is beautiful—I mean, really beautiful…"

"I think so, too, Marissa. My father had quite a lot of competition for her affections when he began courting her."

"But she looks so young."

Meg nodded her head vigorously. She said, "It's very strange to see her like that. She was always younger than my father, but she was beginning to show some age…"

"Uncle John is very handsome, too," added Carrie. "They both look like they're in their early twenties."

Carrie knew John Dearborn was more than a decade older than Aunt Sally, and Meg said the age difference had become a problem for the pair. His injuries had taken a toll on his body, which must have been sad because he was famously athletic. Meg knew him as a man who was old before his time, and now he appeared to be only a few years older than her. Carrie guessed it would take a little time for Meg to become accustomed to the new John and Sally Dearborn.

"Meg's going to be taking some classes with us at school," said Carrie.

"What classes?"

"History, of course. And some physical science courses," Meg said. "I'm going to need a tutor to get up to speed in some other classes, but you'll see a lot of me, I think."

Carrie had driven Meg over to Bainbridge Academy every day for the last two weeks for some tests. Ahearn Industries coordinated the examinations and generously compensated several teachers and administrators from the school for their cooperation. Although she was weak in history, Meg's other scores were unusually high. Carrie knew she'd do just fine.

"You didn't go to high school, did you?" asked Marissa. "Back then, I mean."

Carrie found herself enjoying every word Meg was speaking. Her accent was sort of British but mixed with a Boston affectation. And she pronounced every word perfectly; every consonant was spoken clearly, and each syllable was enunciated with equal attention.

We all must sound like idiots to her, she thought.

"I had a series of tutors and instructors, and my mother was a tremendous help. It was rather lonely, though, and I am looking forward to interacting with others."

"How are you on a computer?" asked Marissa. "Can you navigate the web yet?"

Carrie said, "I'm teaching her how to type and how to get around on the net, but she seems a little nervous about it."

Carrie knew Meg had a lot of questions about the modern world. Meg's own existence proved to her that nothing was impossible, but the idea of stroking a button on a keypad and seeing words or images appear on the screen seemed like witchcraft to her. She questioned Carrie about everything—cars, the wide-screen television that Tom Heath watched endless sporting events on, indoor plumbing (where does everything go?), Carrie's electric toothbrush, light bulbs, and microwave dinners. Everything was so different here.

"Has anybody given you a hard time?" Marissa asked. "About being a little different, I mean…"

"I haven't met many people. Is my background very well known around town?"

"Well, Carrie's dad worked pretty hard to get your father a job at the school. That's one of the rules, right? That he has to have a job? And the principal's daughter is Haley Simpson, and she's got a really big mouth—"

Carrie interrupted. "She's saying that word got around."

Meg smiled confidently and said, "It doesn't matter. It's probably better that people know."

"They call you a *retread*," said Marissa.

"Marissa!" shrieked Carrie.

"What does that mean?" Meg demanded. "Is it an insult?"

Carrie reached up on a shelf and pulled down a thick book. She said, "We can look it up in the dictionary."

She thumbed through the book and finally said, "*A secondhand tire with a brand-new tread on it.*"

"A tire? Like on one of your automobiles?"

Carrie nodded.

Meg thought for a moment. Finally, she said, "I'm the tire. I'm being derided as less than a person."

"I don't know," said Carrie, although she did know.

The girls were quiet.

"I rather like it," Meg said.

"What?"

"It's so perfect. I have a new tread, but the old tire is inside of me—it is so clever."

Marissa said, "I don't think it's meant to be clever—it's meant to be *mean*."

"Well, we shall turn it around on them. I am proud of my *retread* heritage."

Carrie and Marissa looked at each other and laughed. Marissa said, "She's just as incredible as you thought."

"We should look up retreads online," Carrie suggested. "Maybe there are others out there who would like to talk to you. Kids your own age."

Marissa said, "We could start a website."

Meg had no idea what a website was.

Carrie said, "That takes a lot of work."

The girls stopped talking briefly. Carrie had some clothes on her bed that needed folding, and Meg returned to brushing her hair, which had grown two inches in just a matter of days. Carrie looked around the room, which had always seemed oddly cold to her, and realized that there was suddenly a lot of life in it. There was a lot of life in the whole house now, as a matter of fact. She felt a rush of emotion as she realized that her family was finally getting what it deserved.

Marissa said, "I know who could help you with your website, Meg. I know someone who would do just about anything for Carrie."

Meg was a clever girl. She said, "A boy?"

Carrie felt herself begin to blush.

"My brother, Ryan—he's into computers a lot, and I just know he'd do it for you. I'll talk to him."

Meg looked at Carrie, who immediately began to giggle.

9

Running Laps

The Bainbridge Academy football field was located directly across the street from the high school. It was similar to any of the stadiums in the area; the field was bordered by an oval running track, there were seats on both sides of the field, and there was a structure at one end of the field that was used as a locker room for players and coaches.

Tom Heath spent most of his time at the high school. He taught gym class at the main campus, and he developed most of his strategies in his office behind the gym. But he loved the rush he felt when he stepped onto the field of battle. He had known the thrill of football since his playing days twenty years ago, and the feeling hadn't changed much for him now that he was coaching. The only thing more important than football was Carrie. And now, the Dearborns.

"It's actually a game of military tactics—like chess," he said. He was wiping sweat from his brow, as the day's temperature was approaching eighty-five degrees.

John was wearing the usual assistant-coach combination of sweat pants and a T-shirt, but he looked more like a player than a coach to Tom. He said, "I have been reading your manuals, and I think that I am beginning to understand the game. How did you ever convince your superiors that I was a suitable coach for a game that I have never played?"

Tom tossed a bag of balls onto a choppy patch of turf near a bench. He said, "It took some talking, but I pointed out that you were a famous athlete in your day. Plus, you'll be teaching that class on the Revolutionary War, and I think that is what probably convinced my bosses. How many schools have teachers who were actually there?"

Tom called out to a kid halfway down the field. The boy was in shorts and was wearing a jersey emblazoned with the school logo. Tom stood back and stepped into a perfect spiral that hit the kid on the numbers. The kid turned and ran for the end zone.

"Anyway," said Tom. "They're barely paying you to do any of this. The rule was that you had to be working. Nobody said anything about being paid much."

Some of the volunteer coaches were running drills with the kids as the men talked. Tom said, "I need the boys to run some laps, and I was hoping that you would lead them around the track."

John said, "I can do that."

"Have you run track before, John? Carrie says you were quite an athlete in your day."

"I haven't experienced a field like this, Tom, but the principle is the same. You want me to lead the young men around the oval path for a prerequisite number of times called laps."

"That's right—at least ten of them if you can handle it," Tom said. "Remember, you are the oldest man on the field."

John Dearborn's voice boomed as he called the players over. Everyone came, including the coaches, as if drawn by hypnosis. He said, "Follow me, men."

The players and volunteers, even Tom, jumped in line behind John and began to run. He led by at least ten yards most of the way, and the usual noise of a busy football practice quieted to a disciplined rumble of quick-moving feet hitting the track. All eyes were on the leader.

The first ten laps passed uneventfully. Usually a few of the kids, often the O-line guys, would slow to a walk while the better-conditioned players bumped into them or hurled unflattering adjectives at them. John, perhaps sensing that this might happen, turned his head and said, "Continue on, men, we can do this together."

The group continued its rapid pace for another ten laps. There were a few boys in the group who ran track or had engaged in a rigorous off-season program, but most of the men wanted to quit. For some reason, no one could bring himself to stop. Tom hadn't run this many laps since his own high school days. He wanted to puke, too, but he wasn't going to do it.

John looked back again and then cried, "Once more, men, at full speed!"

The assembly of men and boys roared as one, and everyone ran at top speed, but none could come close to their leader. They finished their final lap in a blur and screamed and howled with joy as they reached their goal. Some of the kids ran off to the sideline to throw up, and others ran to the table of water and Gatorade. Everyone was smiling.

Tom had remained somewhere in the middle of the pack. He walked slowly over to his relative and slapped him on the back. John was slightly sweaty but showed no other indication that he had just led a group of teenagers in a race around the track.

Tom was breathing heavily, and his voice was a little shaky.

He said, "I think you'll do fine, John."

10

Male Bonding

"That was a great job today, John," said Tom. "Scary great."

Tom's office was behind the gymnasium near the boy's locker room. There was a wired space that he called *the cage* that was used to store the footballs, orange cones, clipboards, whistles, and all the other equipment used to manage a football team. The boys were all gone now, and the other coaches were in the gym shooting hoops. Tom was sitting at his desk, and John was seated across from him, eyeing the trophies and banners that cluttered the walls and shelves of the office.

"I enjoyed it, Tom," John replied. "It appears that you are a successful coach."

"You mean all the trophies? Sure, we've won a lot, but we've lost some, too. I just enjoy coaching and helping these kids grow up a little."

"You seem to be doing a superb job."

Tom leaned over the desk and said, "It's easier than raising my own kid, that's for sure."

"You seem to have made an outstanding effort in the raising of your daughter."

"I'd like to take credit for that, but I don't know. She's done a lot of it on her own."

John said, "If I may ask—what happened to her mother?"

Tom hesitated, searching for the words that would make the most sense to his friend. Finally, he said, "I'm in the guard, the army guard, and I got called up to go to Iraq."

Dearborn nodded. He said, "You went off to war."

"I had no choice. It wasn't a lot of fun, but I came back after a year, and I still had my job. There was a big party at my house, and everyone hugged me and slapped me on the back and told me that they were really proud of me…"

"It sounds splendid, Tom."

Tom smiled. "Two days later, Katie—that's my wife—told me that she was leaving. She said that she had been thinking about it for a long time but couldn't do anything about it until I got home. She didn't want to leave Carrie alone, but she didn't want to bring her with her, either."

"Anyway, she just left and moved to Seattle, where it rains a lot."

John was listening intently, with his back straight and his hands on his knees. He seemed to consider every word Tom spoke and nodded knowingly. He said, "I cannot imagine leaving my child behind like that."

Tom said, "The funny thing is that we're still married. It's like I just can't let go of that part of my life. I know it sounds silly, but I just don't believe in divorce."

"It doesn't sound silly at all to me, Tom. It sounds noble."

Tom stood up and said, "Let's head out to the car, shall we?"

The two men exited the office and waved to the coaches as they passed them in the gym. Tom reminded them that someone had to lock up when they were done and then led John out the side entrance across the parking lot to his parked Jeep Cherokee. The doors were unlocked because nobody locked their car doors in Bainbridge.

John still had difficulty with his seat belt but was able to secure it. He said, "I'm still rather uncomfortable in these damnable automobiles."

Tom said, "I've noticed that. You'll get used to it."

John almost whispered, "I have noticed the smaller, two-wheeled machines."

Tom laughed. "I should have known that you'd like motorcycles. I have one in the barn, you know—it just needs a few dozen parts. Do you want to work on it together?"

"That would be splendid, Thomas."

"Maybe you could take Sally for a ride."

John said, "I don't know. You may have noticed that she and I don't seem to be communicating as well as we have in the past. Or perhaps we are communicating *exactly* as we did in the past."

Tom knew the Dearborns were having difficulties. Sally seemed to have something to say, but she couldn't seem to get the words out. Meg spoke wonderfully, but there was coldness in her speech when talking to John. Tom was absolutely certain he should stay out of it.

He said, "You guys have gone through a lot. You'll get past it."

John wasn't done talking yet. He said, "And dear Meg has never forgiven me for disapproving of a friend of hers."

Tom said, "A boy, right? It's your *job* to disapprove of her boyfriends! I have no intention of being all lovey-dovey to any of Carrie's boyfriends, that's for sure. They have to know that they have me to deal with."

John continued, "It's quite sad. We were once so close."

"Look, you've got a teenage daughter—well, sort of a teenage daughter—and she's not always going to treat you like a hero. It's just how they are, my friend."

Dearborn seemed to brighten a little. He said, "You are right, Tom. Perhaps my problems are more commonplace than I imagined."

Tom Heath said, "Besides, we have another problem."

"What problem?"

Tom grabbed at his stomach. He said, "I've grown about an inch in my gut since your wife started cooking all the meals. Those porridges and the pies are just too damn good. We have to get her out of the house before I become a whale."

"I haven't noticed a difference."

"You folks have a different metabolism than I do, John. I'm almost forty years old, and my body doesn't burn it off the way it used to."

John said, "What's your idea?"

"I have a friend—a sort of 'lady friend'—and she works part-time for the school as a science tutor. She's actually going to be working with Meg; her name is Carol Simon, and I think that she ought to show your wife around a little."

"I met Miss Simon, and she seemed quite capable," John said. "Does Carrie know that you've been spending time with her?"

"I don't think so, but not much gets past my girl. Anyway, I propose that we get the girls together and see if they form a bond or whatever."

"Sally could use some friends," John said. "Can you believe there was a time I would not allow her out of the house? By what right could I make such demands?"

Tom smiled. "Recognizing the problem is the first step to fixing the problem."

"I was a different man then," he said. "I will be better now."

11

The Body

The grave was shallow.

Initially, Sam used his knife as a sort of shovel, but the earth was soft, so he began using his hands to remove the soil that was presumably covering the remains of an Ahearn team member. He focused his attention on the task at hand mainly because he was a determined man but partly because he could actually *feel* the disapproving looks being shot at him by his friend Oscar. How could he blame Oscar—or anybody—for disapproving? He was practically grave robbing.

"The soil is remarkably squashy," he said. "It's easy to move."

Oscar stood a dozen feet away. "I don't care."

Sam's hands latched onto some kind of fabric. He looked up and said, "I think I've got it."

This time Oscar said nothing. He shook his head and turned away.

"At least keep an eye out for that bear, OK?" Sam said.

After ten more minutes of digging, Sam had more or less unearthed a large object wrapped in something that might have been a thick blanket. He tried to lift it, but it was quite heavy. He gazed toward his bodyguard.

"How about a hand?" he asked.

Oscar did not acknowledge his request.

"Fine," he said. He squatted beside the shallow grave, reached under the package with both hands, and pulled. Sam rolled the package out of the hole before he managed to trip and fall on his backside. He looked over at Oscar and saw no reaction.

He stood up, wiped his filthy hands on the legs of his blue Ahearn Industries jumpsuit, and said, "I'm going to take a look."

Oscar moved another step away.

Sam was pretty sure that there was a body inside the blanket. He pulled at the spot that seemed to be covering the unidentified man's skull. The blanket did not seem to want to move and was much harder than the soil that had surrounded it. Sam picked up the knife and sliced a small hole. Careful not to harm the body, he put his fingers into the torn area and ripped. There was indeed a man's head behind the cloth.

"You recognize this guy?" he asked.

Oscar looked sideways and said, "What do you mean? Isn't it decomposed by now?"

"He looks pretty fresh, like they put him in the ground this morning."

Oscar fumed over to the site and forced himself to look at the face of the man Sam Ahearn had just disturbed. Sam was right—whoever it was, he was young and had the look of a soldier. He probably was one of the original team members.

"I don't know him—do you?"

Sam shook his head. "He's obviously the right age. Oscar, I'm not sure he's really dead."

"Are you nuts?"

"Look at him. He looks to be asleep, maybe, and he's pale, but I wonder if the organism in the mud isn't in this soil also. We are pretty close to one of the holes…"

Oscar said, "You're saying that he's in some sort of limbo—not really dead but not really alive?"

Sam nodded. "That's right. He was probably dead when he was put in there, but he's not really dead now. The process probably takes a lot longer—probably years longer—in this grave."

Oscar said, "This doesn't change anything, Sam."

"The hell it doesn't. You didn't want to help me be Dr. Frankenstein, and I understood your ethics, but we have here a man who is not dead and can be helped. What is your moral obligation now?"

Sam was standing in front of Oscar, staring up into his cold eyes. Oscar stepped back and turned from the terrible sight. Sam knew what his friend was thinking; they had just ripped open the grave of a man well on his way to heaven, and now he had to decide whether it would be OK to stop the man on his journey. No man should have to make such decisions.

"If we left the body here..."

Sam said, "A scavenger would take it; you know that. If we rebury him, then the process will start again, but if he ever does recover, we won't be here to help him. He will be alone."

"OK, I get it. What do you want me to do?"

Sam said, "He's wrapped up pretty good in that thing. You take his feet, I'll take his head, and we'll just carry him to the mudhole."

Oscar said nothing, but he reached down and grabbed the blanket near the dead man's feet. Sam grabbed the other end, and the two headed toward the nearest mudhole, which was only a quarter of a mile to the east. Sam knew it would seem like a much longer walk.

12

The Tennyson Organism

It took more than an hour to reach the green and yellow field. Sam was breathing hard, and his arms were numb from the effort of carrying 180 pounds of dead weight through dense woods. Even Oscar was fatigued, and he was something of a physical specimen. Sam was grateful that the daytime temperature seemed to remain a constant sixty degrees in the Hole.

Too weak to carry the body now, the two men each grabbed a corner of the material and, side by side, dragged it to the mudhole at the center of the meadow. They looked down into the small brown pond and contemplated their next move.

Wiping his brow, Oscar said, "What next?"

"I guess we dump him and wait. He'll probably need help getting out."

Oscar said, "Let's get some things straight first."

"OK."

"Do you know if this will even work?"

Sam shrugged. "At the lab, with the organism watered down and treated, sure. But in this uncontrolled area, anything could happen. The organisms in the mud might tear him apart for all I know."

"What is this organism called?"

"The Tennyson Organism," said Sam.

"Named for that poet or writer, or whatever that guy was?" asked Oscar.

Sam smiled and said, "Named for a drunken construction worker named Bud Tennyson. He was no poet."

"And this organism will do what, exactly?"

Sam said, "It's complicated, obviously, but just remember two things about the process. The mud itself is similar to human stem cells, which have the potential to be turned into almost any kind of cell desired. This mud consists of components identical to those in the human body. Everything that is in you is in the mud."

Oscar nodded. "But the Tennyson thing is in there also."

"Right. When Bud came back covered with this stuff, we found some medical applications right away. He had a wound, a deep one, that was apparently repaired by the mud."

Sam continued, "The Hole was still open, and he led our guys right to a large mud puddle of sorts. The puddle wasn't nearly as large as the mudholes that you and I keep running into, but it was a significant amount."

Sam sat down beside the package and looked past it into the mudhole. There almost appeared to be motion in the coffee-colored muck, but that might just be his imagination. The mire was about ten feet by ten feet and was more square than round. It smelled faintly of rotting flesh, but that, too, was probably from his imagination.

Oscar removed his rifle from his shoulder and placed it on the ground beside the body. He stretched his arms gently and then sat beside his boss. At least Oscar was listening to him, which meant that he was probably not so angry at him.

"Anyway," he said, "when we studied the liquid, we found an autonomous life-form that looked like a little microscopic shrimp. Actually, we found millions of them, and their job seems to be simple: they divide cells, and they replace and repair cells. Use the organism on body parts that require repairs and, voila, dead things come back to life—a natural *Human Regenerative Compound*."

"But these things have their old memories—I mean, they have the memories of the *real* human they are replacing."

"Look, I understand your belief system, I do, but don't doubt that these regenerated people are humans. The program has found nothing fundamentally inhuman about them."

"What about the memories?"

Sam said, "We're not exactly sure. Deep down, memories are stored in actual flesh and blood—perhaps the organism replaces the original material at such a microscopic scale that it is actually able to rebuild the memory cells. Or maybe there is a human soul, and it returns to the body when the body is regenerated. I don't know."

"Is that why retreads are not allowed to testify in court? You're not sure about their memories?"

Sam felt a sting. "Don't call them that, Oscar. But, yes, not enough is known about their memories for them to be allowed in court. But their insight can be a useful tool in criminal cases."

"What happens to these organisms once someone is regenerated? Do they just die off inside a regenerated person?"

Sam said, "They seem to hang around for quite a while. Regenerated humans have tremendous healing capabilities, and we assume this is due to the Tennyson Organisms in their system."

"What happens if you split the body in two—can you make twins?"

"No—that's impossible. For the process to work, we need a mostly intact skeleton and the entire skull. No skull, no regeneration."

Oscar mumbled something and shook his head.

Sam turned his attention to the blanketed man. He used his knife to lengthen his earlier incision enough to remove the man from the blanket. He clumsily began the process of squeezing the dead man from the fabric, starting at the man's head and finishing with his feet. Although the young man appeared quite fresh, he was horribly pungent. A dead man had been placed inside that blanket some time ago.

The flesh seemed almost normal, but the man's clothing was in tatters. It appeared to be a uniform of some type, but the cloth was heavy and wet. Sam thought that it might be wool, but he was not sure. The young man was wearing leather boots; they were a little less damaged than the uniform but were still unrecognizable to Sam. He was now pretty sure that this guy was not one of his men. His uniform was too thick, and the boots looked uncomfortable.

Sam said, "I'm putting him in."

Oscar replied, "I'll help you."

They rolled the body into the muck and watched it sink. The two men stared for a while until Oscar broke the silence.

He said, "I have to pee."

"Go ahead," said Sam. "There's spots all over."

Sam watched Oscar, always a private man, stride over to the edge of the field. He turned away and looked into the mud for some kind of reaction. In the lab, patients were treated slowly in a chamber, and the process took weeks. The subjects woke rested but confused, and there was no strain from the process. Tossing the body into the mudhole would seem to multiply the recovery time considerably, and the patient could be severely affected by the process. Sam wondered if the shock of regeneration would be enough to kill the subject again. Or drive him insane.

Sam heard a gunshot.

A giant brownish shadow was standing over him. The bear was growling, and Sam wondered how he could not have heard the creature approach him. Oscar hollered and fired more shots at the creature. The bullets did not appear to harm the creature, but it was distracted enough for Sam to run for the cover of the woods. But the bear was much faster on an open field than it was in the thick brush that had allowed their earlier escape. The monster was upon him in an instant.

Oscar bolted over, and he again fired at the back of the beast. The bear turned and clubbed him, smashing the rifle from his grasp and knocking him to the ground. Oscar tried to scramble to his feet, but his body was obviously not reacting to the impulses that his mind was sending. His many years inside the ring had not prepared him for the sheer power behind the bear's blow.

Sam stared in horror as the bear lifted its claw to tear into his throat.

A shot rang out and then, after a brief pause, several more. The bear, puzzled, looked to Sam for some kind of answer and then fell down beside him with a resounding thud. The beast's brushy fur was coated in something that might have been perspiration. Brownish-red blood was spilling out from its throat, and one eye seemed to have been blown out of its socket. The creature was dead.

Sam and Oscar both looked in the direction of the gunshots and saw a man in tattered clothing standing near the mudhole. He was tall and lean and was holding Sam's rifle by his side. He looked a little wobbly, and Sam thought that he might collapse, but he didn't. Instead, he tentatively approached Sam and Oscar, who were now standing together, and handed them the rifle.

The man was covered in dirt and mocha-colored mud.

He said, "You shouldn't be in the forest if you can't kill a bear."

From the Diary of Margaret Dearborn:

March 27, 1814, Sunday

Joshua Martel stopped by today. Father and Mother are quite taken with him and with his pedigree. They do not seem to notice his evasiveness when I ask him about Micajer. I fear that Father has some idea that I should marry Mr. Martel, and Mother apparently is in concurrence with this notion. It is an unbearable thought, and I am saddened that their only point of agreement presently is one that brings me such pain.

Do they not understand that I am in mourning?

13

Soccer at Carson Park

Carrie stood at the center of the field. It was the middle of September, and she was shivering from the morning cold. The stands were mainly empty, but there were several sets of parents and other assorted onlookers dressed for the weather standing or seated in comfortable lawn chairs on the track that circled the field. Standing in the center of the crowd were her Aunt Sally and Miss Simon from school. She bristled at the sight of Meg's science tutor.

"Does she think that I'm blind?" she said. "I know what she's doing."

Meg was standing behind her, stretching her legs. She said, "She doesn't mean any harm, Carrie."

"Coming to the game doesn't make her my mother. She's just trying to suck up to me."

"Perhaps," said Meg. "Come on—Coach Daly's calling everybody in."

Meg was not allowed on the school's soccer team. The rules were clear; retreads could not play in school sports. Retreads were not necessarily stronger or faster than anyone else, but their recuperative powers were well known. If Meg were to sprain her ankle in the first half of the game, she might be able to return sometime in that same half. It wasn't fair to the other students who had to bandage and ice their injuries while watching the game from the sidelines.

But the Bainbridge Youth Soccer Association was not concerned with such things. The league was coed and not affiliated with any schools in the area. The coaches and players were mainly interested in playing and having fun, though there was a certain competitive edge to the group. The officials were other players waiting for their own games that were often called out of the stands, and the scores were usually pretty high. The kids played with a physical style, and penalties were not called as often as they would be in a school game.

Carson Park was one of a number of fields in the Bainbridge area. The field was a fifty-fifty mix of weeds and dirt, all of which was peppered with numerous cleat marks that volunteer groundskeepers occasionally smoothed over with long metal rakes. A cracked red clay track circled the field, and there was a basketball court behind the field. There had once been a community swimming pool there, but it had been drained and filled in many years ago. The park, one of many such fields in the area, was almost impossible to locate in the woods behind the old A and A Market Plaza. Only the locals knew where to find it.

Coach Daly was a small guy with a crazy head of black curly hair. Both of his boys played on the team, and both towered over him. He stood at the sideline and surveyed his team. They wore black shirts with the name of a local oil-change business embroidered on the front. Each player had a gold number stitched on the back side of his or her shirt. Meg was number seven, and Carrie was lucky number three.

"Let's have fun out there today," Coach Daly said. "These guys were a real defensive team last year, and they have mostly the same guys this year."

Carrie looked across the field at their opponents. They were wearing orange jerseys, and most of the boys on the team were around six feet tall. Some of the girls were pretty huge, too.

She thought, *What have I gotten myself into?*

The coach continued, "We want to stay out of penalty situations... OK, Meg?"

Everybody laughed.

—◊—

When Carrie suggested that Meg might want to play a sport of some type, she was surprised to hear that Meg had actually played sports her first time around. She described a street game that involved kicking a ball made from animal hide into a marked area while dodging defenders and passing off to teammates. As she attempted to explain the rules of the game, it became obvious she was describing a basic and very violent form of soccer.

Uncle John and Aunt Sally knew nothing of her sporting activities. She explained, "They would not have approved. Father allowed some activities, but he would never have allowed me to play a game of contact—it just wasn't done."

"How did you learn the game?" Carrie asked.

"Cager showed me. He always lived in two worlds, you know—his mother still had means, but he was sort of an outcast among his own kind. So, he made a lot of friends down near the docks. Sometimes I went with him."

Carrie did the research and found an independent league that included players from many towns as well as a few home-schooled kids. The girls were concerned that Uncle John would not allow his prim daughter to become involved in such a thing and ran the idea past Aunt Sally first. Meg's mother reluctantly gave her blessing but agreed that Uncle John might not go along with the notion, though she admitted that he was not as predictable as he had once been.

The subject was brought up over a steak dinner. Carrie, holding a soccer ball, listened as her cousin politely asked her father for his indulgence while she begged a favor. Without mentioning Margaret's history with the sport, she explained that she desired a certain interaction with her peers that she felt was denied her academically. She wanted an outlet for her emotions. She actually talked like that.

Uncle John surprised everyone with an immediate approval. He said, "I think that is a spectacular idea, girls. Tom has told me that youths involved in sports and other after-school events are much less likely to become involved in drug-taking and other destructive activities."

Carrie's father added, "I think that basketball has been a great confidence booster for Carrie."

That was when Carrie dropped her bomb. She said, "I'm signing up for the team, too, Daddy."

"What?" he said. "What about basketball?"

"Coach is going to try to hold my spot, but I just want to do this with Meg. I'd rather she join my team, but she can't, so I'm joining hers. It's not like I've got a potential basketball scholarship riding on this or anything."

"Carrie, you don't even know how to dribble a soccer ball," said her father.

Carrie smiled and bounced the ball with her hand as she would a basketball. She said, "See?"

At the first practice, Meg treated her teammates to a clinic that left some teammates, mainly boys, knocked down, beat up, or spun around. She could score from both sides, and her footwork was dizzying. It was obvious to everyone that she was a rare talent.

"But you have to stop throwing elbows at the defenders," Coach Daly told her. "That is not allowed in this league."

Meg worked hard to tone down her street skills, but Carrie knew she was going to draw a penalty flag or two. Coach Daly was willing to take that hit because he expected her to score a lot of points. He would never say it, but she was probably the best player he had ever coached. Carrie was positive that the coach and the players knew that Meg was a retread, but no one seemed to care. Maybe they were open-minded, or maybe they just wanted to win.

The black team won by a score of five to three. They would have scored more, but Meg only played a few minutes in the second half—Coach Daly held her out to give other players more time and to keep the score down. She only tripped two players, and one of the fouls was mainly accidental. Carrie was still struggling with the new sport, but her competitive nature helped her on defense. Still, it was a great first game, and the girls' teammates were quite taken with them. The coaches insisted that the teams line up and shake hands after the game.

Meg, first in line, shook the hand of the first orange player, a husky girl, and said, "Good game."

The big girl's response was: "You're a *retread*."

She shook the hand of the second player, a tall and thin boy, and said, "Good game."

"You're a *retread*," said the beanpole.

She smiled brightly and said, "Yes, I am. Thank you for noticing."

The third player, another boy, said, "You're a *retread*."

"Yes, I am. How are you?"

"You're a *retread*," said the fourth.

"I am indeed. I hope to have a website up soon."

"You're a *retread*," said the fifth.

"Thank you for showing an interest. You played an excellent game today."

The last few players said, "Good game" and left it at that. Their wills had been broken.

Carrie, standing in line behind her cousin, said, "I was going to trip the last one, but they all gave up by then."

Meg said, "They weren't exactly creative in their insults. They were all copying the first girl, the big one—she was a bit of a *jade*. Here comes my mother."

Aunt Sally and her friend Miss Simon approached the girls. Aunt Sally had on a long blue dress that looked quite stylish; her blond hair was nearly shoulder length now, though she had cut it twice since her arrival. Miss Simon was wearing jeans and a blouse. They were walking closely together and seemed to be sharing some funny joke. Carrie could not even bring herself to look at her aunt's friend.

"You girls were wonderful," said her aunt. "It was an exciting match—Meg, I've never seen you so, um, excited."

Carrie answered, "Meg is great—she's a natural."

Aunt Sally said, "It's almost as though she's been playing for years."

Miss Simon said, "You girls both did very well. Would you like to go with us to the mall now?"

"No," said Carrie.

Meg added, "Marissa and her brother are coming over to the house to help us with our project."

Aunt Sally's eyes narrowed.

"Don't worry—we'll use the computer in the living room. And Father and Uncle Tom will be home from their football match soon."

"I do not want a boy in the house until after the men have returned, all right?"

Carrie and Meg agreed.

Miss Simon said, "Carrie, I thought that you were great today."

Carrie said, "Uh-huh."

"OK, then. We'll see you later, girls."

Carrie watched the two women walk toward Miss Simon's Toyota. Aunt Sally still didn't drive, but she did not mind being driven, and she especially didn't mind being driven around by her new best friend, Miss Simon. Carrie grimaced at the sight of her father's pseudo-girlfriend.

"I don't get what my father sees in her," she said. "Anyway, he's still a married man."

Meg said, "I don't think she's trying to be your mother, and she's not exactly a *jilt*. She just wants you to like her."

"She better not hold her breath on that one," said Carrie. "I don't mind your mom bossing me around, though—it makes me feel like we're family."

"She means well," agreed Meg. "I wish I had more to say to her."

Carrie was quiet as they headed toward her car.

Finally, she said, "And I don't think that Miss Simon is pretty at all. Not at all."

14

The Cozy Kitchen

Carol looked over at her passenger's face and saw sheer terror in her blue eyes. Sally's skin, pale to begin with, was now sheet white, and she was tapping her fingers frantically upon her knees. Carol Simon wondered how her new friend would deal with air travel.

"We're almost there, silly," she said. "You'll be fine."

Sally nodded but said nothing. Carol knew her friend could not understand how people could jump so casually into what must seem like demonic machines and achieve speeds faster than that of the fastest horses, all the while laughing and listening to music. And Carol knew her driving was by far the most terrifying of all. Her driving terrified most people. Even Tom.

She rarely used her turn indicator and only rolled through stop signs. When Sally peered over at the speedometer, the news was predictably bad; Carol was always driving at least fifteen miles over the speed limit. And yet Sally so preferred the company of her fiendish friend to the loneliness of her home life. Why was she so sad?

"I just wanted to show you this site," said Carol. "It's one of several that my husband left me, but I never really knew what to do with it."

Danny Simon had suffered a massive heart attack and died in his sleep on his thirty-seventh birthday. His passing marked the end of life as she had always known it, but Carol was made of strong stuff, and she moved on. Her husband owned several properties and rented them out at fair prices. Carol was a much better and tougher businessperson, and she was able to more than triple her income in just a few years. Not satisfied with simply having money, she returned to school and was soon an accredited teacher.

She found a role at Bainbridge High as a science and history tutor for students of various levels. It was at the school that she met big Tom Heath and knew that she might have a chance at happiness once more. Of course, her happiness would only come if Tom would get off his ass and get a divorce and if Carrie would give her a chance instead of mumbling about Carol not being her mother.

"We're here," said Carol.

The small building was on the corner of Meadow Lane and Main Street. It was an older building, and the remaining paint appeared to be yellow, though it was so faded that it was only a guess. It was a two-story construction that had held a business on the bottom floor and housed a family on the top. There was a sign over the main entrance that was now unreadable. The front steps were accentuated with large columns at the side and led to a large double-door entrance.

"The key's in here somewhere," said Carol as she fumbled through her oversize purse.

"I guess the girls are too busy to come with us old ladies," said Sally.

Carol looked at her beautiful, young-looking friend, the one who was about two hundred years older than she, and said, "They just don't want to be with us, Sally. Carrie hates me, and Meg…"

"Meg blames me for a lot of things," said Sally.

"Here it is," said Carol.

She opened the door to the shop and stepped inside. The power worked, and the overhead lights shone down on a large empty room. The place was gray with dust, with webs, both cobwebs and spider webs, everywhere. Sally said that her skin felt as though insects were crawling on it, but Carol wasn't creeped out at all by the place. She came here sometimes when she missed Danny. This was her happy place.

"Follow me in here," Carol said. "I want you to see something."

They stepped through a swinging door and entered a wide kitchen. There were several large stoves and two sizeable stainless-steel refrigerators that probably still worked, and assorted pots, pans, and plates were laid out on a nearby counter. The room was a dusty mess, but it had potential.

"What is this place?" asked Sally.

"It was called the Cozy Kitchen back when I was a kid. Danny's family owned it, and neither of us ever had the heart to sell the place. It's in good condition, though, and I think that it'd pass inspection if we did a little work."

Sally was wiping down the stove with a rag and looking inside for signs of wear. She turned to Carol and said, "I don't think this stove is good anymore, and the floor's a little cracked."

"Let's look around out back," said Carol.

A screen door led out onto a small paved lot. The back of the building was faded and chipped, and a rusty air conditioner hung precariously from a second-floor window. Carol remembered meeting Danny out here on his breaks and holding his hand or kissing him or both. She pushed the memory away, but not before Sally pretty much read her mind.

"Danny lived upstairs," she said. "The whole family did."

"You miss him," Sally said. They were leaning on the wall near the exit, swatting at gnats that hadn't yet realized that it was fall and time for them to leave. The lot was surrounded by trees, but because the leaves were nearly all gone, they had a lovely view of the mountains.

"You're blessed to have them back, you know," said Carol. "Your family, I mean."

Sally said, "They revived John first. Some of his writings are still in print, and he was quite famous in his day."

"And he was much older than you," Carol said slyly.

"Much. He was such a large figure. You know, I think he's much happier here where he is less celebrated."

Carol pulled out a cigarette and lit it. She said, "Don't tell Tom—he thinks I quit."

Sally continued, "He insisted that we be brought back with him, but the gentlemen at Ahearn Industries were reluctant to revive Meg."

"Why?"

Sally ran her fingers through her long blond hair. She whispered, "They thought that she was a risk."

"A risk?"

"To herself. They didn't want to use the resources required unless they had some reassurance that she would not…"

Carol understood. "That's why she meets with that funny little man every few weeks."

Sally nodded. "Yes. Mr. Johnson."

"Wow. I thought that he was just interviewing her because she is so young."

"That's what she thinks, too."

Carol led Sally over to the far edge of the cracked parking lot. She pointed into the woods and said, "That's where Danny and I used to meet up. My house was down the way a bit, but the trail hooked up right over here."

Sally sighed. "That was not the way that John and I courted. He only visited me while in the company of my parents."

"Tom and I might as well be meeting in the woods. He thinks that he's keeping it all a secret from Carrie, but she knows. Of course she knows."

"Carrie's a little headstrong," said Sally. "But she'll warm up to you over time."

"Maybe," said Carol. "Anyway, that's not why we're here."

"Why are we here, then?"

"I have a business proposal for you."

15

Bear Steaks

"This may be the finest steak I've ever had," said Sam. "And I've had a lot in my time."

He sat near the house on one of the wooden crates from the basement, devouring a jigsawed piece of bear flesh he had toasted in the fire pit blazing hypnotically in front of him. It was dark, and he was nervous that only one of the pits was in use, but their new friend assured them that one massive fire pit was enough to scare off the giant beasts that were likely watching them as they spoke. The massive conflagration used by the last team was, according to the stranger, overkill and probably the result of panic and lack of experience.

Oscar, seated next to Sam, cut a huge chunk of meat from his steak and tore at it. He said, "I feel like a real hunter, Sam. Like a cowboy on the range or something."

Sam grunted.

"Does bear meat always taste this good? It's sort of…sweet," Oscar said.

"I've never had it before. I think a skunk would taste great right about now, though. We haven't really eaten in days."

The stranger was wearing a blue Ahearn Industries jumpsuit. His old outfit, clearly an old military uniform of some type, was worn and filthy. Sam was able to find some hiking shoes in one of the crates that fit him. Although he was a fairly tall man, possibly taller than Oscar, his feet were only a size ten. Out of uniform and dressed as a team member, he looked like any of the scrappy young military men who joined Sam's crew.

Sam said, "We want to thank you again for saving our lives."

The young man nodded. "I thought that you folks were out of luck when I missed the beast. I don't know why I even tried to fire again, but I was astonished to see that your weapons somehow hold more than one ball."

"We were happy, too, son," said Sam. "We'll get you a weapon, and I'll have Oscar show you how to load it—I don't think you need any instruction on how to operate it."

The night seemed even blacker and colder than the last, but the men collected a number of dry branches and roots on their way back from the mudhole, and they had more than enough wood to last the night and much of the morning. The blaze shot up into the sky and crackled loudly with each added branch. Sam was reminded of youthful camping trips with his father on the shore of a particular lake in Wyoming. The company was good, and Sam felt more relaxed than he had since Wallace had vanished.

"How did you come to be buried in that meadow, son?" asked Sam.

The man stood next to the fire, a plate made from a wooden plank in one hand and a sharp knife in the other. He said, "I'm not really sure. The last memory that I have involves crossing the great river; our raft smashed against rocks, and we were forced to swim for our lives. I remember striking many of the stones, and I recall slipping under the water..."

"You were crossing a river?" asked Sam.

"Yes, sir, a great one. We searched for quite a while to find a shallow enough spot."

Sam said, "I guess it wasn't as shallow as you thought."

"The great danger turned out to be the current, not the depth."

Oscar said, "Your friend must have dragged you to shore and buried you. How far away is this river?"

"I wouldn't know, sir; I must have been unconscious. Fendy must have thought that I was dead and must have buried me alive."

Sam and Oscar looked at each other. Oscar said, "Look, about that…"

"We'll talk about that later, Oscar, when…what is your name?"

"My name is Micajer Barclay, sir," he said. "I recently served Major Croghan at Fort Stephenson."

"Well, soldier, I'm Sam Ahearn, and this is Oscar Larsen, and we are delighted to have met you."

Young Barclay looked them over. When his eyes met Oscar's, there was darkness between them, and Sam was sure it might end badly. Sometimes Oscar could be an ingrate. This boy just saved their lives.

"What do your friends call you?" asked Sam.

The young man was lost in his thoughts and did not respond.

Sam tried again. "Mr. Barclay, do you have a nickname?"

"What? Oh, I'm called Cager by most," he said. "There are more scandalous names associated with me, but they are generally not used in my presence."

"Well, Cager, what exactly were you and your friend doing crossing a river in this place?"

"We were separated from our comrades," said Cager, "and somehow stumbled into this new world. We explored much of the region before deciding to cross the water."

Sam grabbed another piece of meat torn from the bear's backside from a pile near the fire and placed it on a thick stick. He carefully positioned it on metal shelving the men had set up inside the pit before they had started the fire. He stepped away from the heat, which was more than gently singing his skin, and bit into his meal. The meat was a little dirty, and there might have been some hair on it, but it was the tastiest piece of flesh that he had ever consumed.

"Anyone see those eyes?" Oscar said.

He pointed to a spot near the edge of the woods. Two twinkling objects that could have been large eyes were indeed staring down at them from a location on top of a small hill. They all watched with interest until the eyes, or whatever, seemed to disappear into the woods.

"Well, Mr. Barclay?" asked Sam.

Cager said, "It was likely an animal, though it was too small to be another bear. It may have been one of those cats that scamper around this place."

"What cats?" asked Oscar.

"They're quite large, though they are not quite the size of a bear. But there are many animals hunting these woods—it could be anything."

Sam said, "But the fire will definitely keep them away?"

"The only animal that will come close to this fire is a human animal."

Sam turned his steak over. It was dark now, but he was sure that the center of the cut was still red, and he didn't want to risk getting sick from undercooked meat in this jungle. He enjoyed the meal, but he knew that a bear-meat diet was not going to prevent starvation in this hellhole. People were known to starve to death on meat-only diets. *That's probably what killed Dr. Atkins*, he thought.

"Are there any edible fruits or vegetables around here? Wild berries, perhaps?" he asked.

Cager sat cross-legged on the grass near the fire. He was staring into the forest and thinking about something more important than his new comrades. He broke away from his memories and said, "Berries? Yes, there are plenty of them and some other plants that are easily consumed."

Sam said, "You say that there is a river, but I have the impression that it never rains here. Where does the water come from?"

Cager shook his head. "We went downriver and wound up here. The current came from the north, or what I think of as north, so I guess the source would be in that direction."

Sam realized that Oscar was sizing up their new friend again. Cager was tall and lanky and impressively fit. His hair had almost completely fallen out, but dark fuzz was already materializing across his skull. His facial features were chiseled in a way that Sam imagined ladies liked to see, but those same features could turn cruel and cold when left unguarded. Something about the man made Oscar wary, but Sam knew that his judgment was questionable where it concerned regenerated humans.

"Why are you looking at me like that, Mr. Larsen?" asked Cager.

"I'll look at you any way I wish," Oscar replied.

Cager eyed him coldly. "Mr. Larsen, how is it that you have no experience dressing a bear? Have you never hunted?"

"What?"

"Perhaps you are more accustomed to preparing the meat than making the kill?" Cager smirked.

"What are you implying?" demanded Oscar. "That I'm somehow weak because I've never gone hunting? I live right down the road from a Shop 'n Save, son. I don't need to hunt—they've got a *meat department*."

"Easy, Oscar," said Sam. He tried to recall another time when someone had actually baited Oscar like that, but he could not come up with any such memory. Only an idiot would willingly cross over to Oscar's bad side, but young Cager Barclay definitely seemed to enjoy toying with him. The kid seemed as though he had a little experience dealing with men like Oscar.

Something in the fire sparked, and the flames danced a little. Sam waited for the fire to settle and then pulled the steak out with his stick and dropped it on his plate. It was slightly burned and was sizzling, and he couldn't wait to tear into it. A part of him did feel like a cowboy on a long cattle drive just roughing it in the great outdoors. He looked up at the starless sky and wondered if he had wasted some of his life.

The big men were still staring each other down when Sam said, "So, you've never been here before?"

"No, sir," Cager replied, still stink-eyeing Oscar.

"Well, where were you when you entered this place?"

"We were in Virginia, Mr. Ahearn. We were avoiding some British and wound up here."

Sam snapped his fingers at Oscar, and the bodyguard reluctantly ended his staring contest with the young man. He pointed toward the field and said, "Oscar, he didn't come through our way—there's another entrance."

"Why is that important?" asked Oscar.

"Well, there's a chance that this hole is closed for good. It only stayed open for a little while this time, and that may be a sign that it's burned out."

"We don't know that it's burned out."

Sam said, "Look, it's an option. I'd like to get out of here as soon as possible—every day we spend here is more than a week Earthside. If Cager can direct us to another entrance..."

Oscar stood up and grabbed Sam's arm, nudging him away from their visitor and toward the entrance to the cabin. He spoke gently into his boss's ear. "We don't know anything about this kid...I know that he's a cocky son of a bitch, and that sets off alarms in my head."

"Weren't you a little cocky when you were his age?"

"Sam, he's about two hundred years old."

"You know what I mean. He saw you looking at him all tough, and apparently, he doesn't respond well to that kind of thing—maybe he's more like you than you know."

"I doubt that, Sam," replied Oscar. "I seriously doubt it."

16

James Wallace's Fate

Oscar slept better and woke up refreshed and excited. The Frankenstein kid was going to be a pain in the ass, but there was some good news. It never occurred to him that there might be another entrance, but the idea seemed obvious now. Why wouldn't there be more doorways spread throughout the Hole? The whole damn world was basically an unstable rift, anyway.

"I'm going to look at the generator this morning," Sam said. "Why don't you guys collect some wood and scout around a little more?"

Oscar felt sick. "I don't need his help, Sam."

There was anger in Sam's voice. "We both need his help. Why are you so ungrateful?"

Oscar said nothing.

Sam changed the subject. He said, "We should cook the rest of the meat now. It will spoil if we don't, and I don't have the refrigerator working yet."

They ate in front of the fire again. The bear meat wasn't refrigerated, and that probably had an effect on the flavor, but Oscar guessed bear meat just didn't taste good in the morning. He never ate toast for dinner, and he never drank whiskey with breakfast. Some foods should only be prepared at appropriate times, and bear meat was one of them.

Still, the men ate all of the remaining steaks. It was clear now that no one was coming to their rescue any time soon, and nobody was opening a Burger King across the street from them. Any available food had to be devoured quickly because there was no telling when the next meal was going to come along.

After a quiet breakfast, Oscar said, "Do you think that you can fix the generator?"

"I don't really know. They had two techs on the team capable of extensive repairs, but maybe something happened to them before the generator died. Maybe they weren't ready for the bears and the cats..."

Oscar looked at Cager. "You want to scout around with me a little?"

"Not really," said Cager. "But I will."

Sam pointed toward the center of the field and said, "You might as well look for Mr. Wallace. Perhaps he's still around somewhere."

Oscar started walking away, and Cager followed him stiffly. They were already walking in an unofficial formation, with Oscar taking the lead. He wondered if the real Cager, the one who was buried years ago, was as cocky as this kid. He probably would have liked that one.

He pointed at the location that used to be the Hole. They walked around the spot and looked for signs of a struggle or a panic. More accustomed to the dim lighting of the Hole, Oscar noted brown stains on the grass that might have been blood. There were only a few drops, and any one of the men might have bled a little when they awkwardly landed Holeside. Still, it was the closest thing there was to a clue about Mr. Wallace's disappearance.

"Do you see the footprints?" asked Cager.

"What footprints?" Oscar replied.

"Right there. Do you see the way the grass bends, and the ground is no longer in balance? A footprint doesn't always bear the shape of a foot."

Oscar could see it now. The grass was sort of off balance in a nonrandom sequence that led away from the cabin and toward the far woods. He checked his rifle to make sure that the safety was off and started down the now-visible path. Cager stood beside him, his gun locked and loaded.

Cager said, "I should lead—I am more accustomed to the area."

Oscar shook his head and followed the trail to the edge of the meadow. He stepped into the brush and felt almost swallowed by the dense collection of plants, trees, and dirt. The mild sunlight was almost completely obscured by the foliage, and he immediately lost sight of James Wallace's trail. He glanced behind him and saw Cager a foot or so behind him; his eyes were gazing in all directions, and he was coolly gripping his weapon with both hands.

"Do you still see the footprints?" he asked.

Cager smiled. "Don't you?"

"Don't be a smartass, son. Do you still see Mr. Wallace's trail?"

"His prints are gone, Mr. Larsen, but there are other, *heavier* prints right here," said Cager. He pointed at the ground, but all that Oscar could see was a few small branches and a flat patch of earth.

"Well, which direction are the heavy prints going in?"

Cager said, "It's that way. Whatever was following your friend wasn't looking to develop a friendship with him…"

"I got it—now let's go," replied Oscar. "You, uh, can lead the way."

It didn't take long to find the location of James Wallace's last stand. His blood-splattered rifle lay on the ground in the center of one of the mini-clearings that the men had run into while mapping the mudholes near the lodge. There was no other sign of struggle, which indicated that whatever beast took him out did so pretty quickly. Oscar hoped that he hadn't suffered too much.

"What did this—one of those bears?" asked Oscar.

Cager started to respond, but his attention turned to something lying on the ground a few feet away from Wallace's weapon. He approached it warily and prodded the dark object with the point of his rifle. It was about eighteen inches long and was covered with dirt, but the two men knew what it was immediately. It was covered in the ripped sleeve of an Ahearn Industries jumpsuit.

"Oh, Lord," said Oscar. "It's his arm."

He bent over and, after a brief hesitation, picked up the appendage and examined it. It was stiff, surprisingly heavy, and was only just beginning to smell. The end of the limb that should have been attached to a shoulder looked as though it had been half incised, half torn from Wallace's body. The hand, though very dark now, looked like any other hand; he could make out the fingerprints and the lines on the hand that a palm reader would have examined to divine his life expectancy.

Oscar pulled the sleeve up a little and examined Wallace's digital wrist watch. It was brightly colored on its face, and the band was black with a silver clasp. It was still working, though it was incorrectly indicating that it was currently five-thirty in the afternoon. The watch had several useful applications that included an altimeter, a barometer, a thermometer, and most importantly, a digital compass. He unhooked the thing and removed it from Wallace's arm.

"Are you a grave robber now, Mr. Larsen?" asked Cager. "That is not your property."

"The only grave that I've robbed lately is the one that belonged to the *real* Micajer Barclay. This watch here is Ahearn property and may help us get out of this hellhole."

"You are implying that I'm not real?"

"I don't know what you are, but I know that you're an abomination before God. You're supposed to be dead, but you come crawling out of that lake of stinking mud like some modern-day Lazarus."

"I am no abomination, sir," said Cager. "I saved your life."

Oscar flung Wallace's arm at Cager's feet. He said, "I'd rather be dead than be beholden to some soulless outrage who calls himself a human."

Cager tossed his rifle aside, slammed his right fist into the temple of the older man, and swung a left at the other side of Oscar's head. Oscar dodged that blow, stepped back, and side-kicked Cager in the stomach. Cager stumbled slightly backward, breathing painfully, then recovered and threw another right straight into Oscar's jaw. Oscar hit the leafy ground but managed to roll out of the way as Cager tried to stomp on his chest.

Oscar clambered to his feet and slipped another roundhouse from his foe. He started throwing jabs to back Cager up enough to have room for a roundhouse kick that landed just above Cager's ear. Shockingly, Cager did not go down but instead tackled Oscar and dragged him to the ground. He was stronger than Oscar but perhaps not as nimble and not as well trained. The pair rolled about, head-butting and kneeing each other in tender spots until fatigue from the battle slowed them.

They pulled away from each other and struggled to their feet; both men were worn, but Oscar felt himself gasping for air. Cager didn't look as tired.

There was motion coming from the bushes, and both men looked around for their weapons. Suddenly, a four-and-a-half-foot animal burst into the clearing and stared at them curiously. Its small head and long neck led down to a massive feathery torso that vaguely resembled that of an ostrich. The blue-and-red-colored bird gobble-squawked angrily at the two men, who were stunned by its arrival, and took a few bold steps in their direction; it appeared to be preparing to attack.

"Is that a turkey?" Oscar asked.

17

Cleaning a Giant Turkey

Sam saw his men moving slowly across the field. They were dragging something very large and were struggling with the weight of the object. *Wallace,* he thought. *They've found the remains of the poor soldier.* As they grew closer, though, it became obvious that they were not burdened with the remains of James Wallace but were instead laboring to pull some large animal into camp.

He went out the door and passed the still-burning fire pit to wait for the men. He raised his arm and said, "Welcome home."

The men looked like hell. Oscar's face was bruised, and a small cut below his eye was still bleeding. Cager's face looked similar, although the wounds were faded, and he was not wincing and limping the way Oscar was. Sam expected that the boy would be better by morning.

"What is that?" he asked as they approached the entrance.

Oscar sounded almost giddy. "We think it's a turkey—a two-hundred-pound turkey."

Cager said, "We wanted to clean it out there, but there are so many wild animals that might want to take it away from us."

"Do you know how to clean a turkey?" asked Sam.

"Of course, Mr. Ahearn," replied Cager. "How can you men *not* know how to do such things?"

Sam said, "We have other talents...watch this."

Sam walked across the grass and up the steps. He reached inside the doorway and flicked the switch for the outdoor light. The bulb glowed nicely in the dim afternoon light, and Sam said, "How's that?"

Cager stepped back and said, "How is that possible?"

"Surely, you've heard of Mr. Franklin's experiments with electricity, son? We've come a long way since then."

"Great job, Sam. Is everything working?" said Oscar, dreaming of a hot shower.

"We're at about fifty percent right now. The boiler's not working yet, but I think I can get it."

"How?" asked Oscar.

Sam said, "The generator wasn't as damaged as we thought. The hydrogen cell wasn't installed properly."

Oscar was reflexively rubbing the cut below his eye. Sam eyed him suspiciously, but he just shook his head. He obviously felt no need to discuss all of the morning's activities with his employer. Anyway, whatever happened out there was between Oscar and Cager.

"We still have some of that mud stuff in the lodge?"

Sam nodded. "Upstairs in the bathroom."

"Is the water running now?"

"The plumbing was turned off from the inside, and the well seems to be working, although the water's a little rusty."

"The toilet's running?" Oscar asked.

"Both of them."

Oscar Larsen almost danced a jig. He recovered and said, "That's great. I'll be right back. Toilet paper?"

"I collected some leaves…"

He strolled into the house and disappeared from view. Sam turned his attention to Cager and said, "Is that really a turkey?"

"I think so, sir," answered Cager. "Or something like it."

"That's great. I found some cellophane, and the refrigerator's working now; we can store the meat for quite a while."

Cager didn't ask what a refrigerator was.

The two men dragged the giant bird toward the side of the house and contemplated the cleaning process. Sam brought a small metal table out from the cellar that was able to hold the considerable weight of the bird, and Cager went to work on it. He sliced the creature open and began removing various disgusting pieces of flesh and gizzards. When he finished pulling its insides out of the body, he asked for a bucket of warm water. Sam got the bucket and the men rinsed the bird's plumage and began plucking its feathers. Sam didn't mind the plucking aspect of the cleaning process, but he wasn't very interested in the more surgical facets of the job.

Finished, Cager began to cut large chunks of flesh, and Sam reluctantly offered to help. His filets were not as professional-looking as those of the young soldier, but he thought that they weren't too bad. Once again, he had the recollection of camping with his dad, and he suddenly remembered that he missed his father. Usually, he kept thoughts of the great man from his mind, as the memories were often so painful.

"So, the turkey beat you guys up, huh?" Sam asked.

Cager paused then said, "The bird put up quite a fight."

"Uh-huh."

Oscar appeared, and he looked as though he had just stepped out of a shower. His hair wasn't any cleaner, but it seemed more controlled, and he had slipped out of a blue jumpsuit and into a gray one. Sam didn't see the point in a cold, soapless shower, but he knew that Oscar liked to stay clean—he was obsessed with hygiene. The big man's puffy face already looked less battered, and Sam knew that just a few more applications of mud would have him looking as good as new.

Cager pointed casually at Oscar. "Mr. Larsen seems to believe that I am not human—is that true?"

Sam shot his bodyguard a look. "Did he call you an abomination?"

Cager did not reply.

"Don't worry—he thinks that two-ply toilet paper is an abomination. He's got to buy a thesaurus and find some new words."

Oscar broke in. "I may have spoken in haste, Mr. Barclay."

Cager stopped carving the turkey and said, "Did you?"

"You saved my life and that of my best friend, and I thanked you by hurling insults at you. You deserve far better than that, and I hope that you could perhaps forgive me."

Cager deliberated for a few seconds and then said, "There is nothing to forgive, Mr. Larsen. It is possible that I may have goaded you on to some degree."

"Why don't you guys hug or kiss or something, and let's put this behind us, OK?" said Sam.

The men were not interested in hugs but compromised and shook hands briskly. Sam tried to remember another time that Oscar had apologized to anyone and could not think of anything. His friend lived his life by a certain code and made no excuses for his actions. Clearly, Oscar felt that he had crossed a line this time, and he was embarrassed.

Sam said, "Look, now that we're all friends again, I think that we have some decisions to make."

"What decisions?" asked Oscar.

"It wasn't wild animals that took all of the equipment from the cabin. I'm guessing that the house has had two-legged visitors. Did you and your friend ever run into humans, Cager?"

Cager shook his head.

"I imagine that all of the damn fire pits probably attracted somebody, and our guys must have gone off with them. Why else would so much stuff be missing?"

Oscar said, "You want to track them down?"

"Maybe," said Sam. "But I don't think there's a hurry or anything. I think that we should stay here for a while and get our bearings. If humans took all of our stuff, then they must have left a trail, and I bet Mr. Barclay here could follow it."

Cager said, "It rarely rains here, and there is no change of seasons to wear away a trail. Any path left by men will last for quite a while."

"Even one that was years old?" asked Sam.

"Perhaps."

Sam said, "I say we stay here for a while and sort of fatten up. If the Hole reopens, then we have a way out. Otherwise, we look for our team, and then maybe Cager can lead us to the other opening."

Oscar said, "You're the boss, Sam."

Sam looked at the young soldier. He asked, "What about you, Cager?"

"I have no other plans, Mr. Ahearn."

"Good. I think we ought to clean up our mess here and get that fire roaring. Night comes early here."

From the Diary of Margaret Dearborn:

May 16, 1813, Sunday

Micajer has not returned, and I have accepted the cold truth that he is gone forever, though my heart insists that he still lives. Father continues to bring Mr. Martel into the house, but I refuse to even speak to the man. My parents may be blind to his lies, but I am not. The terrible silence in this house is almost too much to bear, and I must put an end to it once and for all. There is only one thing for me to do…

18

Sunday Morning Visit

"Mr. William Daly invited me to a movie show today," said Meg.

Carrie, lying on her bed, turned to face her cousin. "What did you say?"

Meg was sitting on the edge of her own bed and was busily filing her nails. Her nails grew at a faster rate than her hair did, and she was running out of nail files trying to keep them under control. *How long is it going to take for her hair and nails to calm down?* Carrie wondered.

She said, "I told him that I'm already involved."

Carrie wrinkled her freckled nose and said, "You can't keep chasing ghosts, Meg. Will is a very nice boy."

Meg shrugged and went back to her nails.

Carrie almost said something else but was distracted by loud knocking on the door. She said, "Come in."

Her father poked his head in. "You ladies have a visitor downstairs."

"Who is it?" asked Carrie.

"It's Mr. Johnson, Meg, and he'd like to speak to both of you."

The girls exchanged glances and headed for the stairs. Carrie knew that it could only be about one thing, but she decided to keep quiet just in case she was wrong. Meg seemed almost uninterested; she liked Mr. Johnson, but she did not like being grilled about every aspect of her life by the man. Who was he to tell Meg how to run her life?

The Heath family room was, like all others in the house, oversize, and was mockingly referred to as the "Great Room" by the family. Tom Heath came up with the nickname after watching an episode of *Lifestyles of the Rich and Famous.* The Great Room was an odd blend of darks and lights, and most people enjoyed the contrast. There were several cushiony chairs and seats and one very long sofa bed. A massive picture window peered out onto the driveway and then into the forest. There were several colorful paintings and some family portraits on the walls and tables, none of which bore the image of Carrie's mother. Her father's pride and joy, after his family, was his impressive seventy-two-inch high-definition television, which he only used for watching his favorite sports teams. Carrie's computer was on a small desk in the near corner of the room.

"Hello, Mr. Johnson," said Meg.

Mr. Johnson was seated in front of the computer, his fingers tapping on the keyboard at an almost leisurely rate. The little man turned slightly to smile at the girls and then returned to the computer screen. He was a well-dressed man with thinning hair and dark skin. Carrie noted that his strong-looking hands were manicured, and she wondered why a man would do such a thing. He was stocky, though, and there was a toughness about him that he always tried to hide. She knew that Meg liked him.

Meg's parents were sitting stiffly on the burgundy-colored couch looking quite confused. Her father stood beside them, a cup of coffee in his hand, his plaid shirt spotted with grease. Carrie glanced at her uncle and saw that he was also wearing a raggedy, grease-splattered shirt and guessed that the men must have been working on the motorcycle when Mr. Johnson arrived. Aunt Sally was wearing a fashionable yellow-and-green dress with a matching bow in her blond hair. She appeared more suited for a television interview than for a lazy Sunday morning at the Heath household.

"I hear you're becoming quite a coach, Mr. Dearborn," said Mr. Johnson.

Uncle John nodded and looked almost embarrassed.

Carrie's dad said, "He comes up with the damnedest plays—he has a future if he wants it."

"What's going on?" Carrie interrupted.

Mr. Johnson swiveled the chair around and said, "I'm sorry to disrupt your Sunday morning, but this is an important matter."

The girls were both in T-shirts and jeans. Meg had finally given in to Carrie and Marissa and had begun to wear comfortable pants on the weekends. She still refused to dress so informally during school hours, but she was now willing to dress down at home. Aunt Sally probably didn't approve, but she didn't object.

"Have we done something wrong?" Carrie asked. Behind Mr. Johnson, through the great window, leaves were blowing erratically, and the flag hanging from the barn was bouncing crazily. *A storm must be coming*, thought Carrie.

"I don't think so—at least not exactly." Mr. Johnson smiled. "Do you girls know anything about this website?"

He pressed a key, and a picture of a Georgian-style colonial house popped up on the screen. The home had three stories, the top one featuring pediment window caps; there were two chimneys on the rooftop, and a bit of smoke seemed to be leaking almost unnoticed from the one on the right. The doorway had small columns on either side, and the door itself was engraved with a type of fruit. Perhaps a pineapple. The house was yellow.

Uncle John said, "The trees behind the house are all wrong, and there were some hills to the north. But the house is very close—very close."

Aunt Sally stood up and stared at the computer. She absently touched the screen and rubbed her finger uneasily across one of the elegant top windows. Her husband was beside her, and he gently tugged her away from the machine. She did not resist his touch. Carrie thought that was odd.

Tom said, "What is that?"

Above the house, the screen read, "Pardon our appearance while we are under construction."

Uncle John said, "That is—that was our home in Stamford."

Aunt Sally asked, "Who drew that portrait of our house?"

"Marissa drew it, Mother," said Meg. "I described it, and she sketched it. She has quite a gift."

"And the website?" asked Mr. Johnson. "Retreadnews.com?"

"Is anyone going to get in trouble for setting up this website?" asked Meg. She didn't want Marissa or her colorful brother to get into any sort of trouble for helping her with the website. Truthfully, she could not imagine why Mr. Johnson was at all concerned about it.

"I don't think so," replied Mr. Johnson. "I'm just trying to get a feel for what's happening."

He clicked on the button marked "Rules for Retreads."

There was a pause, and then the screen was filled with these words:

Ten Rules for Retreads

1. *Retread* must have historical value.
2. *Retread* must have an offer of employment.
3. *Retread* must live with a host for at least two years.
4. *Retread* host must have sole claim of genealogical lineage.
5. *Retread* must renounce all financial ties to family estate.
6. *Retread* minors are not allowed to engage in school sporting events (exception made for intramural and non-school events).
7. *Retreads* are prohibited from joining any branch of the military unless called upon to do so.
8. *Retreads* do not have the right to vote in state, local, or federal elections.
9. *Retreads* are not allowed to testify in a court of law.
10. *Retreads* are unable to conceive or bear children.

Mr. Johnson read the list and nodded. He said, "Interesting. I'm impressed that you remembered so much, though you've left a few things out. And we're not sure about the last one…"

Carrie said, "It's a work in progress."

"Not anymore, Carrie," said her father angrily. "Who did this for you—Ryan?"

Meg said, "This was my idea, my responsibility."

Carrie barked, "That's crap, Meg. We did it together, and I don't see what's so wrong about it—we're just trying to set up an online community."

"May I see the house again?" asked Aunt Sally.

Mr. Johnson brought the screen back to the home page. He looked at Meg and said, "What things are you girls planning to do with this site?"

She replied, "We don't completely know yet. We have discussed something called a *sign-in page* and possibly, um, posting recent photographic portraits to share with people from our past lives."

Carrie said, "Sort of like Facebook for retreads and their friends."

"How did you find out about this site?" asked Tom. "It doesn't seem like they've gotten too far with it."

"Much of our project is in partnership with the Department of Historical Archives, and they pay people to be nosy. This site makes them a little nervous."

Aunt Sally's voice was shaky. "I don't like it at all. I want this *computer house* abolished. Now."

Carrie's father began, "Sally, I don't think..."

"I don't want Margaret to have to relive her past. Don't you understand that she might do something drastic?"

"What are you talking about, Mother?" Meg demanded. "What would I do?"

"I just don't want you leaving me again. I could not bear such a thing."

Meg was confused. "Why would I leave you by looking at a website?"

All eyes were on Meg and Aunt Sally as they talked freely for the first time in centuries. Carrie realized they were disconnected from the others in the room, as if they were in a glass box centered in the room but still separated from spectators. Her aunt, streaming tears now, forced herself to say, "I do not want you taking your own life again."

Shocked, Meg said, "Again? Do you think that I fell from that window on a whim? How could you think that I would do such a thing?"

Carrie, grasping her cousin's shoulder, whispered, "You mean that you didn't, you know, do it on purpose?"

"Do what?" Meg demanded.

Carrie could not bring herself to say the words, but she knew that Meg suddenly understood.

Meg wasn't sobbing, but tears trickled onto her cheeks. She said, "How could you think such a thing?"

Carrie took a breath, then said, "I've been waiting for the right time to tell you."

"Tell me what?"

Carrie said, "I have your diary."

19

The Diary of Margaret Dearborn

Carrie dug through the bottom drawer of her dresser, tossing several sweatshirts and some pajamas aside, and pulled the black leather-bound manuscript from the back. It wasn't particularly large, no bigger than an average hardcover novel, and the dark cover had no visible lettering. Carrie remembered crying over the book so many times and suddenly realized that she didn't want to give it up. Her hands trembled as she handed the journal over to its author.

"I had a goose-feather quill," Meg said. "I sat at my desk late at night and poured my spirit into this manuscript."

Meg sat on the floor between their beds. She looked at her cousin and said, "How did you come across this?"

"When I was little, we used to visit my grandmother in Boston. When I was eight, she came to me and said that I should have it so that I could have an appreciation of our family's history."

Carrie's colorful cell phone vibrated annoyingly. She turned the thing off and put it on her desk without concern for the caller. Anyone important would call back later.

Meg was skimming the pages as old memories physically shook her slender frame. She said, "What did you think of it?"

"I couldn't really understand the words at first—you wrote so, um, lyrically. But as I got older I really came to empathize with it. You were so happy at first, and then your friend..."

"Cager, his name was Cager," said Meg. "I loved him—I *still* love him."

"Yes, he left, and he didn't return, and then you were so sad," Carrie said, "They never found him, you know. They never knew what happened to him or his friend."

"Oh, *someone* knew," replied Meg. "A coward."

The girls were side by side now, each staring into the pages of history together. Carrie had read the book more times than she could remember, but the words always had new meaning upon rereading. The pages were yellowed, but the script was as clear as Margaret Dearborn's memories. Meg put the book down and pushed it away.

Carrie said, "What's wrong?"

"I don't know if it really is mine, do I?"

"Don't be silly, Meg," said Carrie. "Of course it's yours."

"I may look like Margaret, and I have her memories, to be sure, but I'm not really her, am I? I'm just an expensive reproduction of that person—the diary belongs to you, not me."

Carrie shook her head furiously, her strawberry hair flopping wildly into her eyes and across her freckled nose. She grabbed her cousin's arm firmly and said, "I don't know exactly how it works, but I know that you aren't a copy—you're more like a restoration. You have the same frame, but your outside has been touched up a little."

Meg forced a weak smile.

Carrie said, "Look at the last entry in the book. I think that you will understand why everyone thought what they thought."

The last entry was barely halfway through the available pages. When she got to the end, she read the last line out loud, "There is only one thing for me to do…"

Meg nodded as she read the entry again and then smiled. "I guess I can see why Mother—and everyone else—might have gotten the wrong impression."

The room was suddenly quiet enough to hear the voices of the adults downstairs as well as the hum of the downstairs boiler that generously warmed the house. A kind of whistle drifted in from outside that had to be from the crazy wind blowing across the mountain. *The weather fits,* thought Carrie.

Meg said, "I suppose I should go speak to my parents and straighten out this confusion."

Carrie looked away and focused on a photograph of her mother hanging on the wall. Katie Heath was a little taller than Carrie, but there was a strong resemblance, though not as strong as the one between Meg and Aunt Sally. Carrie allowed herself to miss her mother briefly, then pushed the thought away. Forget her and her crazy black room. Today was about Meg.

She said, "Meg, I'm sorry that I read your diary. I haven't opened it since I found out that you were coming here."

"It's OK to read someone's diary if they've been dead for two hundred years, Carrie. I would have done the same thing."

"Meg, can I ask you something?"

"Of course."

"What was he like, really? I picture him sort of like Johnny Depp but not as weird."

Meg looked at her cousin, but she was really peering back into her locked memories of lost love and sour disappointment. Carrie guessed that Meg had no idea she was brushing her hair again; the gentle strokes soothed the sting of her thoughts enough for her to search for the right words. Meg wanted to tell her something, but it was hard for her.

"I'm sorry," said Carrie.

Meg shook her head and said, "He was much brawnier than your Mr. Depp—and younger, too. His dark hair was too long for Father's taste, but the other girls seemed to like it."

"Did he chase you, or did you chase him?"

Meg wrinkled her nose. "It wasn't like that, really."

"Well, how did you meet?"

"We grew up together, in a fashion. His family was wealthy, but his father was belatedly discovered to have been a British collaborator in the war, and he fled the country. Cager never saw him again."

"Maybe that's what happened to my mother," said Carrie sadly. "Maybe she had no choice."

"You'll see her again, Carrie. I'm sure of it."

Carrie said, "What else? Was he quite handsome?"

"I shall describe him to Marissa when I'm ready, and she will paint a portrait."

Meg stood up and walked toward the door. She turned to Carrie, who was now standing, and said, "I want to tell you something that you won't understand."

"OK."

"I never believed that Cager was dead," she said. "I always thought that he would find his way back to me."

Carrie said, "Of course you felt that way."

"Carrie, I still feel that way."

Shaking her head, Carrie replied, "I don't understand."

Meg's voice was almost a whisper. "I still feel him, Carrie. I know you can't understand, but I still don't believe that he's gone."

Meg turned the knob and left the room.

20

Meg's Story

"I'm only going to tell this story once," said Meg. "I want everyone to hear it now so that there is no confusion."

She sat stiffly between her parents on the burgundy sofa as she began to speak. Her mother appeared composed now, though Meg knew she was closer to a meltdown than she would have it appear. Her eyes were glazed and puffy, and her breathing was forced. Meg's father reached across his daughter's lap and grasped his wife's hand.

Mr. Johnson stood beside the computer, sipping from a glass of fresh lemonade, probably wishing there was something strong mixed into the drink. Uncle Tom and Carrie stood awkwardly near the entrance to the room, Uncle Tom's arm firmly wrapped around Carrie's quivering shoulder. Everyone wanted to hear Meg's story, but the truth seemed daunting to her. Her final memories were so private to her, and now she had to tell everyone about that last day.

"I did not jump from the window that afternoon," she began. "I believe suicide to be a mortal sin, and as such, I know that I would be separated forever from my family and from Cager Barclay, my one true love, if I committed such an act."

Her mother said, "But we found you on the ground, and the window was open."

Meg shook her head slowly. She looked around the room and saw that all eyes were raptly focused on her, and it made her profoundly uncomfortable. A pale bird was either flying past the window or was being blown around by the crazy wind. She decided that it was half flying and half blowing and recognized a kindred soul in the bird.

"I did not go to church that day, as was my custom at the time, and instead, I spent the day alone. I remember that I took a brisk walk along the trail that led past that small pond. It was an enjoyable walk; as I remember, the day was quite beautiful—it was unseasonably warm, and the sky was cloudless. I returned home and read for a time," Meg said, speaking of the day as though the events had occurred just a few months ago. She paused for a moment. Were these memories even hers, or were they just chalkboard writings left over from another class? Perhaps she should just clean the board off and move on with her own life.

"At some point that morning, I heard the most horrendous sound, like some strange animal calling for help," she continued.

"Of course, it was no wild creature, exactly, but was instead *Mr. Joshua Martel*, attempting to serenade me." Meg looked directly at her father when she mentioned Joshua. His cheeks burned red at the mention of the name, and a look of realization turned to one of great sadness and, perhaps, guilt.

She continued. "It was, I think, a song by Thomas Moore, though he sang it so terribly that I cannot be certain. And he was dressed as a fool, in frilly cloth, and he wore a strange hat that made him seem even more of a fop. I opened the door, and he stared at me so lovingly, concentrating on the words and the tune. I interrupted him and told him to leave unless he chose to finally disclose the information that he was so obviously keeping from me."

Meg said, "He sort of bowed to me—I remember the movement so clearly—and then he told me that he was ready to tell me of Cager's fate. He said that the price for his truth would be a gentle kiss."

Carrie said, "Oh my God! He was a stalker."

"Maybe, I don't know. I told him that I would determine whether his story merited a kiss of any kind and that he would have to wait to receive his reward."

Her mother turned to her. "You know that was very inappropriate behavior, Margaret. A young lady never offers such rewards to a young man, especially when unaccompanied."

Meg smiled slightly at her mother and said, "I think that you are right about that, Mother. I should have bolted the doors and looked for Father's rifle."

"What did he tell you?" asked Carrie.

"His story made very little sense. He said that he and Cager and another man came upon some invisible cave that just pulled their friend away from them. He said that Cager leaped after the other man, leaving the *courageous* Mr. Joshua Martel alone and confused. He said that the horses were frightened and that they ran away and that in the madness that followed, the cave just went away."

Mr. Johnson wheeled the computer chair closer. "This cave, did he describe it? Was it like a tear in a wall?"

"I'm not sure, Mr. Johnson."

"Where was it? Not Arizona."

"Of course not, Mr. Johnson. I've only just learned about that state. He said that it was in Virginia and that he could show me the exact location if only I would grant him his wish."

Uncle Tom said, "Why is this cave or whatever important to you, Mr. Johnson? Surely, it was just some silly story that he hoped would impress Meg enough to give him a kiss."

"I don't know any more about his tale," said Meg. "I told him that I did not believe him and that it was time for him to go home. He grabbed me and told me that I owed him a kiss and much more, and that was when I realized that I was in danger.

"I tripped him easily, as he was not particularly athletic, and I kicked the side of his knee as I ran into the house. He was much faster than I would have thought, probably because he had experience running away from things, and almost caught me on the staircase. I kicked him again, and he fell down a few stairs, giving me enough time to reach the window at the top of the staircase."

"Stop, please—just stop," said her mother. "I don't think that I can bear any more of this story."

"You wanted to know, Mother."

Her mother said, "The window was open that day because I left it open, and I have been haunted by that memory ever since. Perhaps you would not have climbed through if only it had been left unopened."

"Mother, I almost escaped. I climbed through the window and was upon the ledge when I slipped. It happened so slowly, it seemed; I was wearing shoes that were not designed for climbing, and they just would not grab the narrow ledge by the window. The last thing that I remember from that day was looking down at my feet and thinking that I needed new shoes.

"And then I must have fallen, though I do not recall it at all. Thankfully."

Expecting a dramatic silence, Meg was surprised to see the Great Room erupt in agitated conversation. Everyone was standing now and involved in some sort of discussion with somebody. She saw her cousin speaking hurriedly with Uncle Tom, who had somehow managed to find and open a bottle of Coors Light; Carrie was smiling and crying simultaneously. Meg's parents were jabbering at her, but she was not up for their questions yet. Mr. Johnson was out of his chair, cell phone in hand, heading out the door.

Her father took her hand. "Mr. Martel was a pallbearer, my dear. He visited us often."

Sally nodded. "John left him a considerable sum of money."

Meg said, "You never suspected?"

John answered, "If I had any idea, then I would surely have hanged the man in our front yard. I can assure you of that."

Meg said, "Is it OK if I just go to my room now? It's been an exciting afternoon."

"Me too," said Carrie, who obviously planned to pump Meg for more information.

Meg saw her father looking around and followed his line of sight. She briefly glimpsed her mother near the stairs just outside of the Great

Room. Meg heard the front door open, then close, and she glanced through the window to see where Sally might be going. The wind was still roughly tossing branches and lawn chairs around the backyard.

Her father said, "Of course, ladies, but first…Margaret, may I have a word?"

He led her halfway up the carpeted steps and gave her a familiar smile—a smile from long ago. He said, "So much of your makeup favors Sally, thank goodness, but you have my spirit, the same spirit that proved so useful against fat King George's armies."

"Mother says that often."

His face was pale, and his voice was deadly serious. "I'm so sorry, Margaret. I should have been…I don't know…I should have been different."

She squeezed his hand. "You were doing what you thought was right. In retrospect, I think that what you did and said was right, in a way. How could you suspect that Joshua Martel was so foul or that Cager was so upright?"

"I should have known, Margaret. Especially, I should have known about Micajer."

"I could have told you what happened the day that I woke up in that strange room in Boston," said Meg. "I chose to skirt the subject, and you respected that. I think that we should just start living in the present."

He glanced down the stairway toward the door.

Meg said, "Go talk to her, Father."

21

The Barn

John double-stepped the stairs and headed toward the weather-beaten barn. The wind reminded him of the wild ocean storms he had seen in the Carolinas after the war. Tom's prize grill was knocked over, and John stopped to straighten it. He crossed the driveway and looked into the barn's small side door for some glimpse of his wife. It was dark in there, and he saw no movement.

"Mr. Dearborn…"

He turned and saw Mr. Johnson trotting over to him. His strides were deliberate and had a military gait to them. John had long ago decided that the man was significantly more dangerous than first appearance would indicate. He was thickly proportioned and had the confident manner of a fighter. John decided that the best way to describe the man would be to call him a bulldog.

"We need to talk," Johnson hollered. "Perhaps in the barn?"

John nodded, and the two made their way inside the structure, closing the heavy door behind them to mute the ceaseless beat of the windstorm. The building smelled of grease and oil and was nothing like the barns that John remembered. Sally sat on a folding chair near Tom's old Harley; her eyes were puffy, and her hands were trembling. There was a long workbench that was covered with a variety of tools the men had been using to rebuild the vintage motorcycle. Tom's SUV was parked near the big door, and some camping equipment was piled in a corner beyond the vehicle. There was a second level that was rarely used by the adults but was at one time a favorite hiding spot for Carrie and her friends.

"Crazy weather," said Johnson.

John nodded.

Sally opened up two more chairs, and the men sat down. Johnson said, "I think I may have underestimated your daughter."

"Not just you, sir," said John.

Mr. Johnson had a way of talking that included everyone in the discussion. He looked at the Dearborns and said, "I shall report that she is no threat to herself or to our project. She appears to be a threat only to her soccer opponents."

Sally smiled. "Have you seen her play? I don't remember seeing you at her games."

"The thing is," Johnson began, avoiding her question, "her story about the invisible cave..."

"Well, clearly Joshua was concocting a story," said John. "The bastard."

Mr. Johnson said, "I would like to speak to her about that when she is ready for more questions."

John said, "I don't quite understand why, Mr. Johnson."

"And we don't want to upset her," added Sally. "It has been a dramatic time for her."

"I understand that, Mrs. Dearborn, but I think that she may have information that my company has been searching for. Life-and-death information."

"How could she have such information?" asked Sally.

Johnson said, "What do you know about Sam Ahearn, Mrs. Dearborn? Have you heard his name?"

"Of course," she answered. "He is the reclusive president of your company. We heard many stories about him while in hospital."

Sadness crept across Johnson's weary face. He said, "He's not reclusive, Mrs. Dearborn; that's just our, um, cover story. He's gone missing, and I think Meg may be able to help us."

"That seems unlikely, Mr. Johnson," said Sally.

"I know, but you should know that my company is unique in that most of us are quite close, closer than family sometimes. We lost some good men a few years ago, and your daughter might be able to help. I know my story sounds unlikely to you, but we would do anything to find them again."

"I promise you that we'll talk to her soon, Mr. Johnson," said John. "But not today."

"I appreciate that, Colonel."

John stood as the smaller man walked toward the exit. He shook John's hand and then turned to shake Sally's. He said, "You have a remarkable daughter, Mrs. Dearborn."

He opened the door, marched across the yard, and climbed into his car. The vehicle backed up slowly and turned onto the dirt road that led back into town. A tornado of dirt and dust surrounded the car as it moved away from them. John wondered how the man could even see to drive.

"What an interesting man," said Sally. "He would have been closer to normal height in our time, I think."

John said, "Don't underestimate him, my dear; he is a good man."

Sally grasped his hand. "So are you, John. You are a very good man."

Shaken, John replied, "I'm not certain about that. It appears that I was wrong about everything, and as a result, I may have been the cause of my daughter's death."

"You were trying to protect her. Everyone found Joshua's manner quite impressive," said Sally. "Myself included."

"Not Margaret."

"I think there is probably enough blame to go around, my dear. I just wish that we had been able to overcome the grief…"

John remembered his rages and the finger-pointing. He said, "I was so angry."

"I blamed you, John, and you knew it. Could you ever forgive me?"

Tears were slowly working their way down John's cheeks. He ignored them and said, "You were correct to blame me. You were right to stop..."

"Stop what?"

He paused, then said, "You were right to stop loving me. I was bitter and jealous..."

They were still standing near the door, and John took a step as though he were leaving. She grabbed his arm, which coursed with his familiar strength and passion. John halfheartedly attempted to pull away, but he knew that he did not want to be away from her. She wrapped her arms around him, and the two embraced.

"I think it's time that we stopped living in the past, my dear," she said. "I think it's time that we live up to our promise."

John said, "I want to be the man that you thought you married. I could not bear to lose you again."

Sally was crying and sort of laughing, too. John drank in her beauty as he had when he spotted her surrounded by young men at a masquerade ball so long ago. She knew of him, of course, but she had been such a lovely surprise, and he had chased her and practically bullied her family into allowing him into their home. She was so much younger than he, but she was like nothing he had ever seen before.

She reached for the back of his neck and then pulled his face toward her own. He placed his hand on her cheek, pushing her long locks to one side, and stared deeply into her eyes. She shook her head and kissed him ardently, and he returned her enthusiasm in kind.

John pulled away. "Do you want to go for a ride?"

"What? On the *motorcycle mobile?*"

He smiled. "Of course."

"In this weather?" Sally asked.

"Well, if you don't feel comfortable about it, we could do it another time."

"No," she said. "I only feel safe when my arms are around you."

He walked over to the big door and pressed the button for the automatic door opener. John pushed the Harley toward the exit and kick-started the machine until it erupted with a fury. She climbed on gracefully, wrapping her arms snugly around his waist, and whispered something into his ear. He couldn't understand her words, as they were competing with the roar of the engine and the howling of the wind, but he knew that they must be beautiful words.

Part II
(Living for the Present)

22

Game Trail

"I could use a shower," said Oscar. "A hot one."

Sam knew his friend hated the perspiration saturating his body and staining his blue Ahearn Industries jumpsuit. Oscar's hair was unkempt and long, though not as lengthy as Cager's crazy locks, and the growth of his facial hair was stemmed by the use of his very sharp knife. His body looked fit, though, thanks to frenzied training with his protégé and to the group's back-to-basics diet of fresh meat, berries, nuts, and roots.

"No showers for a while," said Sam. "You'll be okay."

The Ahearn men had lived safely for weeks in the lodge, but it was time to go. All of the mudholes had been mapped, and there were no repairs needed on the house. Finally, Sam declared, "The Hole isn't going to reopen anytime soon. It's time to look for Cager's entrance. Maybe that one's not burned out."

The men were hiking in a rough triangle formation down the game trail Cager had discovered while on a hunt. The hard soil was covered with slippery green vegetation and branches of various sizes that had fallen from the trees. Each was carrying a makeshift backpack of blankets, weapons, and plastic containers filled with water. They hoped to find springs along the way that would allow them to refill their crude canteens before they ran out.

The path widened and narrowed with regularity but was, on average, about fifteen yards wide. Invisible to Sam and Oscar, but apparently evident to their friend, were markings and faded footprints to and from their cabin that led deep into the woodlands north, if north even existed, of their home and onto the long path that led somewhat easterly toward…something. Sam worried that following a trail left by thieves might be a mistake, but hiding in the lodge was no sound strategy, either.

"This trail that we're following," Sam asked. "You think it's our stuff being hauled away?"

"I see signs of workhorses or, perhaps, oxen," Cager replied.

"Maybe some of our men have survived," said Sam. He hoped to find at least some of the men alive and in good health, but he feared the worst. If they had left of their own volition, then they would certainly have left a note or some hint of their plans.

Sam led, holding one of the torches directly in front of him. He had been able to forge a strong soap from lye and lard, taken from various wild animals Cager had killed. The leftover animal bits were used to create strong oil that burned protractedly and efficiently. The torches would hopefully scare off the enormous predators that hungrily prowled the woods. Hopefully.

Cager was marching closely beside Oscar, his rifle at the ready, scanning the forest at his side for anything that might be a danger to them or a clue about the missing men. Often, the foliage was so dense on either side of them that it was a virtual wall blocking them from any avenue of escape should they be attacked. At night, when they set up camp, they always made certain there was a nearby exit in case the campfires were not enough to scare off the natives. Of course, there was always the chance that an intruder might use that same exit as his entrance to their camp. The men slept in shifts and watched the forest intently.

"No decent person should have to wallow in sweat and dust like this," said Oscar. "I hate it."

"It's too late to turn back now, Oscar," said Sam, annoyed. "Maybe we'll find a lake or a pond somewhere."

"It's not the same," grumbled Oscar.

Cager continued scanning his flank. He said, "I've only seen the great river in my time here. I've found some small springs, and our well proves that there are underground currents, but I've never seen any real bodies of water other than the river."

"And we're running sort of parallel to the river now, separated by a few miles?" asked Sam.

"I think so," said Cager. "But I don't know how far Fendy and I traveled after my injury."

Cager had recently begun having memory flashes that led Sam to believe that the young man had traveled for quite some time after being injured. He spoke of his friend's arm propping him up and of the man's determined words of encouragement. Mainly, Cager spoke of an overwhelming sadness for being a burden to his friend.

"Stop for a break?" asked Sam.

The others agreed, and they paused to drink from their canteens. After all had finished, they sat down with their backs to one another in a close circle. The temperature was always cool in the Hole, and miles of hiking tended to tire even strong men. Sam knew that he would one day look back and relish the time spent with his friends as they explored the strange world, but that wouldn't be for a while.

"How long do you think this trail goes on for?" asked Sam.

Cager said, "I don't know—forever, possibly."

"It probably leads straight to the people we're following, Sam," said Oscar.

"No," said Cager. "It's a game trail of some kind. Occasionally I see faded markings on the soil. Something big used to run this trail."

Sam stood up. "Looking at the grass, I'd say it's been a long time since anything like that has traveled this path."

Cager said, "I agree."

Oscar wondered, "Why is the grass so wet? It hasn't rained in all the time we've been here."

"The plants seem to absorb the water from the fog, like in a cloud forest," answered Sam. "At least the moist air keeps the temp down."

The men resumed their triangle formation and started back down the path. Their military-style boots were top of the line and had been designed for terrain such as this. All conversation was kept to a minimum, as their ears were needed at least as much as their eyes. Sam glanced back at Cager and silently thanked God they had been fortunate enough to literally unearth the man. They weren't going to survive without him.

"You're going to work for me when we get back Earthside," said Sam. "Oscar and I are going to need you there."

"I'd be honored, Mr. Ahearn—just as soon as I've checked on Margaret."

The girl was never far from the poor boy's thoughts, Sam knew, and he could not help but admire the devotion. Ahearn had married once and had since soured on the whole template of marriage and family. He had decided to construct his own family from trusted friends such as Oscar, Mike Standish, Rufus Johnson, and a few others connected to the company. His Ahearn family would never disappoint him in the way that his own father had ultimately been a letdown. That was something that he had in common with Cager; it was clear that his father had betrayed a lot of people when he scurried across the ocean to live in England. Sam's father had avoided punishment, too.

"Margaret is John Dearborn's daughter?" asked Sam.

Cager nodded. "Yes, sir. He is a great man."

"I own a few of his books. *Courage and the Day* is quite an inspirational book...I learned a lot about leadership when I read it. Was he really so bold?"

"The colonel is the most valiant man I have ever met. He was quite kind to me before Margaret and I grew close."

Sam smiled. "Fathers don't like having that line crossed, Cager."

Cager cocked his head. He said, "Do you hear something?"

Oscar pointed straight ahead. There was a dark dot in the far distance that appeared to be slowly ambling toward them. The men squinted and twisted their heads as they watched the dot grow larger.

Sam wished that the sun was brighter and distant objects were clearer in the Hole. He thought that the whole damn world resembled an old black-and-white movie.

Cager calmly mentioned that the tree line was knotted with close-quartered vegetation. There was no room for them to slip into the woods, and there was nothing to use for cover. He pointed toward the nearest side and then slowly walked toward the impregnable forest. Sam held the torch up high, which either made them an obvious target or obliquely protected them from a dangerous animal.

The bull-like creature approached at an impressive speed. It was at least eight feet tall at the shoulder, and its enormous head was covered by what looked like a giant black wig. Sam thought that its three-foot-long horns resembled those of a Texas steer; they pointed sideways and turned up slightly at the tip. Its black tail stood straight up, which might just be a sign of anger, Sam thought.

"Bison," said Cager. "Biggest…"

The creature was almost upon them as Sam waved his torch and the others fired their weapons into the air. The buffalo adjusted its pattern slightly and ran past them without a second look. Oscar grabbed his arm and saw blood bubbling through the sleeve.

Sam looked at him, and Oscar mouthed that he was OK.

The noise did not fade but, instead, grew to a clatter. More dots were streaming toward them, followed by an oversize black mark that Sam knew could only be the bulk of the herd. The dark mark seemed to trail off into a vanishing point in the distance. Several more animals whipped past them, and the rumbling from the stampede was beginning to overwhelm them.

The ground was shaking violently, and Sam fell awkwardly onto his ass. He reached up to Oscar, and his bodyguard pulled him up. Oscar was talking, but the words could not reach Sam's ears, drowned by the roar of the stampede. Sam looked toward the black mark, which was now a sea of buffalo faces and horns.

There appeared to be no end to the line of charging animals.

23

Heavy Traffic

Dust and sod clouded the air, and the men gasped for breath as the beasts crashed past them. At first, the animals seemed to notice them and apparently adjusted their course enough to avoid contact, but soon the bison were filling the path to capacity, and the margin for error narrowed. The forest behind the men shook but not enough for them to push their way into the matted woods and safety.

Cager struggled to turn amid the oncoming wave and seemingly fired his weapon over the heads of the creatures. Sam was confused and tried to say something, but all words were lost in the thundering storm. Cager stood back as something huge landed at his feet and then fired once more into the crowd. A second buffalo crashed lifelessly and silently atop the first as Cager waved his friends over.

Most of the bison avoided the fallen creatures, and the men huddled beside the oxlike cadavers, but some trampled over their comrades, and others tripped and were themselves stomped to death by the riotous herd. Cager killed several more over time as the first members of his makeshift barricade were trampled and squashed into dark, carpet-like puddles of flesh. Sam and Oscar pressed against the inflexible wall of thin trees as their friend calmly stood perhaps a foot away, his rifle relentlessly firing into the crazed drove. Sam wondered how this remarkable young man could have been so unappreciated in his own time. He should have been as famous as Daniel Boone—and he probably would have been if he hadn't gotten lost in the Hole. History's loss was Sam's gain.

Sam realized that Oscar had protectively angled himself in front of him as though his comparatively puny frame would stop one of the creatures from reaching Sam. Sam gently nudged his friend to the side and watched the show in front of them. Although not as stoic as Cager, Sam felt cooler than Joe Montana facing a blitz. He felt alive.

It became clear the herd was thinning when the noise began to subside. There was too much mulch floating around the trail for them to guess the number of animals that passed them, but clearly, the stampede was dying down. The earth was no longer shaking, and the trees and bushes were trembling less excitedly. After a few moments, only an occasional bison shuffled past.

Sam took a step toward Cager and fell dizzily to his knees as the adrenaline rush began to subside. He said, "I feel like I just got off a roller-coaster ride."

Oscar rubbed his ears and said loudly, "Those things were buffalo?"

"Bison," replied Cager, still looking down the path. "Twice the size of any that I have ever seen and hopefully twice as flavorsome."

Sam looked at Oscar. "How's your arm?"

"Stings a little, but I'll be all right."

Sam began looking around for his torch and found it almost untouched and unlit a few feet away. He picked it up and sniffed the top for oil but could only smell the dirt and death that permeated the air around him. He reached into his pocket for his lighter.

He said, "Those things are long extinct Earthside."

"Like the bear?" asked Oscar. "And that turkey thing?"

"Exactly. The entrance to the Hole must have been much larger once, allowing for massive migrations."

Oscar said, "And now it's closing up—maybe for good."

Sam nodded. "Maybe."

Cager pulled out his knife and began to carve flesh from the carcass of one of the least-trampled bison. Oscar pulled a long piece of cloth from his backpack and held it out for his friend. Cager placed the first steak carefully onto the cloth and began slicing another. Neither had eaten, and both were ready for a fresh meal.

"Cager, in front of you!" yelled Sam.

The wolf was larger than any Sam had ever known. He thought it was at least five feet long, and it probably weighed upward of two hundred pounds. It looked sort of like a gray wolf, but the face was different, and the legs seemed to have different dimensions. It was snarling at Cager as it approached the dead buffalo.

"Get your own meal!" hollered Cager.

Sam heard more snarls and saw that he had one of the beasts slowly moving up on his side. Soon, others had joined the crowd of wild dogs, and all of them seemed ready to spring upon the men. Cager pointed his rifle at his chief antagonist but did not shoot, as he feared the wolves would panic and pounce upon them.

"We should just leave," said Oscar prudently. "We should let them have their dinner."

"This is our dinner," said Cager. "Not theirs."

The gray-black animals circled around the men. They were growling and barking and seemed to be working themselves into a frenzy. Cager's wolf suddenly lunged at him and caught several bullets for his trouble. It fell upon the corpse of the disputed bison without a whimper. The other animals were unfazed by the gunfire and instead closed in on the men. Oscar, rifle in hand, looked around and counted at least a dozen dogs and saw no chance of surviving this battle.

Sam stepped past Oscar and stood by the bison carcass. His torch was lit, and he waved it at the creatures, which reluctantly backed away. Floating pieces of grass and other debris sparkled when they made contact with Sam's torch as he waved it a little more wildly at the retreating canines. The sizzling sod fragments lit up the sky, which had apparently turned to night during the time of the great bison migration. The wolves moved away a little more as they growled and howled at Sam and his men.

Sam said, "Cut some steaks so that we can get out of here. Big ones."

24

An Old Friend

Meg saw Gertrude Samson standing at the entrance to the Cozy Kitchen. It was only May, but it was hot, and the fans weren't installed yet. Trudy stepped over a thick piece of lumber that used to be part of the door and cautiously called into the darkness. Meg could see Gertrude, but Gertrude couldn't see her.

"Trudy," Meg called. "Come on in."

Meg sprinted across the cluttered room and grabbed her playfully. She looked her over and said, "Well, you look a little like my old friend…"

Trudy's hair, which was nearly as long as Meg's, was a frenzied mix of pink, purple, and black dye. She had some odd piercing over her left eyebrow and another one on the side of her nose. Trudy spun around for her old friend and flashed a daring tattoo strategically located just above the top center of her pale lowrider jeans. Meg thought that she looked thoroughly modern.

A tall man approached. He was young, in his early twenties, and was wearing work clothes. He had a tool belt strapped mannishly about his waist, and he wore a yellow hard hat to protect his head. Trudy stared at him as he walked over and then covered her mouth.

"Colonel Dearborn," she squealed. "You look amazing."

Meg's mother came from a side room. She was dressed in baggy clothes and wore no makeup, but she looked impeccable. Sally touched Trudy's arm. "My goodness, Trudy, you are a miracle to my eyes."

"Sally, you are stunning," she said. "I am so glad to see you again."

Meg smiled as Trudy looked around the place. Drywall covered most of the walls, and knotted wire hung from cutout sockets here and there. The floor was covered with rubble and dust, and the room was lit with industrial flashlights. She wondered what her friend thought of the chaos in front of her.

"What's going on here?" Trudy asked.

Meg smiled. "Mother and her friend are opening a restaurant soon. Carrie and I will be working here when we have free time."

"When shall I meet your friend?" asked Trudy.

"She's in the kitchen, I think. Let's go look."

Meg strode toward a side door that led to a room that was more chaotic than the one they had just left. There were large holes in the wall where major appliances had once been mounted. Metal fragments and broken glass were scattered randomly across the floor, and what appeared to be a dead mouse was lying peacefully atop the nearest counter. The mouse jumped up and ran into the shadows.

Carrie entered from the back door. She saw her cousin and her friend and danced over the shards to hug them both. She said, "I'm so glad to meet you, Trudy. Meg has been so excited about your visit."

"Me too, Carrie. Where can we go to talk?"

"It's pretty warm out—we can go sit outside," Carrie replied. She looked around and said, "Hey, where's the dead mouse?"

Meg smiled. "It wasn't really dead, Carrie."

Trudy said, "Maybe it was a retread."

The girls moved into the back parking lot. There were no chairs, so they sat on the hood of Carrie's car. They gazed back into the restaurant and watched Meg's parents as they entered the kitchen. Her father looked around for witnesses and, seeing none, reached down and kissed his wife on the neck. She turned and smiled and prepared to return his kiss when Meg called out to them.

"We can see you!" she cried.

He looked out at the girls and waved. Meg's mother gently pushed him away as she whispered something that made him laugh. The pair marched back into the darkness of the larger room. Meg shook her head as she watched.

"Are they always like that?" asked Trudy.

"Pretty much," said Carrie. "Ever since…"

"Since when?"

Meg said, "Since they discovered that my death was an accident initiated by Joshua Martel. Or Margaret didn't end her life—you know what I mean."

Trudy said, "I stopped worrying about such things, Margaret. I have only this life now, and I'm going to do the best that I can with it."

"Is that why you are not with Andrew?" asked Meg.

Trudy said, "I was so happy to be alive and with Andrew at first…"

Meg patted her friend's hand. "You don't have to explain anything to us."

"I'll just say that your parents have a very special connection, Meg. I think that you understand."

"I do, Trudy," said Meg. I'm so glad to see you."

Trudy said, "Me too, your website is such a wonderful thing. Have you heard from many of our old friends?"

"Just you and one other so far. Do you remember Martha Nicholson?"

"I remember her," said Trudy. "She moved away soon after you had your accident."

Meg said, "She said that she might be in the area soon."

"I think you girls will have great success as news of the website spreads," said Trudy.

Carrie said, "We hope so—we've got fifty or so members already, and we're told that there are hundreds of retreads out there somewhere. Maybe more."

"Have there been any problems?" asked Trudy.

"A few people have left terrible comments, but they seem to be in the minority. Generally, the experience has been positive."

Carrie said, "And we're being monitored by the Department of *Hysterical* Archives. Apparently, they have nothing else to do."

"That's to be expected, I guess," said Trudy. "They've made quite an investment in us retreads."

Meg said, "We've already been contacted by a potential advertiser—a tire company. We're hoping to gather more as news spreads."

The conversation lulled, and the group stared into the empty forest. It was almost spring, and the bare trails would soon be covered with greenery and shaded by enormous overhead trees. There were still patches of snow here and there, but the rising temperatures would soon take care of that.

"You look quite contemporary," said Meg. "You've embraced current fashions with full steam."

"Yeah, I was always kind of, um, trendy," she said. "I can't believe you're wearing jeans."

Carrie said, "It took her a while."

"Are you dating?"

Carrie said, "She went on a double date with me a few weeks ago. A boy from our soccer league asked her out."

Trudy winked. "But he was no Cager Barclay?"

Meg climbed from the hood of the car and stood apart from her friends. She said, "My heart tells me…it tells me to wait a while longer."

"And nobody understands about Cager—not even you, Carrie," said Trudy. "But I remember him."

"What was he like?" Carrie had to ask. "I mean from your viewpoint—was he as wonderful as Meg remembers?"

Trudy thought for a few seconds and then said, "The only person I could compare him to would be Colonel Dearborn. He was so large a person, and I don't just mean physically, but he was large in *spirit*. I never believed that Cager was dead—I always expected that he would turn up one day. His story was never meant to end so soon."

Meg said, "Perhaps it hasn't."

"Perhaps not, Meg," said Trudy. "Yours is far from over, to be sure."

"What about you, Trudy?" asked Meg. "Where do you go from here?"

She cleared her throat uncomfortably. "I'm moving out to California. I've met a gentleman, and he wants me to visit with him for a while."

Meg said, "What gentleman?"

"He's a doctor. Actually, he was one of the doctors who worked at the clinic…"

Carrie blurted, "Does your husband know about this?"

"He knows," said Trudy. "He wasn't as upset as I would have thought. And he's not *technically* my husband."

"What?"

"Yeah, it seems that there is some legal disagreement about the validity of retread marriages. You might want to broach the subject with the colonel and your mother."

Meg said, "Do you mean that they may be living sinfully?"

"I just think that they might want to look into it and perhaps renew their vows."

Carrie said, "How long are you here for?"

"I only have a couple of hours, and then I return to Boston. I have to pack my few possessions for the flight west."

Meg said, "Well, let us show you around before you leave."

"I can't," said Carrie. "I'm picking up Ryan, and we're meeting Marissa in Manchester."

Meg watched Carrie's cheeks turn red at the mention of his name. The crimson hue dulled the freckles that spotted her cheeks and briefly gave her the appearance of an older woman. Meg tried to imagine life without her inimitable cousin and decided that she could not have landed in a more fortunate spot. *She's more a sister than a cousin,* she thought. *A true sister.*

"I am so glad to have met you," said Trudy. "Margaret could not ask for a more wonderful family—I'm actually quite jealous."

Carrie said, "Maybe your new family is waiting for you in California."

"Maybe," said Trudy doubtfully.

Meg and Trudy stood back as they watched Carrie's Toyota wheel cautiously through the parking lot and then screech madly onto the street. She honked and waved wildly as she zipped out of town. The music from Carrie's radio blared and then faded as the car disappeared from their sight.

"She's quite nice," said Trudy. "Quite nice."

"I love her," answered Meg. "I love everything about this place."

Trudy looked at her old friend. "I always thought that you deserved so much more…that fate had been so cruel to you."

Meg said, "Things have worked out, Trudy."

"Your family is so extraordinary," Trudy started, "and I am so happy for you, but…"

"What?" asked Meg. "What is it?"

"I just think that it might be time for you to move on a little," Trudy replied. "I think that Cager would want you to live this new life to its fullest."

Meg's forehead wrinkled slightly as she considered her friend's suggestion. She smiled and said, "You're right, of course."

Trudy said, "Have you visited the old home yet?"

"Stamford? Father bristles at any mention of the town."

Trudy almost whispered, "Colonel Dearborn lived quite a long life after you were gone, but his disposition hardened considerably when you…left."

Meg said, "I know that he outlived my mother."

"He was saddest when she passed—and cruelest. I heard people in town talk and say things about the colonel and his coldness, but I knew them both. They just struggled with their loss…"

Guilt washed across Meg's mood. "It was all my fault."

Trudy shook her head. "It was all the fault of Mr. Joshua Martel."

Meg said, "May he rot in hell."

"Did you just swear?" Trudy asked, shaken by her friend's words.

"Don't tell my mother," said Meg, only half joking.

Trudy said, "Well, maybe you are moving on, after all."

25

Blizzards and Kisses

"What was Meg's friend like?" asked Ryan.

The Manchester Dairy Queen had some customers, but nobody was staying inside to eat. How the restaurant stayed in business was a mystery to Carrie. The parking lot was generally empty, and there was a Wendy's across the street and a McDonald's just a few lots down for competition. Hardly anyone she knew came here to eat anymore, and the ice-cream season ended around September.

Carrie and Ryan were the only ones seated at a table, and that was just fine with her. They sat across from each other and held hands while she sipped her Sprite and Ryan struggled to spoon out his M&M Blizzard one-handed. The cup kept rocking and moving, but he refused to let go of Carrie for the sake of his treat. Maybe that was why she liked him so much.

"She's real nice, but she's not like Meg," said Carrie.

Ryan looked at her, and she almost blushed again. His eyes were brown—he called them his "pools of mud"—and she loved to stare into them when they were talking. She knew he was really listening and not just nodding like most boys do. Carrie didn't care if he wasn't as big as some of the boys or that his hair was so long. He was perfect for her.

"What do you mean she's not like Meg?" he asked.

Carrie explained, "Well, she's got a tattoo and some piercings, and she talks like everybody else."

"You mean she's adapted well," Ryan said with a smile. "She's moving on with her life."

"I don't know. I think she's just trying a little too hard—Meg doesn't do that."

"Your cousin's unique," said Ryan. "Does her friend walk really, um, *straight* like Meg?"

Carrie saw a movie once that showed young ladies walking around with piles of books on their heads and wanted to ask Meg if that was how she had learned to walk. Her cousin had the straightest spine in southern New Hampshire. Her posture was possibly genetic, as Sally juggled pots and pans and cleaned obsessively, all the while appearing to be standing still.

"She's definitely graceful, but she doesn't *shine* the way Meg does," Carrie said. "I think Meg was always a standout."

Ryan said, "She's not the only one."

The door opened, and some high school kids walked in. Ryan and Carrie didn't know many kids in Manchester, but they checked them out just in case. Most were dressed in baggy jeans, and all of them wore Manchester West shirts. The boys were noisy and disruptive, and the one skanky girl laughed really loud at everything the boys were doing. Carrie was afraid that the kids would sit in the dining area and make a racket, but they left quickly. She wondered why so many kids felt a need to show off when their parents weren't around.

"When's Marissa getting here?" asked Carrie.

"She'll be here any minute. One of the girls she works with is dropping her off."

"She really likes working at the bookstore," said Carrie. "I was hoping she'd want to work at the restaurant with us, but she's too happy there."

"As long as we're all working," said Ryan. "We're gonna need money to keep the website running."

Carrie said, "Trudy says that Retreads.com is going to pay for our college eventually. She thinks it'll take off like Facebook or something."

Ryan said, "Maybe, but our chat room seems pretty depressing so far. I can't get myself to even look at it anymore."

"I know what you mean," Carrie said. "There's a lot of talk about loneliness and isolation. I think chatting helps them, though"

"Maybe, but it creeps me out."

Carrie looked at him and whispered, "Can I ask you something?"

"OK," he said.

"When do you think we're going to…kiss?" Carrie asked, her cheeks burning.

Ryan was quiet for a few seconds while he looked for the words. Finally, he said, "I really want to but…"

"But what?"

He fidgeted a little.

"Do I have bad breath or something?"

He shook his head.

"Then what?"

He gave her the look again. "Well, I was always a little intimidated by your dad, and then I met your uncle, who's maybe the scariest man ever—"

Carrie snorted.

"Don't laugh at me, Carrie," he said. "They just make me nervous."

Her free hand reached over to his cheek. "They already think that you've kissed me, and you're still alive. They won't kill you for kissing."

The door opened again, and this time it was Marissa, letting in the cool spring air. She scrutinized the hand-holding, face-rubbing pair and rolled her eyes. Carrie wondered how Marissa could be so understanding about her brother and her best friend dating. It must be tough taking in sickening scenes like the one in front of her.

Her hair was mainly purple, but there were hints of pink here and there across her dome. She was wearing an oddly rhinestoned denim jacket and a light pair of corduroys. She had a blue Converse sneaker on her right foot and a white Nike sneaker on the other. Marissa wasn't wearing socks, as far as Carrie could determine, but she did seem to have some kind of gold chain wrapped twice around her left ankle.

And it all looked good on her.

"Well," she said. "What was Meg's friend like?"

Carrie and Ryan shared a look.

"What?" asked Marissa. "Did I say something wrong?"

Carrie said, "No, I was just explaining to Ryan that she was a lot different from Meg."

"How so?"

"Well, she talks like us, and she dresses a lot like…you."

Marissa said, "Nobody dresses like me."

"Well, it doesn't look as good on her, that's for sure. But she's real nice and everything."

Marissa sat down beside her brother. She was carrying a book bag and pulled out a paperback copy of *Emma* by Jane Austen. She said, "I got this for Meg—I think she'll like it."

Carrie smiled. "Oh, thank you. She reads books so easily, like she's watching TV or something. I think she wants to write."

Marissa said, "I think we both know what she'd write about."

"Cager," said Carrie. "An eight-or nine-hundred-page book about Cager Barclay."

Marissa grinned. "Right. And that would only be volume one of a ten-volume series."

Ryan got up to throw his empty cup away.

Carrie said, "Trudy's all crazy about him, too."

"What do you mean?"

Carrie leaned over to her friend. "She says that Cager was just like Meg says. I think she half believes that he's still alive, too."

Marissa said, "He must have been amazing—maybe Meg can help me paint a portrait of him."

"I know she plans to one day," said Carrie. "When she's ready."

Carrie almost wished that Meg was wrong about Cager. If he had just been some normal guy Meg had known a long time ago, then letting go would be easy, over time. But it sounded like her cousin had lost something that could never be replaced. She looked at Ryan standing beside the red trash can and wondered about their future.

Hopefully, their future would include a kiss sometime soon.

26

Mountain Men

It was late afternoon, which meant darkness was coming fast, and the temperature was beginning to drop. Sam was looking around for twigs and branches to start a campfire. He watched his friends circle the clearing while pointing their rifles skyward. A surprisingly large squirrel population had been providing the men with fairly tasteless meals for several days, but the rodents were not to be found this day. The larger beasts seemed to have disappeared, too, but Sam knew that there would be more monsters soon enough.

The squirrels were no larger than those that Sam had grown up with in northern California, though their fur was dark and stripeless, and their noses were long and blunt. Cager was able to shoot the animals without noticeably damaging the meat, whereas Oscar was prone to vaporizing the poor creatures with his high-powered rifle.

Oscar walked past him, rifle in the air, mumbling quietly to himself. Sam could hear the jingle of the cartridges in Oscar's backpack as he passed by. His blue Ahearn Industries jumpsuit seemed impossibly neater than Sam's. He thought that Oscar looked good, though; he was sleeker than ever, and his dark hair was fuller and no longer peppered with patches of gray.

Sam reached for his own hair. He knew it was long now, but he hadn't seen a mirror in quite a while. He said, "Oscar, how does my hair look? Does it look like it has more texture than before?"

Oscar put his weapon down and turned back toward Sam. "What?"

"My hair. Does my hair seem to have a lot of body to it now?"

"Sam, I'm not comfortable with this line of questioning."

"I'm serious, Oscar. Your grays are gone now, and I can't help but wonder if I'm experiencing the same effect—is it coming back?"

"I don't know, Sam," Oscar said. "Here comes Cager—let's not freak him out with your beauty tips, OK?"

Cager was gazing at the empty canopy of branches and leaves above as he approached them. His jumpsuit was gray, though it may have been blue before his battle with the bison had stirred up so much dirt and grass. His rifle was pointed at the ground now, and he looked disappointed. He rarely came back to camp without dinner; it was a point of pride for the young man.

He said, "I'm sorry, gentlemen, but even the squirrels seem to be gone. I saw some berries off a ways, though."

"It's not your fault, son," said Sam. "I'll sleep better if I don't have to worry about the big animals."

"I found more wagon marks heading that way," Cager said, pointing possibly easterly. "We're on some kind of trail, obviously, but it is hard to guess the parameters of the pathway."

Sam took a sip from his canteen. The oddly shaped leaves that were so common in this world often held small drops of moisture at daybreak, and the men had learned to drain the liquid into their canteens as early and as often as possible. The water was vaguely bitter, but they no longer noticed.

Sam pointed at the tracks. "How much stuff do you think they were dragging?"

"Their wagon was fairly large, I'd say, and it was being pulled by some beast that was not a horse."

"But you don't think they could have been pulling the machinery and tools that are missing from the cabin?"

Cager shook his head.

"What does that mean?" asked Oscar. "Maybe they weren't the only ones stealing from us?"

Sam said, "I think they probably just took the scraps."

"Where did the rest of our equipment go, then? Our men had ATVs and snowblowers, for God's sake. Where is all that stuff?"

"I have a theory," said Sam. "Maybe—"

"Pick up your rifles," Cager calmly interrupted. "We are being watched."

"What? Another bear?"

"Humans, Mr. Ahearn. Two of them."

Cager appeared undistracted but for his eyes, which moved slowly from his far right to his far left. He said, "There are two of them, and they are approaching very quietly."

"What does that mean?" asked Sam.

Oscar said, "That means they're stalking us."

"I will get the one on my left, while you two take cover and distract the other one," said Cager.

"No, we stay together as…" Sam started before realizing that Cager had slipped into the dark forest.

"How's he do that?" asked Oscar.

The first rifle shot hit the ground in front of them and the second sailed way high, accompanied by a scream. Oscar and Sam hit the ground and began to fire in the general direction of their man. Sam spit out some twigs and a bit of dirt, then fired several more rounds. Oscar was more deliberate with his shots, and Sam was sure that his bodyguard had returned fire accurately.

Shots rang back as the men retreated behind a nearby oak tree. The tree stopped several bullets, but wooden splinters sprayed the area in every direction. They fired several more volleys and waited. Sam peeked out and saw nothing but was reluctant to move. He had been firing blindly to begin with and had no clue as to whether their attacker was still around.

Cager's call loudly broke the silence. "Over here."

Sam and Oscar looked at each other and then trotted in the general direction of Cager's voice. After some effort, they found him in a small clearing about twenty yards away from their freshly blemished oak tree. He was standing over the still body of a hairy man wearing clothes made from animal furs. The man appeared to be dead, but Sam wasn't sure.

"What happened?" asked Sam.

Cager said, "I struck him with my rifle as he began his ambush. I think the blow to the head killed him."

Oscar said, "Why didn't you just shoot him?"

"Dead men are incapable of talking, Oscar," replied Cager. "And I think we'd like to know who he is."

"Where's the other one?" asked Sam.

Cager sighed. "Didn't you men hear him as he fled? I could hear his footsteps from here."

Sam smiled. "Yeah…I thought I heard something like that."

"Me too," said Oscar.

The dead mountain man was tall and lanky, though he was probably smaller than Sam had originally thought, as the pelts that covered his torso were quite bulky. His hair was as long as Cager's, and he sported a beard that fell to his chest. His head was bent slightly as a result of Cager's strike. Dark liquid was bleeding onto the leaf-covered dirt beneath him. One eye was still open.

"Is he really dead?" asked Oscar. "Should we use some of the mud on him?"

Cager said, "His friends will return for him at first light. If there's a mudhole around, they'll bring him there."

"How do you know that?" asked Sam.

"Wouldn't you?"

Sam nodded.

Oscar wiped his brow. "Then his friends will be here soon enough. We should get out of here."

"I agree," said Cager.

"His rifle is one of ours," said Sam. "I wonder how he got it."

Oscar rolled the body around and checked for pockets. He found a cloth bag tied into the man's shirt that contained five bullets. He said, "Did we win the fight, or did they run out of bullets?"

Cager said, "They probably saw our rifles, but they must not have expected the quantity of bullets in our possession."

Oscar added, "We keep getting in fights like that, and we won't have many left. Then how do we stop the giant bears?"

"Take his bullets and smash his gun, Oscar," said Sam.

Oscar took the small bag and found two more in the rifle. Then he bashed it unsuccessfully against a tree several times. He said, "These things don't break."

"Well, either take it or throw it."

"Then we get the hell out of here, right?" asked Oscar.

Sam shook his head. He had turned and was looking in the direction that Cager had indicated. Sam wished that he could see the marks in the trees and the soil that his young friend could so easily detect. He felt so vulnerable sometimes and hated himself for it. *I'm supposed to be the alpha male,* he thought.

"What, Sam—do you want to stay and fight?" asked Oscar. "I don't think it's worth the risk."

"Of course not, but…"

"But what?"

Sam turned back to Cager. "If we dropped back a distance and made it seem like we left—could you track this guy's friends?"

"Hunt the hunters?" asked Cager.

Sam nodded. "They have our weapons, so I'm going to assume that these are the guys we've been tracking."

"I can do it, Mr. Ahearn, but I should go alone. You two would make too much noise."

"We're a team, Cager," said Sam. "I don't like breaking up the band."

Cager said, "You know that I'm right, Mr. Ahearn. We should find a position and wait for his partner to return. I'll follow them and double back as soon as possible."

"And what are we supposed to do while you're gone?" asked Oscar.

Cager smirked. "Perhaps you could discuss the texture of Mr. Ahearn's hair. I think it is quite striking."

"I knew you were listening," said Oscar. "I knew it."

27

Shadows

Cager didn't mind the dirt. There were no insects in the soil, and his blanket of leaves and brush kept him warm enough. He had spent several years, apparently, in this world's earth and had come out a stronger man. Cager saw his emergence from his grave as an affirmation of his faith and was somewhat puzzled that Oscar seemed to disagree. *Ashes to ashes, dust to dust…*

At sunrise, such as it was in this colorless world, he heard men approaching long before they appeared in the little clearing that held the remains of the hairy man. Cager had run across men like this before, and he doubted they would allow their friend to remain dead for long in this world. He was surprised at the accompanying noise as they made their way to their comrade. They were brazen in their commotion, as though they were daring Cager to attack.

There were four bearded men, dressed in furs and leather; three appeared to be fairly large, and all seemed pretty young. Cager knew that guessing a man's age was an impossible task in the Hole, but he still found himself doing it. Oscar and Sam were looking younger by the day, and yet he still saw their age in their footsteps and in their banter. He wondered how old he should consider himself and decided that he still felt like the nineteen-year-old boy who was injured crossing the great river all those years ago. Of course, Oscar probably thought that he was only a few weeks old and that his memories were false.

He was hidden among the fallen leaves beneath a large tree that might have been another oak but for the strange leaves and astounding size. He was less than fifty yards away from the men, but he knew they did not see him. He saw a large shadow slowly trudging through the woods beside them and smiled to himself.

The tallest of the men was giving directions and pointing, and all of the men were laughing enough to make Cager suspect they had been drinking. Two of the men rolled the corpse roughly onto a kind of stretcher made from branches and leather. They strapped him tightly to the contraption but did not immediately leave. One of the men produced a small flask, and they all drank from it. The two men tending to the corpse began to push at the smallest man of the group, and all cackled as he fell over. He jumped up quickly, cursing, and was roughly knocked down again.

Cager watched the horseplay with some amusement but mainly concerned himself with the fifth member of their group, who was quietly moving about among the trees. The man was good, Cager thought, but was overconfident in his approach. These men were not accustomed to being the hunted, Cager decided, and suffered from a lack of discipline.

Finally, bored with their roughhousing, the men set off. The smaller man, who may have been the one Oscar and Sam had swapped bullets with, picked up one end of the makeshift stretcher and followed his associates into the woods. Cager did not move, as the shadow man was still lurking nearby. He considered capturing the man and then following the others, but the shadow man was probably expected back soon, and Mr. Ahearn wanted Cager to simply observe these men. He was not supposed to be noticed.

It took less than ten minutes for the shadow man to tire of his task. Cager quietly rolled out from his mantle of leaves and followed the man into the darkness. His jumpsuit blended easily into the dark shades of the jungle, and his boots made no sounds as he followed the man. His legs were stiff from inactivity, but they loosened with every step. He felt so strong these days.

The shadow man moved quickly through some dense areas but soon brought them out onto a hunter's trail. It was less than two feet across and was often blocked by young saplings and fallen branches, but it was undoubtedly a trail. Cager, barely sweating, made his way through the woods and tried to remain parallel to the path as much as he could. Occasionally, he had to move deeper back, but he always made his way to a spot near the trail.

Finally, they caught up with the shadow man's friends. The larger man was leading, and his two subordinates were in the middle, pushing and punching at each other, while the smaller man struggled behind them as he pulled his heavy load. The little one was probably ten yards behind the others, and the shadow man said nothing to him as he passed him. Cager, from the woods, could hear the little man mumbling and grumbling to himself.

The shadow man called out to the larger men, and they stopped briefly to talk. He took a sip from his friend's flask, and the two men chatted. He shook his head several times and said something that made the big man laugh. The group started back up just as the little man pulling the stretcher arrived. He slowed down briefly but speeded up as the large man yelled back at him.

Cager tracked them for another hour as they headed farther away from the great trail. As the compass Oscar had removed from the dead soldier's arm did not appear to function correctly, the Ahearn men had begun to map objects by their proximity to the great trail. Traveling up the trail, away from their cabin, was now *uptrail*, and moving downward was now *downtrail*. If a map showed these directions on an up-and-down line, then all movement to the right would be *overtrail*, and all movement to the left was *undertrail*.

They were now heavily undertrail and farther away from his friends than Cager desired. He remembered longer exercises than this, though, and he was confident he could make his way back to Mr. Ahearn quickly at any time. He used the quiet moments to think about his new life and his lost life with Margaret. Mr. Ahearn always seemed to want to say something whenever Cager mentioned her, but he always stopped himself. Cager was no fool, and he understood that it seemed impossible to Sam and Oscar that she was still alive, but her heart still beat inside his chest, and he knew what he knew. One day, they would be together again.

He saw that the larger men had stopped at a small clearing. They called out to the small man pulling the cadaver, and he hurried up a bit until he reached his comrades. Cager looped around the site and positioned himself behind a thick bush. He dug and clawed at the soil under the shrub until he could see the men clearly. He was only twenty-odd feet away, and he could hear their words plainly. Cager heard something else coming from the rear, but it was subtle and far away.

The mountain men were walking across the grassy clearing to a small mudhole. Cager was hardly surprised to see it, as the men's mood indicated a level of enjoyment he rarely saw at funerals. The big man grabbed a handful of mud and smeared it all across the gaping hole above the dead man's ear. He wrapped something around the dead man's head, possibly an overly large leaf, and then began roughly removing the man from the stretcher.

"Mr. Bonneville here appears to have enjoyed his meals," said the big man. "He is far too fat to be wearing these garments."

The shadow man, who was slim and blond, said, "I remember when he was no larger than this whelp."

The little man who had pulled the corpse through the jungle said, "Mr. Sanders, I don't appreciate—"

Sanders slapped the little man across his right ear, much to the enjoyment of the others. "You begin to collect this stuff and rub it across his body—and I mean everywhere across his body. Get to work."

The small one rubbed his ear and looked angrily at the one called Sanders. He then went to work removing Mr. Bonneville's clothes and then slowly applied the mud to every portion of the dead man's body. Cager remembered awakening inside the brown liquid and struggling to his feet. He decided that he preferred that method to one that included mud rubdowns on every pore of his dead body. It appeared to be too much of an intrusion on his privacy.

Finally, the little man said, "I'm all done, Mr. Colter."

Colter said, "Then go round us up some firewood, Willy. We're gonna be here awhile, and night is coming."

28

Old Cemetery Hill

The brick-stone path led down through an odd cluster of aged grave-stones. Carrie, leading the way, was studying her MapQuest printout as she walked and was mumbling as she moved along. Ryan walked with her, his hand comfortably glued to hers while still somehow texting with his free hand. Meg followed but often fell behind, as she frequently stopped to read names on the stones. Carrie knew she was looking for familiar names and was afraid she might change her mind. It must be horrible to remember people so vividly and to know that they were long dead. Maybe that was why God made old people so forgetful.

Meg once reluctantly promised they could make this trip after school was out, and it was one promise Carrie wasn't going to let her weasel out from. They completed their finals before noon and headed out as soon as Ryan could meet them. MapQuest led them into Massachusetts and, after a while, down through the narrow streets of Stamford. The roads were being worked on all over town, forcing frequent detours, and it seemed that the number of red-vested street crews outnumbered the actual locals. After a while, Carrie and her friends arrived at Old Cemetery Hill.

Wikipedia told her that the graveyard was one of the most pictur-esque in New England and was the final resting place for several dozen Revolutionary War soldiers. It wasn't a bad spot to be buried, Carrie decided, especially in the summertime. The view of the harbor was awesome, and the small town wasn't loud enough to disturb your sleep.

Carrie already knew she didn't want to be cremated, and now she knew she wanted a small-town location. She was going to have to put all of these thoughts into writing someday.

The chilly breeze from Stamford Harbor made her shiver, and Ryan reflexively pulled her closer. Meg, the sensible one, wore a light jacket over her colorful sundress and seemed not to notice the cold. It was bright and sunny, and the temperature was in the low seventies inland. Carrie hadn't thought about the coastal winds.

"These stones are freaky," said Ryan. "The pictures look like gargoyles."

Meg stopped to look at a slate-gray gravestone. "It's a skull and wings—and this small panel here is an hourglass."

Ryan made a face. "Why would they put those things on a tombstone?"

Meg answered, "For good luck, I think."

They trudged past more dark headstones with epitaphs such as "Too sweet alas for mortals here, their Saviour called them home" and "As I am now so you must be, prepare for death and follow me." Many of the graves held infants, and Carrie realized how lucky she was to have been born in an age of medicine. If not for antibiotics, all of her ear infections and her early bout with whooping cough could easily have put her in the ground when she was a baby.

They crossed over a hill and saw an even larger cropping of graves. Beyond that lay the blue harbor that Margaret Dearborn had learned to swim in centuries before. Not long ago, there had been yachts and large sailboats dotting the bay, but the wealthy had moved on to towns like Marblehead, and now the small harbor was largely empty except for a handful of fishing vessels. Carrie wondered if the town was dying.

A shirtless teenager was mowing the blue-green grass near a large and faded obelisk. He was dark and handsome and looked very strong. Carrie looked at him discreetly and exchanged a look with her cousin as they passed him. The girls often knew what the other was thinking and sometimes finished each other's sentences. Carrie had never felt as close to anyone before, even Marissa.

"It's supposed to be down at the bottom of the hill," said Carrie. "I think we're getting close."

Ryan took the map and sprinted ahead. Carrie watched as he bounced around and over the plots until he finally stopped and hollered to the girls. She couldn't understand what he was saying, but she knew that he must have found what they were looking for. Her hand felt warm suddenly, and she realized Meg was gripping it. Together, they hiked down the trail toward Carrie's excited boyfriend.

He was pointing at a large stone. "This is it. This is it."

Carrie was expecting a large family column with family members listed in order, but there was nothing so grand in the plot. There were three stones, the smallest belonging to Colonel John Edgcomb Dearborn. Aunt Sally's spot was immediately to his left, and Margaret's was to his right. Uncle John's headstone merely gave his name and the dates of his birth and death. Carrie knew that her uncle had outlived her aunt by many years, but he had been a wreck following the deaths of Sally and Margaret.

Margaret's marble stone was stained now, but the intricate carving was still legible. It listed all of her vital information and ended with:

Freed from the mischiefs Sin hath wrought
From pain & tears & all their Springs

Aunt Sally's stone was at least the equal of her daughter's in size, but it gave no real epitaph. Uncle John had been ill at the time of her death, and her funeral was rushed. She was not even forty years old then, and he had not seen it coming. Carrie once read that he burned the house down, rebuilt it, and burned it down again after her passing. She had trouble reconciling the bitter old man that John Dearborn had been with her wonderful uncle. Growing old wasn't fun, she guessed, and it changed people.

Ryan said, "You can't even tell they dug up the grave."

The dirt and grass surrounding the plot definitely seemed to match the others in the graveyard. Aunt Sally's stone was slightly sunken, and Uncle John's was crooked, but most of the other stones were warped or bent or something else. It was impossible to tell that the Dearborns had been exhumed, leaving the graves empty and incomplete.

"Daddy was here when they got Uncle John," she said. "They wouldn't do it without him."

Meg widened her eyes. "Really?" she asked.

"He had to sign for him," Carrie said. "I think he almost changed his mind."

"Sign for him? Like one of those delivery vehicles?" asked Meg. "That's very cold."

Carrie nodded. "That really bothered him, I guess. But I'm glad he went through with it—I'm glad you're here."

Meg said, "I feel the same, though with some guilt."

"You should feel guilt," said Ryan. "Apparently, your sins wrought a lot of mischiefs."

Meg snorted indelicately. "Ryan, that's so very funny."

The shirtless boy turned off his mower and began to approach them. Carrie said, "I hope we're not trespassing."

"It's a public spot," said Ryan. "We have every right to be here."

The boy smiled as he approached. He said, "Are you here for Margaret Dearborn?"

Meg looked at him. "How do you know about Margaret?"

The boy began to speak but found himself briefly muted by Meg's gaze. After a few seconds, he said, "People start showing up here at the beginning of summer to visit."

"What are you talking about?" asked Meg.

"You know," he said. "They all read about her tragedy, and they drop off flowers and notes. Believe me, it's a pain to clean up."

Carrie said, "People drive here to see her grave?"

"Right," he said. "And to see the ghost."

Ryan had been examining the stones, but he was listening. "There's a ghost?"

The boy smiled. "Well, that's the legend. She comes out when the moon is full to look for her lost lover."

Carrie said, "For real? I mean, not that ghosts are real, but people really think there's a ghost?"

He brushed back his thick hair and said, "You guys aren't here for the ghost?"

"We are now," said Meg.

29

The Ghost of Margaret Dearborn

Carrie drove along Route 19, reversing direction several times, searching for the path that led to the remains of the Dearborn estate. Most of the construction work was done for the day, but intrusive orange cones were everywhere. Finally, she spotted cars parked at the side of the road and guessed that they might belong to other kids coming to see the ghost. She parked the Toyota by the other cars and saw a bare spot that must have been the pathway leading toward Meg's old home.

"Too bad Cager's not here," said Meg as she climbed from her seat. "He was quite good at following tracks and such things."

Ryan said, "I don't think we'll need him tonight. The path looks pretty big."

The trail was easy enough to follow. The moon was almost full, and the stars were abundant in the cloudless sky, making the heavily traveled pathway surprisingly well lit. They could hear the murmur of a small crowd of kids grow louder as they pressed on. Carrie was carrying a blanket from Big Lots, and Ryan was shining a flashlight in all the wrong directions. Meg followed quietly and seemed to be looking for some familiar sight.

"Was this path here before?" asked Ryan. He was breathing heavily.

Meg shook her head. "No. There was a long gravel road that led toward the town, but I guess it's gone."

They crossed over a hill and saw a large group of kids huddled around a sparking bonfire. The air was filled with smoke and steam, and Carrie flashed back to camping trips with her parents near Lake Barron in southern Maine. Her parents seemed *forever* back then, and the world was so much simpler. She wondered if any of the kids had brought marshmallows. Her parents always brought marshmallows.

Meg took in the sight. "The skyline looks sort of familiar, but there are so many trees now…"

Carrie grabbed her hand and led her toward the pack. There were at least a dozen kids, mostly girls, mingling around the fire. Nobody was toasting marshmallows, but some were sipping from plastic cups. There was a half-empty wine jug on the ground, and Carrie realized that that was what they were drinking. Sometimes she wished she was cool enough to be one of the kids who drank and got stoned, but her father's voice was always in her head, talking her out of trouble. He wouldn't think these kids were cool.

Someone rose from the assembly, and Carrie recognized him. His name was Charlie Whitehouse, and he was the dark-skinned boy from the cemetery. Charlie was wearing a shirt now and a leather jacket that made him look sort of like a biker. Carrie glanced at her cousin and saw that she was smiling. *Maybe she's finally found someone*, she thought. *Maybe she's ready to move on.*

"I'm so glad you guys made it," Charlie said. "This is always a fun time."

Ryan said, "When does the ghost show up?'

"I've never actually seen her. The ladies all say that they've felt her or they've seen a shadow or something," Charlie said. "I don't know exactly what they're seeing."

"I knew it," said Ryan. "Your parents are gonna be pissed when we get in after midnight, and I don't even see a ghost."

Charlie glanced at Meg. "I have a good feeling about tonight, Ryan. I think Margaret will show up."

Meg said, "Why would you say that, Mr. Whitehouse?"

"Call it a hunch. Come over and meet my friends."

—〰—

Charlie's friends were actually cool. Nobody mocked them for not drinking, and they were included in the conversation. Someone had brought marshmallows after all, and they were toasting them on the ends of long sticks that Ryan had found at the edge of the clearing. He kept burning his, perhaps intentionally, but Carrie browned hers perfectly. Meg enjoyed the marshmallow squares, but her hands became too sticky, so she refrained from overindulging.

"When, exactly, does this ghost arrive, Mr. Whitehouse?" asked Meg.

She was sitting beside Carrie, close to the flames. Her back was straight, her shoulders perfectly even, and she looked as though she was carefully posing for a portrait. Most of the boys were looking at her, and some of the girls, too. Meg never seemed to notice the attention, and she was too focused on her ghost to care about much else.

Charlie was sitting beside Meg. He threw a stick into the fire. "Could you please just call me *Charlie*? You make me nervous when you call me *Mister*."

Meg said, "Of course…I'm sorry."

"And I don't know when it'll happen. I just get a kick out of this whole experience."

A girl named Amy piped in, "Margaret usually appears as the moon crosses over the house."

"What house?" asked Ryan.

Amy was a pretty girl and a talkative one. She sighed and said, "Margaret's house was right over there."

She pointed past the campfire toward a tall bowed birch tree. A patch of fog covered the ground around the tree, and it sparkled eerily in the moonlight. Amy said, "You can almost see into the past when the moon lights up the area. Sometimes you can see Margaret walking past you, looking for her lost lover. Once in a while, she'll look right at you, but then she goes right back to searching for Victor."

"Victor? Who is Victor?" asked Meg.

"Victor was her lost love. He was a Revolutionary War soldier—his ship sank in the harbor."

Carrie said, "I thought Meg died in 1812?"

"That's right. During the Revolutionary War."

Amy looked serious. She was a nice enough girl, Carrie thought, and she had generously given them all some of her marshmallows. Carrie said, "And Victor never came back?"

"No." Amy was near tears. "Poor Margaret had to live with her abusive parents until she finally threw herself out of a window. The doctors said that her heart stopped beating before she even hit the ground."

Ryan asked, "How would they know that?"

"I don't know. I'm not a doctor, am I?"

Charlie edged closer to Meg. "What do you think?"

She smiled softly. "I don't think the house was there. I think it may have been farther up the hill, and I think she and her parents might just have been fighting like we fight with our parents. I don't know that it was…abusive."

Amy said, "No offense, but I think I know the story better than you kids. I grew up with it."

Someone said, "Shh, look…"

"At what?" asked Ryan.

A girl mumbled, "Boys never get it."

Carrie and Meg looked at each other and smiled. *What an awesome night,* Carrie thought.

After a moment, the crowd started talking excitedly. Most of the girls had seen something that must have been a sign from Margaret Dearborn. Amy said that she glimpsed Margaret's glowing white dress, which was being blown about by an ancient sea wind. Two girls thought they heard horses, which had some meaning to them, and another girl was sure that she heard stifled sobs that would never end. Most of the girls were crying.

—⁓—

The group quickly began to thin out after the shared experience. The wine was gone, and the marshmallows were mainly in Ryan's stomach. Carrie sat by her boyfriend, their blanket wrapped tightly around them, and ran her fingers through his hair. Amy approached her and asked for her cell number. She gave Carrie a half hug and ran off with her friends.

Meg stood by the bent birch, looking into the woods. Charlie was fake boxing with a friend on the other side of the fading bonfire while another friend laughed at the sight. Their breath was visible in the air above them, looking like wordless comic-book talk bubbles. After a few minutes, his friends did some kind of hand-bump good-bye with him and walked away. An owl was hooting somewhere, and the wind was pushing most of the leaves around in the trees overhead. Carrie wondered how long kids had hung out in this spot, hoping to catch a glimpse of their local ghost. She would have to look it up later.

Ryan said, "We're gonna have to leave soon, Carrie. Your father's gonna kill me if you don't get home."

Carrie reached into her bag and tapped a button on her cell phone. She said, "It's only nine-thirty, Ryan. We'll be fine."

"It's more than an hour home, Carrie," he said. "We have to get going."

She nodded. "You're right—I'll go get her."

Carrie stood up and brushed most of the soil off her butt. She walked across the weeds and dirt to her cousin and grabbed her gently by the arm. Meg turned to her and nodded without having to be told. Carrie squeezed her hand and hugged her gently.

"It's just so odd," said Meg, brushing her hair back with her free hand. "So very odd."

"I know."

Meg tapped herself on the temple. "It all seems so recent to me, but...I can't even decide where the house really was. Everything is different now."

Carrie said, "We should just get going."

"You are right, Carrie. Our fathers will be waiting for us."

Carrie wrinkled her nose. "I know—I love that about them."

They walked slowly back toward the bonfire. Ryan and Charlie were the last of the crowd, and they were talking about the "Insane" level on *Gears of War*. Charlie looked like a jock to Carrie, but apparently, he had his nerd side, too. He played video games and hung out with ghost hunters on Saturday nights.

"You guys have to get going?" Charlie asked.

Meg nodded.

Charlie said, "What do you think those girls would have thought if they'd known that Margaret was sitting beside them all night?"

"What?" asked Carrie.

He grinned a little. "I've worked at the cemetery every year since I was fifteen. I know all about those government guys coming in and digging things up."

Meg said, "Mr. Whitehouse, I really don't know what you are talking about."

Charlie said, "My mom used to have an old painting of two blond women sitting across from each other in this big hallway. There was a big flower pot sitting beside the older one."

Meg brightened. "Do you still have it?"

He said, "I think she sold it at a yard sale or something. The portrait wasn't very good, but I recognized you when I saw you this afternoon—how could I not? And your name is Meg—short for Margaret."

"Well," said Meg. "Thank you for not informing all of your friends about my presence."

"They would have been OK with it. They just would have asked a lot of questions."

Ryan interrupted, "Meg, we have to get going."

Charlie said, "Listen, I'm going to school at Southern New Hampshire University this fall."

"In Hooksett?" asked Carrie.

"Right. I'm a Penman now. A business major."

Meg said, "I have heard wonderful things about the school."

Charlie lowered his voice. "Would it be all right if I called you this fall?"

Carrie was sure that Meg was blushing, but the darkness covered it well. She said, "I would like that, I think, Charlie."

"Great. Maybe you could come to a football game there or maybe a movie…"

Meg exhaled and said, "You should know that I may not be looking for the same thing that you are."

He frowned. "Is there someone else?"

"Yeah," said Ryan. "Victor."

Meg gave Ryan a look much like one her mother had given him when she caught him holding hands with Carrie. She said, "Ryan is sort of right, I'm afraid."

"I guess I understand, Meg," Charlie said. "I would still like to see you, though."

Ryan was firm. "We have to get going, guys. I'm afraid of your fathers—you both know that."

Carrie said, "It's my car, Ryan. How can they be mad at you if I get in late?"

Meg touched Charlie's hand gently and slipped him a small sheet of paper. She smiled and then started back down the pathway leading to the street. Carrie and Ryan followed her, while Charlie remained at the site. A few embers were still glowing, but the fire was mainly out. He kicked some dirt on the few remaining glowing orbs as he watched his new friends ramble slowly down the pathway that led back to Stamford.

The fire was out, but he was in no hurry to leave.

30

Father and Daughter

Meg sat beside her father on a long wooden deckchair. They drank lemonade and watched familiar insects dance crazily around the front light. The farmer's porch reached entirely around the house, but the town lights could only be seen from the front of the structure. The full moon was not as bright in Bainbridge as it had been in Stamford, but the streetlights, small bonfires, and even bug zappers combined to light up the area in a way that made it appear that the stars had left the sky and had landed across town. Meg never tired of the view.

John was wearing work pants and a heavy shirt. He swatted at a fly and said, "How was your evening, Meg?"

She smiled. "Very interesting, Father—Stamford has changed quite a lot since our time."

John said, "I believe that *now* is our time."

"I guess I quite agree," said Meg. "I just meant…"

He nodded. "I understand. It is hard to put old memories away, but I do try to press them aside as much as I can."

Meg took a small sip from her glass. "It is almost as though the town we knew has vanished from history. The people are still quite wonderful, though."

He said, "My most vivid memories of our old town are not happy ones."

Meg looked at him. He sat regally in his chair, his fingers kinetically tapping the arms as he glanced casually into the woods, then down to the city, then back to the forest. She wondered if he half expected the British Regular Army to burst from the trees and demand his immediate surrender. Even in Margaret's last days, she had known that the war had never really ended for Colonel John Dearborn.

"Do you miss it?" she asked.

Her father ran his fingers through his black hair and thought for a moment. Finally, he said, "These last few months have brought me more happiness than I have known in both of my lives. I could not imagine a life away from here."

"So, you don't miss any of the old times? I just remember that you were so important and so intense."

"God gave me a second chance that I truly did not deserve, my dear," said John. "I was a terrible husband and father, and I became even more unbearable upon the terrible events that took you from me."

"Well, we're all together now. We have Uncle Tom and Carrie, and you and mother are so happy now."

John smirked. "I will be happier when I am allowed to see the inside of my bedchamber."

Meg almost snorted her drink from the shock of her father's unexpected comment. He was now sleeping in one of the smaller rooms near the Great Room, and he was not particularly enamored with the situation. Her mother was planning a late-summer wedding and had no plans to allow her husband back in until their union was indisputably legal. Father said he remembered taking his vows vividly and saw no reason that he could not be allowed inside his own dormitory. But Sally Dearborn ruled the bedroom firmly.

Meg said, "She is quite serious, you know. She would be more comfortable with you completely out of the house."

"I told her that I would not sleep in the barn," said her father. He was grinning, and the look suited him. He was such a handsome man, and she could see why her mother had fallen for him. According to Carrie, many of his young students had eyes for the youthful man who sat beside her. She shook that disturbing thought from her head and remembered a time when he had been the hero in her life. A time before Cager had begun stealing her attention away from him.

"It will work out, Father," she said. "She deserves this."

"And more," he agreed.

Something flew by, and Meg jumped from her seat. "What was that?"

He laughed. "That was a bat, my dear. They are all about."

"I should not be so jumpy around such things," Meg said. "Carrie would try to make a pet out of the filthy creature."

"She might at that," he said. "She is quite at home in the forest."

"Uncle Tom takes her deer hunting in the fall," she said. "I cannot imagine such a thing."

Her father said, "For a time, I took young Cager with me on hunting trips. Until things took such a bad turn."

"He was quite good, wasn't he?"

He nodded. "He was better than almost anyone. He could track anything, and he never lost lead."

"Better than you?"

"I don't know, Meg," he said. "He came closer than anyone."

Meg whispered, "He admired you so much."

"I should have treated him better—he just wanted something that I could not give him."

Something ran across the front lawn, but this time Meg said nothing. Her father would have reacted if the creature was anything dangerous, and he remained in his thoughts. Still, she kept a wary eye out for another such animal. She had never shared her father's love for the outdoors, at least not when wildlife was involved. She just had a logical aversion to dirty beasts rooting around in their own filth while baring their sharp little fangs at her.

When the silence became uncomfortable, Meg said, "Perhaps you should talk with Uncle Tom about the way he speaks to Ryan. Ryan is a fine young man."

"Tom means no harm," said John. "And he isn't so cruel to the boy as I was to young Cager."

"But Ryan is afraid of him."

John said, "I think that your uncle has a lot more respect for the young man than you think. He allows him in the house, he trusts his daughter to travel out of the state with him, and he trusts Ryan to ensure Carrie's safe return."

Meg looked surprised.

"What is it?" her father asked.

"Then you trust him to look after me when I am out of state as well?"

"Of course," said John. "He is a fine young man."

"I should have a talk with him, then."

"About what subject, Meg?"

"I shall tell him that you two respect him and that it is all right for him to finally kiss Carrie. At least on the cheek, but I doubt she will allow him to stop there."

Her father shook his head. "If you give her such advice, I fear that Tom Heath will evict me from this house tomorrow. Perhaps we can push this part of our conversation from all memory."

Meg's eyes flashed mischievously. "We'll see…"

31

Camp Mountain Man

A small branch snapped across Sam's face, and he controlled the urge to cry out. He could almost feel the welt healing as the pain quickly subsided. The mark would be gone within the day. He was part of the world's ecosystem now, and the Tennyson Organism was in his blood. *How long will I live in this world?* he wondered. *Will I even age?*

Oscar was a few steps ahead of him, peering into the forest, looking for any sign of Cager Barclay. Both men were holding their rifles and looking about nervously. They knew that they were soft targets for the mountain men and the giant bears. Sam felt the panic, of course, but the thrill of the Hole was in its cruelty. This world was not for the feeble, and Sam occasionally wondered if he was deep down a weak man. *Am I the man I pretend to be?*

Sam said, "Do you see any tracks?"

Oscar looked upset. "Plenty from the mountain men—nothing from our boy."

Sam looked around and saw only wild foliage and giant trees. He said, "He had to have left something."

"Our boy's a ghost, Sam, you know that."

"Well, where'd he go?"

"What do I look like, Daniel frickin' Boone?" snapped Oscar. "He doesn't leave a trail, Sam—you know that."

Sam shrugged. "Well, we're making too much noise looking around—let's just follow the hillbillies and assume that he'll turn up."

Oscar nodded. "It looks like they'll be easier to follow. I think they're practicing for Macy's Thanksgiving parade."

"You've noticed, too?"

"Cocky bastards," said Oscar. "Just daring anybody to chase after them…"

Sam brushed his hand across the fading welt on his cheek. Why should the mountain men have any fear if they could not be truly harmed or even killed? They must feel like gods. Foul-smelling, drunken gods.

Sam said, "Distortion."

"Excuse me?" Oscar replied.

"These boys have died and been resurrected dozens of times, I bet. I don't think it's healthy to repeat the process that many times."

Oscar agreed. "Cager's just about what he was two hundred years ago, but these bastards have been, um, *demented* from the process?"

"That's right," Sam said. "Too many reboots will result in some level of distortion."

"Or they're just a pack of assholes," Oscar offered.

Their tracks were obvious even under the dim lighting and the camouflage of the world's crazy vegetation. One of the men had defecated near the trail, and another had cut down a branch near the edge of the trail. Cager would think these men were amateurs or worse for leaving such an obvious trail. Sam was grateful for the help.

There were at least three sets of footprints and some continuing tears in the soil and greenery of the little pathway that Sam thought might be from a makeshift stretcher. Cager had been right about these guys coming back for their friend as soon as they had reinforcements. Sam wondered what kind of friend he was to let Cager go off on his own like that. They were all supposed to be a team—*more than a team.*

They followed the dark corridor wordlessly, stopping only to drink from their dwindling cups, and concentrated on their mission. Oscar led while Sam followed, lost in a storm of contrary thoughts. He heard the jingling of the bullets and cartridges that half filled his satchel and wondered if there was a way to stop them. A slight breeze seemed to be moving in from behind them, and he hoped that the rustling of the branches might cover up the sound of the bullets and of his own footsteps. He thought they might as well be wearing cowbells.

Oscar stopped. He turned and whispered, "The trail's opening up…"

Sam suddenly realized that his rifle was at the ready, and he was walking sort of hunched over, like a soldier in a war movie, ready to duck or dive. Oscar was walking the same way, but he looked bolder and badder to Sam, as though he had done this before. He felt sweat dripping from his nose and wiped it away. He was taking deep breaths and focused on inhaling through his nostrils. Sam wondered if that would make his nose sweat even more.

Oscar held his hand up in a sort of fist, which Sam took to be a *stop* sign. He froze as his bodyguard stepped out from the woods and into the clearing ahead. Quietly, as quietly as possible, he followed his friend into the open. Oscar stood a few feet away from him, and he was chuckling.

Sam stepped around him and looked at the small clearing ahead. The opening was only a few yards apart at its deepest, and the tall grass and shrubbery were at least knee high. At the far end of the gap lay a small pool of mud, and Sam thought that Oscar was perhaps laughing at the sight. He looked around again and realized that some knees were sticking out from the fauna. Focusing, he realized that a man was lying near the edge of the forest, his head shaded by the darkness of the woodlands. The man's head looked out from behind its dark veil and smiled at Sam.

"I've been waiting since daybreak for you men," said Cager. "How long does it take you two to follow a simple trail?"

Thrilled, Sam said, "We've been extra-cautious, Mr. Barclay. We didn't want to make a racket."

Cager stood up and brushed his jumpsuit off. He walked over to Oscar and patted him on the shoulder. Oscar shook his head. "So, I guess we didn't surprise you, son?"

"You gentlemen have been making a bit of noise all day," said Cager. "But not enough to catch everyone's attention."

Sam was standing with his friends now. He said, "I'm not sure they'd care if they did hear us. They seem pretty bold."

Cager nodded. "Foolhardy, I'd say. Nevertheless, I followed them to their camp, and I'm certain we can get there without notice. They are even bolder and drunker when home based."

Oscar said, "Maybe we should rest for the night and scope this place out in the morning."

"Their drunkenness will keep them from rising early," said Cager. "Perhaps we could investigate a few hours before dawn."

Sam reached over and wrapped his arm loosely around Cager's shoulder. He said, "We stay together from now on, son. I know we're not as ninja as you, but we are as loyal, and we can be pretty capable."

"It was my mistake to suggest that you were not, Mr. Ahearn," said Cager. "You are two of the bravest men I've known, and I should never have hinted otherwise."

Oscar slapped Cager on the back. "You talk awfully old for such a young kid."

Sam laughed and said, "It's like he's a little old man at the VFW or something. He uses words my grandpa wouldn't know. Did everyone talk that way back in your day, Cager?"

With a smile, Cager said, "I speak as all of my friends spake, Mr. Ahearn."

"Of course you do," said Sam. "Let's set up here and get some sleep. We're getting up early."

32

Underwhelming Gratitude

"It's a dump," Oscar whispered in the darkness.

Sam couldn't really see his friend, as the sun wouldn't be up for another hour, but his eyes were getting used to the dark of the Hole, and his other senses were stepping up. He saw a rough shape in front of him that he knew to be Oscar, and his hearing, which was sharp lately, helped his mind paint a picture of him. Sam's sense of smell hadn't improved much, though he knew that none of them should turn down a bath anytime soon. They were all getting a little ripe.

Cager led them a few miles downtrail from their mudhole campsite until the path abruptly turned into the mountain men's little shantytown. The sudden end to the pathway reminded Sam of a dead-end alley, and he felt a level of claustrophobia settling in. Not only was he lost as hell, but there was really no place to go if the bad guys started shooting. The last time he had been boxed in like this had been the day of the giant bison stampede, a day he did not wish to relive. These bison were armed.

Sam expected some sort of rudimentary settlement and instead found a small clearing within an entanglement of heavy trees. By his count, there were seven huts, each built by carpenters of varying skills, and a large campfire near the front of the compound. There was only one way into the site, as the oaks created a formidable barrier around the place, and the fire made surprise entrances unlikely. He saw a variety of bodies lying about the small gathering place near the fire. He could hear snoring from his spot among the bushes thirty yards away and knew that the men would be nursing hangovers in the morning. He wondered how they made their alcohol.

The forest stunk of smoke, rotten food, and human waste. Sam couldn't believe these men would isolate themselves in such a way, and he wondered if they were living in such filth to avoid the bears and other colossal creatures or if there was some other kind of animal to be avoided. Either way, he thought, there must be a better way.

Cager whispered, "Look close to that shack—the one over there."

"The one closest to the woods? What about it?" Oscar replied.

"Quiet, Oscar, our voices carry in the silence," said Cager. "Look closer—someone's sitting in front of the hut."

Oscar looked again and finally nodded. Quietly, he said, "Is that guy tied up?"

"I believe so," murmured Cager. "He's dressed differently, as well. His clothes have been sewn, and his boots look like they belong to Mr. Ahearn."

"How can you possibly see all that, Cager?" asked Oscar.

Cager said, "Just trust me on this."

Sam said, "We should probably get a closer look at that guy, but I don't think we want to go all Navy SEALs on this campground."

"Stay right here, Mr. Ahearn," said Cager. "Cover us if we must quickly retreat."

"Who's *we?*" asked Oscar.

Cager smiled. "Come on, Oscar."

Sam watched them slip out of their safe spot among the bushes and onto the semi-lit trail. The jumpsuits blended adequately into the shadows, and both men crept cautiously into the hillbilly compound. Oscar stopped near the fire and seemed to be covering his friend while he checked out the prisoner. Sam could see Oscar's rifle slowly swaying back and forth as he looked for any signs of consciousness among the passed-hooligans. Sam lifted his rifle and readied himself for action.

Cager reached the hostage quickly and seemed to be shaking the prisoner to wake up. He stopped and pulled something from his waistband, probably his knife, and made some quick motions with his hand. Sam lost sight of them and focused on Oscar, who was now backing slowly away from the camp. He relaxed his grip on the rifle slightly and breathed in anxiously. The rescue seemed to be working.

He heard a muffled snap behind him but did not react. There were many sounds in the Hole, and almost all of them were perilous in some way. Darkness meant little to him now, and sometimes it helped him to see what he needed. The noise could mean only two things: he was under attack from an animal, or he was under attack from a human. Time in the jungle had taught him what footsteps sounded like, and his life now depended on his ability to recognize such noises. He waited for another footstep.

The next step was more muted and much closer than the first, and he knew that he could not hesitate. He swung around quickly, slamming his rifle butt into the abdomen of a rangy mountain man. The man made a gurgling sound and pointed his own rifle toward him. Sam stepped to the side and slammed the butt of his weapon into the man's ribs, and as the man doubled over, he struck him again atop his skull. His attacker dropped wordlessly to the ground. Sam kicked the man's weapon away from his hand and turned his attention back to his friends. He squinted into the darkness but could not immediately see anything.

Eventually, he saw shapes approaching from the wooded complex, their outlines highlighted by the red-yellow flames behind them. He looked down at his own injured prisoner and saw that the man hadn't moved and hoped that he had not killed the bastard. Sam pointed his weapon in the direction of the approaching figures and exhaled as he recognized them. Cager was carrying something large, presumably the prisoner, on his shoulder, while Oscar followed several steps behind. Oscar was looking back toward the camp, and both hands were on his rifle.

He watched as the men ducked into their safe spot alongside the small trail. Cager looked at him and at the mountain man on the ground and frowned curiously. He said, "I see you've met Mr. Sanders."

"Let me help you put this guy down," said Sam. "Is he all right?"

Sam grabbed the man's arm, and the two gently placed his still frame beside the other unconscious stranger at their feet. Cager said, "This man is a friend of mine."

"Which one? Sanders?"

"No, this one. I have spoken of him before."

Oscar backed into their den and said, "Jesus, Sam, who's this?"

"He snuck up on me while I was covering you guys."

Cager said, "I watched Mr. Sanders at great length yesterday, and he's a good tracker. I'm quite impressed with you, Mr. Ahearn."

"Me too," said Oscar proudly. "But not surprised."

Sam beamed slightly then shook off the compliments. He said, "So, who is your friend, Cager?"

Both strangers were lying side by side. Cager's friend was stirring, while Sanders was still motionless. Sam could see something dark caked onto the man's hair and face and guessed that it was blood. He turned his attention to Mr. Sanders's wrist and found a healthy pulse. Satisfied, he focused on Cager's man and saw that his eyes were open but perhaps not aware. Sam stood over both men for a moment, then walked over to Oscar, who stood near the entrance to their hideout. He was watching the camp closely, and Sam knew he wanted to get going.

"You all right?" Sam asked. "You did a good job over there."

Oscar said, "Yeah. Most of those guys aren't moving for a while, Sam. They have some kind of still made from scraps of metal over there—God only knows what they're brewing. I think they may have taken apart a washing machine or a dishwasher or something to make the thing."

Sanders groaned.

Sam pointed his rifle at the man and said, "Are you all right? I doubt your friends are sober enough to come to your aid."

Sanders sat up. He rubbed his head and coughed several times before he spit blood onto the ground at Sam's feet. He said, "This ain't over between you and me, stranger."

Cager's friend stood up. He was almost as tall as Cager and a bit stockier and looked unsteady on his feet. His light hair was long, of course, and thick, and his features were sharp and almost cruel. He kicked angrily at Sanders, missed, and fell clumsily to the ground. Cager tried to help him back up, but he pushed Cager away disdainfully. He snarled, "Stay away from me, *monster.*"

"Monster?" repeated Cager. "I just liberated you from those men, Fendy."

The man shook his head. "I don't know you."

Sanders chuckled. "This Burner doesn't seem all that grateful. Perhaps you should give him back to me, and we'll all forget about this."

Sam looked at Sanders. "What do you mean *Burner?*"

Oscar grabbed Sam's shoulder. "Sam, daylight's gonna spring on us in minutes. We should get out of here."

Sam turned to Cager's friend and said, "What's your name, son?"

"My name is Fenderson Heal, and I was a friend to the *actual* Micajer Barclay. You should know that this is not a man standing beside you but rather some *daemon monster* living within his bones."

Oscar winced. "I guess all of his friends really did talk that way."

33

Last Penny

Sam Ahearn was in heaven. Every day he was eating new and tasty game, only to set up a new camp the next night and be rewarded with an even better meal. Each evening's campsite smelled like an exotic restaurant, and he half expected to be seated by some primping French waiter every time he shuffled over to the fire. Sam hoped to escape from the Hole eventually, but he knew that the best days of his life were these ones. Food would never taste the same, and friendship would never be so important Earthside. He loved it almost as much as he hated it.

The rescued captive was almost as good of a hunter as Cager. Fenderson Heal brought down some kind of giant brown-and-white elk back on their first day overtrail, and the sweet meat would have been enough to fill their stomachs for days if not for the boar-like creature Cager killed the very next day. Its meat sort of tasted like ham, but it had a fresh flavor to it that Sam did not recognize. It was an actual *new* taste to him, and one that he liked but could not adequately describe. None of the men could guess what the creature was, but all, even Fendy, knew that it was succulent.

Their new friend, armed with the rifle taken from Sam's would-be attacker, led the men on a slow, essentially overtrail path toward his home, and Cager followed behind, his rifle always at the ready. The air appeared slightly drier as they moved farther away from the trail, and the softer, spongier soil made little sound beneath their feet. The giant oaks were slimmer, and there were small saplings jutting out from the ground. Their footpath eventually opened up onto a larger trail that would lead to Fenderson Heal's home.

Sam and Oscar felt almost spoiled by their guides and wordlessly agreed to stay out of the rivalry. Fendy generally refused to speak to the man he called a monster, though he competed intensely with him. Cager, furious with his old friend for his disloyalty, simply made it a point to outdo him at any challenge. Neither showed an interest in conciliation.

On the fourth day, Fendy told Sam that his settlement was near. Sam had a little difficulty understanding his words, as a dull noise began to permeate the air. Cager told him that he knew the sound—it was the sound of the great river that had taken his life years ago. The noise was little more than a whistle, but it was constant and annoying. He guessed he would get used to it just as people who live near airports or train stations learn to block out those sounds.

"Your friends won't mind us barging in?" asked Sam. "I'd hate to get shot for saying hello."

Fendy said, "All *true* men are welcome at Last Penny, Mr. Ahearn. I think that you will enjoy your stay."

The two men stood over the cooling remains of a campfire as the sun made its morning flash across the sky. Sam said, "Do you ever get used to the odd sunrises here?"

Fendy shook his head. "It is the way of our world, Mr. Ahearn, just as the frightful bears and bison are part of our world."

"You've grown accustomed to the bears?" asked Sam, who knew that he would never get used to such creatures.

"I prefer them to the big cats that thrive on the other side of the river."

Sam knew Cager bristled at the mention of the cats, and it seemed that young Mr. Heal had similar sentiments. He did not look forward to running into the beasts, but he knew that it might happen. Cager's exit from the Hole was on the cat side of the river.

"Where is Oscar?" asked Fendy, his eyes scanning the bushes on either side of their camp.

He was wearing an outfit strikingly similar to the Ahearn jumpsuits Sam and his friends were wearing. There was no logo on his outfit, but Sam knew that he recognized it from somewhere—maybe from the boys at Exxon? He was wearing seemingly new Larry Bird Converse sneakers and white crew socks. Fendy explained that Last Penny had many such items claimed from abandoned or absorbed camps located all over the Hole. Sam had a lot of questions for the good people living at the fort.

"He and Cager went out for a while," explained Sam. "I think they just wanted to talk about something."

Fendy said, "It would be best if you did not mention your friend's history to anyone at the fort."

Sam nodded. "Would they harm him if they knew?"

"Immediately, Mr. Ahearn," Fendy replied. "With no regret."

"OK. Have you ever mentioned his name to anyone at the fort?"

Fendy paused. "I have spoken of Cager Barclay with my family there. Cager, *the real Cager*, was a great man and a good friend."

Sam started to answer but was interrupted by the rustling of leaves and familiar voices joking and laughing. Oscar popped out from the woods, followed by Cager, and headed over to Sam. Cager glared at Fendy, who would not return the gesture. This was a familiar ritual now, and Sam was impressed that Cager seemed to strike fear in a fairly rough kid every time. He saw a smirk form on Cager's face and felt the urge to smile. He remembered Cager baiting Oscar on the first day of their acquaintance. The kid could be the cockiest bastard of all time when he wanted to be. It was almost an endearing quality.

"Your friend says that you would be in danger at the fort if they knew who you were," Sam said. "Perhaps you could stay behind while Oscar and I get a look at the place."

Cager shook his head. "Together from now on, Mr. Ahearn. Remember?"

Sam smiled and said, "I remember."

Oscar stepped closer to his friends. "Well, then, we need a new name for you, Mr. Barclay. How about *Daniel Boone* or *Kit Carson*?"

"Some of these people may be familiar with those names, Oscar," said Sam. "Let's just use a name that we know—why not Mike Standish? I think we can remember that."

"OK—and he is part of our team?"

Sam said, "Right. We are all from the same place, and you both work for me. Can you remember that, Cager?"

Cager nodded. "It's essentially true."

Oscar looked at Fendy. "You seem like a good man, Mr. Heal. You really do. Can we trust you with Cager's secret?"

Fendy returned Oscar's frosty gaze and said, "I owe you gentlemen my life…"

"No," said Oscar. "You owe Cager…I mean you owe *Mike* your life. He saw you, he saved you, and he didn't kill you when you insulted him for his effort."

"I do not apologize for that, Oscar," said Fendy. "But I repay my debts."

Oscar stepped closer to Fenderson Heal. Fendy was tall and stocky, but he recognized Oscar Larsen's kind of danger, and he felt the heat from Oscar's glare. He took a small step back.

Oscar said, "You'll answer to me if anything happens to Cager. You can bank on it, my friend."

"OK," Sam interrupted. "He gets the point. I know we can count on you, Fendy."

"You can."

"Good," said Sam. "I think we should get going."

The men put on their bags and resumed their familiar march. The long walk would take most of the day, and Sam wanted to get there before sundown. Fendy probably spoke for the population of Last Penny, but Sam wanted to see the place in daylight before he showed up with his hand out. Anyway, his newly young legs were craving the hike now, and he wanted to start moving. He could not remember a time that he felt stronger, and he wanted to make the most of the experience.

The path seemed to expand with every step until Sam suddenly realized that they were no longer in a forest but were passing over a large weedy meadow. The grim forest never went away, though, and Sam expected that it would again absorb the greenlands sometime soon, and they would be right back in the thick of it. Sam noted that the noise from the river was growing to a rumble.

"How far away is this river?" he asked.

Fendy said, "Ten miles or more, Mr. Ahearn."

Stunned, Sam said, "And we can hear that noise all the way over here?"

Cager called out from his position behind them, "It is quite a large body of water, Mr. Ahearn."

Fendy pointed and said, "The fort is just over that hill."

The men increased their pace and climbed the rough knoll as quickly as they could. It was steep and peppered with stones and loose gravel, which Sam and Oscar repeatedly stumbled over. Their backpacks jingled as they moved upward, and Sam thought that he felt a cool breeze snaking around the treeless summit. At the top, they stood side by side and stared down at the buzzing settlement several hundred feet ahead. Sam knew the colony was tiny compared to the smallest towns that he had lived in *Earthside*, but it seemed enormous to him now. His stomach fluttered as he looked down on the small reminder of civilization before him.

Last Penny was a mammoth development, rectangular in shape, more than a half-mile deep in every direction, and surrounded by a wall made from hundreds of twenty-foot trees. The outer wall nearest them had an open gate, and Sam saw two armed men standing to one side of it. Inside, he could see wooden structures and dirt streets. Grayish smoke was coming from small chimneys atop most of the structures. Most of the houses appeared to have small vegetable gardens out front or in the backyard. A small group of men played a game sort of like soccer in a field near the center of the fort.

And there were people, lots of people, bustling around the lively compound as though they were clamoring home from work at the peak of rush hour. Many of the figures were wearing long dresses, and Sam dared to hope that they were indeed women. He missed women.

Oscar said, "It's like Grand Central Station down there."

Sam nodded.

Each point of the rectangle seemed to be part of a tower, or maybe a tree house, and Sam could see men staring into the distance. Realizing that the nearest sentry was looking straight at him, Sam said, "I think they see us."

Fendy stepped forward and waved.

Oscar said, "Sam, do you see that building at the center of the town?"

Sam looked. It wasn't the largest structure in the compound, but it appeared to have a bell on top of it. He said, "Oscar, I think it's…"

Oscar's voice was shaking. "A church, Sam. A church."

"Where'd they get that bell?" Sam asked. "They couldn't have made it."

Oscar shook his head, "I don't care, Sam. I think we might be home."

Part III
(Living for the Future)

34

Ahearn Industries

Rufus Johnson stopped to examine the stylish building in front of him. It was three stories high and heavily windowed. The glass was tinted and looked thick and bullet resistant, which he knew it was. A T-shirted landscaper was pushing a lawn mower across the thick blue-green grass elegantly framing the edifice. Rufus followed the shadowed stone path past a large marble stone to the double doors of the home office. "Ahearn Industries" was chiseled boldly into the stone, and he smiled sadly at the sight. The place had once been so *familiar* to him, but now it was just another place he dreaded. Like an airport or the Hall of Records.

Menlo Park was home to Ahearn Industries, and he could think of no better location. Rufus could smell the San Francisco Bay from the parking lot, a benefit of the constant breeze that oscillated between the two points. And there was excitement in the area; high-tech companies still popped up almost monthly in the town, and every now and then, one of them hit it big. Ahearn certainly had.

The sunny town was a "tree city," and the streets were lined with a variety of colorful California trees. Ahearn Industries was surrounded by its fair share of neatly pruned green trees, some of which were as tall as the three-story structure that he would soon enter. The town had strict rules concerning the care of the trees, and an improperly trimmed tree could cost the company thousands of dollars. The landscapers were paid well to prevent such fines.

The streets were clean and the people friendly, but he rarely visited Menlo Park anymore. This was perhaps his third trip since Sam's disappearance nearly a decade ago, and already he wanted to turn and run. Menlo Park was home to him at one time, but that was long ago. The only thing he missed about the town was the constant weather. The temperature rarely rose above eighty degrees or dove under seventy. It was perfect. Things would be better here if Sam hadn't been so reckless. Why did he have to climb into that damn hole?

The girl at the desk was new, at least to him, and she was California beautiful. Blond, blue-eyed, and tan—the usual. She was dressed for the weather and was showing a lot of leg. He tried to stretch a little taller for her but knew that his kind of short couldn't be stretched. She was too young, anyway.

She smiled. "You must be Mr. Johnson."

"I am indeed," he said. "I'm afraid I haven't been here for quite some time."

She handed him a pen to sign in with. "We've done some remodeling lately, but I'm sure you can find your way up to Mr. Standish's office."

"Top floor still?" he asked as he signed.

"He hasn't moved, sir."

He glided down the hall and stopped at the elevators. They looked new, and the doors opened as he approached. He stepped in, and the elevator spoke to him, "What floor, please?"

He looked around for a panel, but there were no buttons to press. He said, "Excuse me?"

The automated voice was coming from a camouflaged speaker on the ceiling of the elevator. "What floor, please? Do you know the name of the person you are visiting?"

"Engine Room, please," he said. "I have a shipment of dilithium crystals for Mr. Standish."

"Mr. Standish is on the fourth floor," said the voice. "We will arrive in less than a minute."

He scratched his head and waited. *Why are automated voices always female?* he thought. *It would be much cooler if they all sounded like James Earl Jones.*

The door opened a few seconds later, and he stepped out onto the fourth floor. The front desk was unmanned, and he passed it as he headed down the low-carpeted hallway to Mike's office. The walls were bare and clinical. He wondered if he should be wearing a clean suit like those used in the labs at the other facilities.

He passed several offices, including one that bore his name, and stopped outside Sam's office. The nameplate to the side read, "Samuel Ahearn, President." He shook his head faintly and continued toward Mike's office. He stopped and knocked.

Mike Standish opened the door. "Come in, R.J."

Mike was dressed stylishly, of course. His suit was charcoal, and his tie was some kind of blue-tinged creation that had a name like *magic teal* or *Caribbean azure*. The shoes looked vaguely like the ones that O.J. Simpson had claimed he didn't own. Rufus was wearing a two-hundred-dollar suit from Men's Wearhouse.

Mike was getting older, but he looked like he still hit the gym. He wasn't tall, but he towered over Rufus, and his chest must have still measured more than fifty inches. His hair was almost gone now, and the wrinkles sprawling across his face were telling. Mike led him to one of two sofas and handed him a scotch. He said, "Nice trip out here?"

Johnson said, "Sure. I knew most of the flight attendants."

Mike nodded knowingly. "Well, you travel a lot."

Mike sat on the opposite sofa. He sipped from his scotch and said, "You look good, R.J. You should stay out here and have me find something for you to do."

Johnson shook his head. "Maybe when Sam comes back."

"How'd you like the talking elevator?" asked Standish. "Pretty cool, huh?"

"Sam would love it. A little disturbing, though."

Mike chuckled. He said, "Has the Dearborn girl said anything more about her magic cave?"

"We've spoken about it," said Johnson. "I don't know that she ever believed Martel's story."

"And you do?"

Rufus Johnson crossed his legs as he knocked back the scotch. He looked at his friend. "Maybe it's wishful thinking, but it just sounded right when she said it. It sounded the way someone from her time would describe an entrance to the Hole."

Mike nodded. "We've set up an office in Virginia, just in case, and we've been discreetly checking around for any oddities of history that may point to a second hole. Our partners at the DHA are ready to find a Native American burial ground or the remains of a lost colony at any time. We'll step in and buy up any land attached."

Rufus nodded.

"It's funny that we never considered that there might be other entrances to the Hole," said Mike.

"We thought we were special, I guess."

Standish got up and grabbed a bottle from the bar. He splashed some more in both of their glasses and sat down. He said, "Damn, it's good to see you again, R.J. When was the last time we talked in person?"

"Christmas party, I guess. Not last year but the one before."

Mike frowned. "Long time…long time. You look good, though, like you could still go a few rounds if you wanted."

Johnson said, "About the girl."

"The Dearborn girl?"

"Yes," said Johnson. "She's quite special. The whole family is…"

"Her father's coaching football now? The great Colonel John Dearborn is tossing footballs to a bunch of teenagers? Seems a waste."

Johnson smiled. "It's amazing what people do with their second chances, Mike."

"I guess," Mike said doubtfully. "But it seems like he's squandering his talents. You'd think he'd at least write a new book or go fight in some war. He was supposed to be such a hardo—"

"You may be surprised, Mike. He's not just good at coaching football—he's especially gifted at it."

"And his wife?"

"She's opened a restaurant with a friend."

"I don't know, R.J. They sound so...*ordinary*," Mike sounded disappointed, and Rufus knew why. Sam had been such a fan of John Dearborn, and it seemed that Sam's legacy was somehow tarnished by his star retread's lack of accomplishment. Dearborn should be fighting for the French Foreign Legion or something. Instead, he was a boring old family man. Or so it seemed.

"I'll introduce you to him one day, and you'll change your mind, Mike," said Rufus. "I promise you."

Standish waved his hand almost dismissively. "And the girl is still in high school?"

"Sort of," said Rufus. "She's going to be taking concurrent classes at her high school and some advanced stuff at UNH."

"She's pretty smart, then?"

Rufus nodded. "But all of her friends think she's a little crazy. She's convinced her boyfriend in the invisible cave is still alive. Her cousin is the only one who seems to believe her, and even she has her doubts."

Mike added, "And you think the girl may be right?"

"Of course, but how could I tell her such a thing? I'd probably be giving her false hope."

Mike nodded.

Rufus glanced around the room until his eyes focused on a portrait of a young Linus Ahearn smiling handsomely down at him from the far wall. He said, "The old man really screwed Sam over, huh?"

Mike looked at the portrait and nodded. He said, "Alzheimer's is a bitch, R.J. It would have been nice if he'd told somebody when he got diagnosed. Sam cleaned up a mess."

"But everyone thought Sam was the bad guy."

Mike said, "Let's get out of here. I know where we can get a good steak..."

Rufus paused and then said, "Maybe next time, Mike."

"OK," Mike sighed. "Maybe next time."

"Have you looked into this Joshua Martel character? Did he leave any writings, any hints?" asked Rufus. "He might be the key to bringing Sam back."

Mike's face turned flush. "There seems to be a little problem with Mr. Joshua Martel."

"What kind of problem?"

"We can't find him. History says that he was quite the philanthropist, but he must not have spent much on his own funeral."

Something like desperation crept across Rufus Johnson's face. He stood up, his knees bumping the underside of the table, and barked, "Just dig up the whole graveyard—do whatever it takes to find the bastard."

Mike shook his head. "There's at least five old graveyards in Stamford, and that's working on the unsubstantiated conclusion that he was even buried in the town. One of the graveyards had a flood about a hundred years ago, and some of the graves were moved around. Joshua Martel is lost to history, R.J."

"That's just bullshit, Mike. Bullshit."

35

Back to Stamford

Marissa sat on the hood of her father's white Chrysler LeBaron. She wore casual shorts and an oversize Jimmy Buffet T-shirt. Her glasses were real, and she wore dark clip-ons to fight the rays of the early August sun. Meg stood in front of her, staring hopefully down the dirt road that led to Stamford's main drag. She wore a white-and-yellow sundress and some uncomfortable sandals. Meg was pacing.

Marissa said, "How long should we wait?"

"Charlie promised he'd be here," said Meg firmly. "He had no reason to lie."

Marissa said, "We have all day, Meg. I don't have to be anywhere else."

Meg turned away from the road. She looked at Marissa and said, "I'm so grateful for your help, Marissa. This is quite important to me."

"Anything for you, Meg," said Marissa. "But I don't understand the secrecy."

Marissa told no one of the trip into Massachusetts, not even Carrie. The phone call from Meg had come only a day before, and Marissa only half understood her friend's delicate whisperings. Meg was on some kind of mission, and who was she to refuse her? She knew Meg would do anything for her.

"So, this was your town, huh?" asked Marissa.

Meg said, "As I remember."

"Why do you always have to qualify your answers about back then?" asked Marissa.

Meg frowned. "I don't know. I guess I'm just not sure about who I am—what I am..."

Marissa said, "You're a teenager, Meg. You're not supposed to know all that yet. Your parents don't seem all that worried about it."

Three cars left dirt clouds in their wake as they blasted past the white house. There was a faded "For Sale" sign planted at the end of the dirt driveway. Most of the other houses on the street had similar signs, and some looked abandoned. The road was bumpy and didn't seem to be getting any of the renovations that other areas of the town were receiving. Most of the drive through town had been hampered by annoying construction crews and slow-moving detours that led to more detours. Maybe Charlie's street was next on the list.

His house was a Cape Cod design—a broad structure, one and a half stories, no frills, and a big chimney jutting up from the center of the roof. It seemed to Marissa that every other house in New England had a similar design and could be easily captured by her paintbrush. The bright green front yard smelled like freshly mowed grass and seemed almost professionally cut. The backyard, bounded by a cute white picket fence, was much smaller but was equally well groomed. Marissa remembered that Meg's friend was a landscaper or whatever someone who dug graves and stuff was called. The smell of sea salt permeated the air.

"Anyway," said Marissa. "I like you exactly as you are."

A smile crossed Meg's face.

Marissa said, "Your dad was famous when you were a kid, right?"

Meg climbed beside her friend. "Oh, yes. People came from all over to talk to him, and he wrote several books about military tactics and such."

"When I Googled him, it listed his books, but they were mostly out of print. I have some friends who are collectors and come into the bookstore, and I think that I might be able to track a few down. I don't think they'll be very expensive because...well, hardly anyone remembers him now."

Meg said, "I think he enjoys his anonymity."

Marissa looked doubtfully at her watch. "We've been here for almost an hour."

"He'll be here soon; I promise."

"Did your father know any other famous people—like Benjamin Franklin or Paul Revere?"

Meg smiled. "No one has ever asked me that. I think he knew Mr. Revere, but he knew him more for his work as a silversmith than for his patriotism. Father once dined with Benedict Arnold, and he knew General Washington."

Stunned, Marissa hopped from the hood of the car and leaned into her friend. She said, "Your father was friends with the father of our country?"

"Not friends, exactly, but he was under General Washington's command at times, and they did occasionally correspond over the years…"

Shaking her head, Marissa said, "Did you ever meet him?"

"I would have liked to, but no."

"What was he like?" Marissa asked, a cloud of colors forming into a vague picture somewhere in the back of her mind. *Maybe I'll ask Mr. Dearborn to help me paint a portrait of President Washington,* she thought.

Meg said, "Father told me that he was quite tall, and he had the largest hands. He said that no man could swear as well or as often as the general."

"President Washington swore?"

Meg said, "He was the great man of our generation, but he wasn't perfect. He owned slaves, Marissa."

Marissa said, "He did?"

"He was a man of his time, I guess."

Marissa had a terrible thought. "Did you own slaves, too?"

"Lord, no," Meg said. "Father infuriated so many of his contemporaries with his views on the subject. He once beat a fellow officer for striking a young slave."

An old Ford Explorer chugged down the road and slowed as it neared the driveway. The woman behind the wheel turned cautiously up the paved driveway and parked beside the girls. A young man sitting beside her in the passenger seat was holding a large rectangular object. He stepped out, and Marissa realized that the object was a poorly framed painting. She also recognized that Meg's friend was absolutely gorgeous. He was wearing cargo shorts and a cut-up Patriots T-shirt. His body was muscular—like a swimmer, not a bodybuilder—and he was very tan. His face was angular and strong, and he had a crooked smile, sort of like a younger, less weird Tom Cruise. Was Meg here for the painting or the boy?

Charlie Whitehouse said, "I'm wicked glad you're here, Meg."

Meg didn't immediately get up. She said, "It's good to see you again, Charlie. When do your classes start?"

"In just a few weeks. Is it still OK for me to call you? I'll be in Manchester soon for early practices."

"Of course, Charlie," said Meg. "Charlie, I'd like to introduce you to my dear friend Marissa Robinson. You met her brother, Ryan."

"Hi, Marissa. Your brother's a pretty protective kid…"

Charlie looked into Marissa's eyes, and she felt a flutter of excitement. If anyone could make Meg forget her bicentennial boyfriend, it was this guy. She said, "It's good to meet you, Charlie. What sport are you practicing—soccer, like Meg?"

"No, I play lacrosse," Charlie replied. "I didn't know you played soccer, Meg. Are you going to play at UNH?"

Meg sighed and said, "I'm not allowed."

Someone cleared her throat, and everyone looked at the thin woman with graying hair standing beside Charlie. She was tall and leathery tan and looked tired. Charlie said, "Everyone, this is my mother, Janice."

Meg carefully climbed from the hood of the car and said, "Mrs. Whitehouse, I'm Meg Dearborn, and this is my very close friend, Marissa Robinson."

"It's nice to meet you, ladies," Mrs. Whitehouse said. She looked both of them over and said, "How do I get some of them purple streaks in my hair?"

Marissa had heard this before. She said, "I'm sorry if you don't like them, I…"

"No, dear," said Mrs. Whitehouse. "I'm serious."

Charlie said, "She is. You should see her high school yearbook—she had some really, um, *eighties* hair."

Marissa looked the woman over with a keener eye. Charlie's mom was lively and still kind of pretty in an older person way, and her lines weren't as pronounced as she first thought. She was wearing black pants and a white dress shirt; she looked like the hostess of an Applebee's or a Ruby Tuesday's. A few tweaks here and there and Charlie's mom could be *old-lady hot.*

Charlie said, "Why don't we get out of this heat and head on inside. You guys can look this picture over in the house."

The front door was unlocked. A narrow front foyer led directly to a carpeted staircase. Charlie and his mother led the girls into a small, light-colored parlor to the left of the stairs. The interior of the house was nice enough, but the rooms were missing color and luster and seemed plain and uninteresting to Marissa's sensibilities. She wanted a house with secret rooms, fire poles, and wishing wells. One day, she hoped to invent a new color and use it to paint her bedroom.

Marissa counted a dozen photographs of Charlie nailed to the walls and came to the conclusion that Mrs. Whitehouse was quite fond of her son. There were no photos of Charlie's parents or of anyone else, for that matter. Marissa didn't see a television or radio, and the only sound she could hear was the strained coughing of an aging central air-conditioning unit. There was a small piano near the far wall, and Marissa wondered if it was Charlie or his mom who played it. Maybe it was there for decoration.

The girls sat on an old brown sofa, while Charlie stood in front of them, gently tearing newspaper wrappings off the portrait in his hand. Mrs. Whitehouse sat on a nearby love seat and watched her son. He wrestled briefly with the paper, then handed the picture to Meg. She stood and placed the portrait against the edge of the couch and stared at it. It wasn't the highest-quality painting Marissa had ever seen, but it was definitely a portrait of an older Sally and a slightly younger Meg facing each other from separate wooden chairs. They were wearing formal-looking dresses and attractive shoes, and their long blond tresses were fluttering in some breeze. Both were smiling and holding hands as light streamed in from a large window behind them. A vase or pot holding blue and yellow flowers sat on a table beside Sally. The frame was cracked and bent, and a small light rectangle indicated a spot that must have given the name of the picture or perhaps the artist.

Meg twirled the picture toward Marissa and said, "What do you think?"

"It looks old—that's for sure," said Marissa. "Let me look a little more closely. Are you sure you never posed for this?"

"I think I would remember, Marissa."

Marissa put her glasses on and eyeballed the picture for a few moments. Finally, she said, "It's absolutely an oil painting; it seems to have lost a bit of texture, and the colors have faded. It's definitely not professionally done."

"How do you know that?" asked Charlie. He was hovering curiously over her shoulder, and she could feel the heat from his breath against her. Goose bumps were forming wherever the soft mist wandered across her neck. Marissa glanced back at him and felt her cheeks burn when he smiled at her. She inched away from him even though part of her didn't want to. Charlie didn't seem to notice.

Marissa decided to concentrate on the mysterious picture. She said, "The details, I guess. The hands don't seem to have fingernails, and the facial structures are good, obviously, but too identical. There's no signature, but I'd say this is the work of a talented amateur."

Meg crinkled her nose. "Could you do better?" she asked.

"I don't know, Meg. Probably. Maybe."

"Would you help me restore it? And frame it, too?"

Marissa said, "Of course."

"I want it to be our secret for a while."

Marissa nodded.

Meg turned to Charlie's mother and said, "How did you come into possession of this painting?"

She replied, "I *came into possession* of it, I don't know, twenty years ago. It was in my grandmother's attic when she died. I don't have any idea where it came from, but I know she liked flea markets and yard sale-ing."

Meg brushed her hair back. Marissa had initially envied Meg's long blond hair—actually, she had envied most everything about Meg's beauty—but her opinion had changed about the hair. It grew even faster now than before, and only Meg's determination with her many brushes kept the locks from Armageddon. She was still secretly jealous of almost everything else about Meg, though. Almost everything.

"Did you have to pay your friend to return the painting?" asked Meg.

"I gave it to Myra last year, and she just put it in her closet. One look at you and I can see it belongs to you."

Meg said, "I cannot tell you how much I appreciate your gesture."

"Just let your friend here help me with my dye job, and we'll be square," said Mrs. Whitehouse. "I want to be trendy."

"You've got a deal," said Marissa. "I think you'd look amazing as a redhead."

"A redhead?" Janice mused. "Sure, but I still want the purple streaks."

36

Breakfast at the Shapeway Home

For a moment, Sam thought he was back in his apartment in Menlo Park. He was comfortably sprawled across a king bed and covered by a layer of thick blankets. But the bed, though a welcome change, was lumpy, and the room was almost frighteningly dark; there were no streetlights, no digital clocks lighting the room, and no sign of those annoying California birds chirping outside the window. *God,* he thought, *I miss those damn birds.*

The room was silent except for the snoring coming from some other part of the room. Sam recognized the labored breathing and knew that Oscar was somewhere near. Oscar was always nearby—he even went on vacations with Sam. He wrapped his arms around his pillow and closed his eyes. Sam rarely fell back asleep after waking, but he gave it a try, anyway. After a while, he sat up and waited for the sun, which came quickly.

He stretched, then looked around the dim room. It was empty, except for the bed, and uncarpeted. Fendy's mother-in-law, Mrs. Shapeway, had given them fresh clothes last night, and Sam was eager for a change. All the outfits were jumpsuits like the one Fendy was wearing, and Sam quietly tried his on. It was snug, comfortably so, and he liked it. There had been a patch, probably an emblem, on the chest of the suit, but it was gone. Where had it come from—Exxon or another oil company? There was a company in Arizona called Fusion Industries that was always poking around in Ahearn's business—they'd like to look around the Hole and see if there was anything to steal.

A knock on the heavy door brought Sam's thoughts back to the here and now. He stepped over Oscar and opened the door. Fendy was on the other side. He was dressed in clean clothes and looked like he had washed up somehow. He said, "Breakfast is just about ready—why aren't you men up yet? Mother doesn't like waiting."

—m—

"Thank you so much for breakfast, Mrs. Shapeway," said Sam. "We've been eating charred meat for months now. This porridge is quite an improvement."

"You may call me Alice if you wish, Sam. I believe we have a similar number of years behind us, don't we?"

Sam smiled at the woman seated across from him. She wore a dark, pilgrim-y dress and had her hair tied up inside a white bonnet. Her face was as young and perfect as anyone living in the colony, but her eyes hinted at her age. They were blue and attentive and a little bit wary. Sam imagined that she had seen a lot. He said, "Well, Alice, I think you may be right."

It was daylight now, but the oil lamp on the table was still lit, brightening the shadows of the dusky chamber. The room seemed tight, and Sam realized that the iron stove near the far wall took up almost a quarter of the room by itself. There were no windows in the room, but Sam recalled seeing a glass one on the main wall of the receiving room.

That room, much larger than the dining room, seemed to be the main room of the downstairs. A fire roared in the corner stove, and Sam welcomed the warmth. There were comfortable seats and a larger community table centering the room. Clearly, that was the entertaining room, the room where Sam and his friends had been welcomed into the Shapeway household.

Fendy, seated beside Sam, said, "Mother is one of the *Originals*, Mr. Ahearn. She and her husband were among the first to arrive here."

"Is that why your house is larger than the houses farther back in town?" asked Sam.

Alice nodded. "We had no fence when we first arrived, and we had such a large clearing to build on. My husband and I—and so many of our friends—built wonderful homes for our families. The trees were so large and plentiful, and we had a collection of tools and nails that we all initially shared."

Sam said, "And then things got rough?"

She smiled but not happily. "The gateway closed suddenly...the only way home...and suddenly we had no more tools or weapons and no natural ores to fashion new metals."

"No metals at all? Besides that wonderful razor Fendy loaned me earlier."

She shook her head. "That was just a leftover item that belonged to my husband, Sam. Of course, this scarcity of tools and metals caused some amount of squabbling among the settlers, but we overcame our problems when the animals arrived."

Fendy said, "Mainly the bears, but we've run into other creatures that seem to have a taste for humans. Luckily, the cats stay on the other side of the river—I expect they might be able to climb the walls around the town."

Sam said, "What of Mr. Shapeway? Is he..."

"He was the first to meet one of the bears, Mr. Ahearn," Alice said coldly. "The first to go."

"I'm so sorry," said Sam. "Those creatures are..."

Alice sort of waved him off with a gesture and a smile. "It's been quite a while now, Sam."

Sam ate a little more porridge from his wooden bowl and gulped down a deliciously creamy liquid that was not milk or ale. Perhaps a kind of cider?

Cager stepped into the room, soon followed by Oscar. They were both dressed in clean jumpsuits identical to Sam's. The clothes had no tags, but Sam was now sure they had once belonged to the Exxon guys.

Their suits were quite similar to Ahearn suits but were colored more dully. The tags had been removed, but Sam knew he was right.

Oscar said, "This house is bigger than yours, Sam."

"I think so, buddy. Why don't you guys grab a bowl and sit down?"

Alice said, "Mr. Larsen, why don't you gentlemen sit down, and I will bring you your breakfast."

Cager muscled in beside Fendy, while Oscar sat across from them. Fendy looked annoyed, but he said nothing. *They are so alike,* Sam thought, *and they don't even see it.*

Cager said, "What's the plan, Mr. Ahearn?"

"Well, *Mike*, I'm supposed to meet with the town manager after breakfast, and I was hoping Mr. Heal would show you two around the town—kind of give you the lay of the land."

"Mr. Mallory is stopping by this morning?" asked Alice. She had apparently served the boys and seated herself without anyone noticing. Sam thought her voice sounded a little odd as she asked the question.

"Is that OK, Alice? Apparently, he was occupied when we arrived last night."

Alice said, "Mr. Mallory is always welcome here."

Sam was unconvinced. He gazed at Fendy, who only shrugged.

The men ate quickly. Oscar said, "I have never had soup for breakfast before, but I like it."

Cager nodded. "The porridge is quite good. What meat is in it?"

"Whatever Fenderson brings home. He is one of the town's best hunters."

Cager coughed.

Oscar said, "Does everyone have a job? I noticed there were some crops deeper into the city, and I saw some shops."

"Each household is expected to make some contribution. I often help my neighbors, but I am not required to so long as Fenderson hunts."

Oscar said, "And Fendy is your son-in-law?"

The men looked at Alice, but she did not answer immediately. Fendy said, "The passing bell rang for my wife recently…"

Sam thought Cager was going to speak, but he stopped himself. He moved his chair and gave Fendy a little more room at the table. Sam wondered if he should say something.

Alice Shapeway said, "The good Lord has challenged us in this little world, but we believe His tests shall make us stronger in the end."

"Amen," said Oscar.

37

Mallory

Sam thought Alice was an intriguing woman. She was tall and fair-skinned, her brown-red hair was partially covered by an odd white bonnet, and importantly, she was easy for Sam to talk to. Alice turned her head often from embarrassment or excitement, almost snorting when she laughed, and her nervous smile reminded him that he'd been spending too much time with Oscar. She spoke with an odd mix of southern twang and British aristocracy. Fendy's widowed mother-in-law was one of the oldest citizens of Last Penny. Sam believed her stature as an Original gave her considerable influence in the fort. Such a woman would be quite prized in a place like this. In any place, really.

Sadness crept into the conversation when the subject of family arose. Alice spoke confidently, happily even, but her eyes gave much away to Sam. He saw the loneliness of a woman who had outlived her loved ones. They turned dull, and the smile waned, when she mentioned her late husband and daughter. Sam saw the pain that youthful camouflage would not conceal. He carried a bit of it himself.

"I am the only woman to give birth to a child here," she said. They were seated on the wooden front steps to her home, probably the largest traditional house on the compound, talking politely, a discreet foot and a half of empty space between them. The perpetual hum from the faraway river went almost unnoticed by Sam, as did the odd, cool breeze that circled the compound. The brighter sunlight was the only thing that seemed to bother Sam in this part of the Hole. The difference was slight, but it made Sam's eyes ache.

Alice said, "William and I were so happy at the time. How could we know that she would have no friends to grow up with? She was always the youngest."

"She must have been lonely," said Sam. "The ultimate only child."

"She was," Alice answered. "And then her father died…"

They retreated into comfortable silence.

Sam watched a midsize man with dark, medium-long hair and a polished, almost cocky carriage approach. He seemed to float across the stone walkway, stopping at the bottom step. The man was dressed practically, in comfortable work pants and a durable long-sleeved shirt. Alice had found similar clothing for Sam to wear, and he was chafing a little bit from the fabric. He was, however, enjoying the feel of his new Larry Bird Converse sneakers. He'd had enough of the boots.

Alice was still wearing the pilgrim dress from breakfast, and Sam liked it. He thought he would describe her look as *retro Puritan*. Interestingly, she was wearing sneakers, too. Men's sneakers.

"It is wonderful to see you, Alice," said the man. He turned his gaze to Sam, who was now standing. "And you must be Samuel Ahearn; it is a pleasure to meet you."

They shook hands.

Sam said, "I hear great things about you, Mr. Mallory."

Mallory replied, "Please, call me Lark."

Sam realized that he and Alice were following Mallory toward the street. The eight original homes were constructed near the main entrance of the compound and were all older and somehow brighter than other houses in the city. There was even a small patch of grass, or something like it, covering her front yard. Mallory turned leftward, away from the entrance, and headed toward the bulk of the town.

"The village is more than a half-mile long and nearly the same wide," said Mallory. "It may seem small by your standards, but it was quite a bit of work to construct."

"It's simply amazing," said Sam. "How long have you lived here?"

Mallory removed a piece of cloth from a pocket and wiped his brow. He said, "I arrived here just before your friend, Mr. Fenderson. I was hungry and tired, and I was sure the town was just some wild hallucination."

Sam knew the feeling. He said, "Where are you from? You carry yourself like an Ivy Leaguer."

Mallory looked down and kicked at the reddish soil. "I came from a place where God and family are not looked upon with any favor."

Sam smiled. "Los Angeles?"

"No," said Mallory. "I do not know that place."

Alice said, "Mr. Mallory is a deacon in our church and is looked to for guidance in our city."

Sam couldn't get over the people, male and female, walking past him. No one seemed to acknowledge them except to occasionally glare at Alice. Even Lark Mallory, unofficial mayor of the fort, seemed to escape the notice of most passersby. Either he was not important to them or the locals were afraid to talk to him. Sam doubted that he had been advised to meet with Mallory his first day in town because the man was unimportant. And Alice's manner had grown cooler since Mallory was around. Sam reminded himself that it was none of his business. He was just a guest in the town.

He said, "I didn't realize how skinny my friends and I have gotten until this moment. This low-carb thing works wonders."

Mallory laughed. "We'll fatten you up a little, Samuel."

Alice said, "You'll gain some weight here, Mr. Ahearn, but not too much. There are no obese people in this town."

"Will your friends be joining us today?" asked Mallory.

Sam shook his head. "They're going to visit the church later today. My friend Oscar is quite devout."

"And Mr. Heal—is he about?"

Alice said, "He hunts today."

"Of course," said Mallory. "I was delighted to hear that he had been rescued from those criminals."

They approached the church as they spoke. It was large and shapeless and seemed purposefully drab. Early Americans never gussied up their churches, Sam remembered, and considered most sacraments of the Catholics and the Church of England to be man-made and not divine. He wasn't sure if they even celebrated Christmas and Easter. They were kind of like the Jehovah's who seemed to knock on his door once a week. He missed them, too.

Alice said, "The bell is a new construction. We have no metal ores in the region, but the blacksmith was able to fashion metals recovered from other sites."

Sam wondered if his dishwasher was one of the recycled metals. Was there a Maytag logo somewhere on the bell? He smiled at the thought.

Alice said, "The church has always been a part of our lives, and Pastor Tremaine has been with us since the beginning."

Houses began to jam together, and bustling townspeople began to press around them. None of these people were wearing fancy sneakers, and their clothes had a distinct hand-me-down look to them. Alice looked a little uncomfortable as the unwashed masses banged against her, but Mallory was oblivious to the crowd. The street smelled of refuse and squalor like in any other slum that Sam had visited. He made a mental note to call this part of town *the South Side* on his map. The south side is always the toughest part of town.

Sam remembered his pricey neighborhood near Menlo Park and pined for its solitude. The nearest house was more than one hundred yards down the road. He had almost forgotten just how much he hated crowds until now. It was easy for him back home. He sent assistants out to do his shopping, and Mike Standish, the real Mike, handled many of his calls and meetings. Sam hated malls and parades and even drive-in theaters. Nothing about the Hole had changed his mind about that.

They passed the church and walked by dozens of smaller homes, most of which had gardens to one side. A few of them had small structures, maybe barns, in the back. None of them had a driveway or a satellite dish, though many had wells, and most had little houses with carved-out moons erected somewhere on the property. No house was painted, though there may have been a kind of sealant covering the walls. Sam felt icy stares and occasional bumps from the locals and tried to brush it off. He reminded himself again that he was just a visitor.

The houses began to diminish in number until only a single stone structure remained. It was only ten or fifteen feet long and much less than that in length. Two long pipes jutted crookedly from the level rooftop. The dark wooden door was thick and malformed and was covered with large black clouds.

"A crematorium?" Sam asked.

Fendy called those mountain men Walkers, Sam thought. *They called him a Burner. What exactly do they burn here? And what's a Walker?*

Mallory said, "We rarely use it."

Sam looked at Alice, but her thoughts were her own. He said, "Where are the relics that I have been hearing about?"

Mallory nodded. "We are nearly there. The third shed is all but full now, and we may have to build a fourth."

The storage huts abutted the heavy wall at the end of the compound. Each one was the size of a small garage, and all were placed roughly at the foot of a lookout tower. There was a large enclosure set up across the street from the sheds that looked like a large animal pen, probably for the oxen used to move relics and treasures from around the Hole.

Sam looked up and saw a man standing on a platform at the top of the tower. He held a rifle in both hands and appeared to be paying very little attention to them. Sam suddenly understood why Mallory had seemed so unfazed by the obvious hostility they had encountered in the South Side. The man was thick and black and familiar-looking. Sam said, "I swear I know that man."

Mallory replied, "I believe you do. His name is Jason Keith—do you remember him?"

Sam remembered. "Of course. He works for me—at least he used to. May I speak with him?"

Alice said, "Mr. Keith will be joining us for dinner tonight, Sam. He and Fenderson are great friends."

"Great," said Sam. "Now what's in the sheds?"

Mallory said, "Lots of things, Samuel. You know about the fabric and the footwear, but we have much more. We have clothes, tools, and weapons. Some that belong to you, I believe."

"Why is everything stored in this, um, colorful part of town?" asked Sam.

Mallory pointed his chin upward. "Mr. Keith and the other sentries are quite capable, Samuel."

"My company hires the best."

Mallory led them to the largest building and said, "Mr. Keith has been helpful with some of the objects we've recovered. He said you have a greater understanding of mechanical devices."

Sam shrugged. "I have a bit of knack, I guess. Let's see what you've got."

Mallory opened the unlocked door, and they stepped inside.

38

Backyard Picnic

"Most of the stuff was junk," said Sam. "But this is interesting."

He held up a tile-shaped piece of plastic. It was opaque, not clear, and little lines ran through it in all manner of directions. Sam dropped it on the table in front of him and watched Oscar pick it up, his index finger tracing the lines. Oscar could never just look at anything; he always had to touch things.

"What is it, Sam?" he asked.

Alice's backyard was spacious, and the neatly cut grass, or green-blue weeds, reminded Sam of his lost life of affluence. Who cut the grass, and what tools were used for the job? Perhaps one of the locals ran some kind of landscaping service for the fancier houses in town.

Neat shrubbery dotted the backyard but could not quite take Sam's attention away from enormous sections of the great wall that permanently shadowed the yard. He knew that the fence initially guarded the original eight, and the rest of the compound had expanded slowly over time. Most of the additions to the fence were shaded differently, and Sam felt he could judge the age of the neighborhoods as he would read the rings on a tree stump. Alice's house would be the middle ring.

They ate near the house. It was warmish and breezy, and Sam imagined it to be some company picnic with the real Mike and Rufus and some of the others on their way over. In his mind, the ringing of the great river was perhaps the hum of the pool filter or a static-y radio that no one felt inclined to turn off. And Alice was not just somebody's mother-in-law. He saw her in a different role.

A bright cloth cover was draped over a large wooden table, and everybody sat on matching chairs. Sam and Cager sat on one side with Fendy and Oscar on the other. Jason Keith had not yet arrived. Alice came in and out of the house, carrying various foods and more of the ale, which he realized had alcohol in it, out to the men. She carried herself well, and he could not help but stare at her.

"I think it's a solar panel, Oscar. I think it's designed specifically for the Hole."

"Who would do that?"

Sam shrugged.

"Can you hook it up?" asked Oscar. "Like to this house—put in some lights or something?"

"There were some lights in the shed, but I think all of this stuff is just leftover. They must have found an abandoned site, kind of like ours, and brought back some shiny, useless stuff. Intriguing but useless. I doubt I could figure it out even if they had more."

"What do you mean?"

Sam took a bit of bread and soaked it in some oil. He took a bite and said, "That technology is way ahead of me."

Cager said, "How could that be? You and Oscar have only been here for a few months. How long would that be back home?"

"Maybe a decade—not enough time to make such leaps in technology, I don't think. I don't even recognize this material. If you look at the panel, there's some kind of cloudy liquid that moves about as if by its own will."

Oscar said, "Then where'd it come from?"

"I don't know, buddy, but I've never been convinced that these holes only open to our world."

"You're saying aliens?" Oscar looked alarmed.

"No," said Sam. "But Mallory said he came from a place with no God. Maybe he wasn't exaggerating."

Alice placed a plate of warmed vegetables onto the table. She left for a while, then returned with a larger plate that was covered with sliced meat. It looked to Sam like venison, but he didn't ask. He was just grateful for food now.

"Would you care to say grace, Mr. Ahearn?" she asked as she sat beside him. "When Mr. Keith arrives."

"Of course, Alice," Sam said. "What did you boys do today?"

Oscar said, "We looked around. This town's got some serious class warfare going on—did you know you need a special pass to visit this end of town? One of Mallory's men stopped us when we were heading back here."

Sam looked at Alice. "There must be great resentment about this."

She shook her head. "No person has ever complained about the rules *before* they were allowed to move in. Only after admittance."

Cager said, "We also visited the church. The pastor there sure likes to talk."

"About what?"

Oscar glanced at Alice. "Perhaps another time."

"I am no child, Mr. Larsen," said Alice. "You may speak freely in my presence."

Cager took over, "He mentioned that your daughter fell in the house and that the damage to her skull was too much for her. He said that she was with child at the time, the only person ever to conceive in this town."

Alice moved her jaw slightly. "Yes, well…Pastor Tremaine does indeed speak a little too freely."

Cager pressed, "What was her name?"

Fendy stood up.

Cager stood, too, and the men eyed each other. Cager repeated his question, "What was her name?"

"Her name was Mary," said Fendy. "I don't wish for you to speak it. Ever."

"Everybody calm down," said Sam. "Sit down."

"Did you burn her in that damnable incinerator? What did you do with the body of your wife and child?"

"She is buried near town," Alice said, her voice muffled. "Why do you speak this way to Fenderson, who has been your friend, or to me, the giver of this meal?"

Cager's words exploded. "Is she in a casket? A sealed casket?"

Alice's tone was even. "I have had enough of this, Mr. Standish. Please leave here immediately."

Fendy said, "You heard my mother—get out of here, or..."

"Do you know that I dream about my time in the ground, Fendy? I dream about the dark, the loneliness, the stench. I dream every night about these things because I spent so much time, so many years, in the soil, unable to move or really to think, but I still dream about it. Part of me was alive all the time I was there."

Fendy said, "Cager..."

"Cager?" repeated Alice.

Sam took her shoulder and pulled her away from the confrontation. He said, "Calm down, Cager—we can figure this out. We really don't need the neighbors knowing our business."

Cager looked at Alice. "Do you ever wonder why nobody ages in this world? Even without the mud, nobody ages because we all eat what comes from the soil. Even the trees don't die but instead grow into the clouds."

Fendy said, "I should never have allowed you here, *creature*, and I certainly won't have you judge us on our way of life and our decisions."

Cager tagged him with a right from across the table, and Fendy staggered. Sam was impressed that the kid didn't fall. He shook his head a little, stepped onto the table, and sprang upon Cager with impressive speed. The two wrestled briefly, but Cager was the stronger of the two, and he quickly took control. He had one knee on the ground and the other on his former friend's chest when Oscar pulled him away. Sam ran around the table and checked on Fendy, then looked at Oscar. Not long ago, Oscar may have been on Fendy's side, but there was no chance of that now. He looked like he wanted to take a pop at Fendy, too.

Cager said, "She's alive, you bastard. She and your unborn child are lying in a hole under some rock in this godforsaken jungle, and you sit here drinking ale. *You're* the *abomination*, and I wish that I hadn't saved you from those fetid men in the jungle. You deserved whatever they were going to do to you."

Fendy stood up and glared at Cager.

Alice Shapeway said, "Samuel, how could you have brought this to my house? You bring this Walker into my home, and he…he…"

She stormed into the house, passing Jason Keith, who stood in the large doorway. He looked at Sam, and said, "I missed something, didn't I?"

Sam said, "You missed a little. Have you met, um, Mike Standish?"

"I have," he answered. He pointed at Cager and said, "But who is this big man right here?"

Fendy rubbed his jaw. "His name is Cager Barclay, Jason. We were friends once."

Jason was a lanky man who always looked ten years older than he really was. Even after all this time in the Hole, he looked damned near middle-aged. He said, "First you say this guy is a stocky bald man I used to work for, and now you say he's a dead man that just punched you in the face. Which is it?"

"My name is Cager Barclay," said Cager. "And I have had enough of this place."

"You and me both," said Jason. "Do you guys know a way out?"

Sam said, "We've given up on the one near the lodge."

Jason said, "Me too. When I last visited the place, it was a ghost town, and the damn bear monsters were trying to eat their way in. I'd rather work in this Amish village than wait to die in that place."

"Where did all of the tools and equipment go, Jason? We assumed it was all here, but only a few pieces seem to have made it to Last Penny."

"I'm sorry, Mr. Ahearn. I was sent out on a hunting detail, and we ran into a pair of those bears. When I got back to camp, the only survivor, there wasn't a soul in sight."

"It's not your fault, son," Sam said, "How far have you gentlemen scouted around here—have you found any more holes?"

Fendy shook his head. "There are a few muddy bogs near the great river. And some empty campsites."

"I have something of a map going in my journal. Could you append it for me?"

Fendy replied, "Mr. Martel was our cartographer, Mr. Ahearn, but I think I can scribble something down for you."

"I thought there were only two of you," said Sam. "There was another?"

Cager smiled. "Joshua Martel would not have followed us here. He did not actively seek out adventure."

Fendy smiled, then winced, at Cager's words. "I don't know how long it took him to crawl back into the fort after Major Croghan drove the Red Jackets all the way to hell to Canada."

"You were at the battle of Fort Stephenson?" Sam asked. "Did you see Tecumseh?"

Fendy said, "We saw him, Mr. Ahearn, but we couldn't shoot the man to save our lives. He just walked across the battlefield as if he was taking a stroll through town, everyone shooting at him and screaming, and then he sauntered into the woods as though none of it was real."

Cager added, "Our only hope was for him to trip over Joshua as he hid behind some log."

Alice was back. She placed her hand at the small of Sam's back, which gave him a thrill, and said, "Perhaps we could all sit down and talk more rationally."

Her eyes were puffy and sadder than usual. Sam wanted to embrace her, to soothe her, and more. Instead, he said, "Alice, I never meant to lie to you."

"Of course you didn't, Samuel," she said, sniffling. "You were protecting your friends."

Cager said, "I am sorry for my words, Mrs. Shapeway. I can leave whenever you wish."

"That won't be necessary, *Mr. Standish*," she said. "I believe you've been through enough hard times. You are welcome here always."

Oscar said, "Let's eat, then, and stop all the squawking."

Alice sat beside Sam and held his hand as he said grace.

39

Martha Nickelson

"So, you just gave away a perfectly good boy," Carrie said, exasperated, "to *Marissa* of all people? I am so mad at her…and just a day before the wedding."

Carrie's face was red between the freckles, and she was sort of snorting. Meg had to look away, fearing a laughing fit. She said, "Carrie, they have spent some time together helping me with Father's gift. It was quite evident from their first meeting that they have an attraction. His mother seems to like her, and that takes a lot of doing, let me tell you."

"You don't steal a friend's boyfriend—that's the rule," Carrie explained. "Everybody knows the rules."

Meg didn't want this conversation. Carrie knew full well that her heart was affixed to only one man, and his name was not Charlie Whitehouse. Charlie was sweet and handsome, and she was quite happy to see Marissa finally get serious with such a boy. Anyway, Meg was more interested in the much-delayed visit from her friend Martha Nickelson. Most of the summer had been spent with canceled plans and last-minute snags. Finally, she was coming.

"Marissa did not steal anything from me, Carrie. She was so downcast about the obvious, but she never would have acted on her feelings; you know that. It was my doing, and I'm glad I did it."

Carrie hesitated, her brow furrowed. "Well, she does deserve a good boyfriend. Did it take a lot to convince her that it was OK?"

"Oh, yes," said Meg. "She argued with me, but she knew I was right just as you do. Charlie deserves a girl who isn't chasing a ghost."

Carrie shrugged. "Well, you know best, I guess, but I'm still mad. Anyway, where did you put the portrait—the one that cost you a boy-friend? It better be worth it."

"It's in the Great Room right now. I hoped that we could hang it in their room after Martha arrives."

The front lawn smelled of cut grass and was covered in morning dew. It took Uncle Tom hours to mow it in its entirety using a riding lawn mower, and he usually drank beer while doing so. Her understanding of modern law was that this was not illegal, but she wasn't sure. So much about the world had changed since her childhood.

A cool late-summer wind circled the hill and brought neighbors' voices and breakfast scents back to Meg upon its return. She wondered if the neighbors could hear bits and pieces of her conversation. Perhaps they gossiped about her. Of course they gossiped about her. She lived in a family of retreads.

There was a small vegetable garden near the old barn that mainly held tomatoes but also had small patches of peas and carrots. Her mother spoke of planting a cornfield, but that would be closer to the house that she and her father were going to build across the street. Uncle Tom owned the land, and her father planned to clear it and build a new house not so far away from this one. Meg realized that no member of the Dearborn family had any plans to move far away from Uncle Tom's house. She certainly wasn't leaving her room unless she and Carrie got an apartment of some sort together. But this would always be home to her, not Stamford or some college dormitory and perhaps not even any other place that her future brought her to. This was home.

This had been the most enjoyable summer of Meg's life, and that included Margaret's long-ago memories of privileged youth and lost carelessness. She and Carrie spent several weekends in a quaint coastal Maine town with some of the girls they had met that night in Stamford. Their friend Amy DeCicco and her sister, Ally, worked in a lobster restaurant and had plenty of room in their cluttered apartment. Meg could never bring herself to eat the ghastly sea insects served at the restaurant, but there were other meals on the menu for her. Carrie tore the red bugs apart with an insatiable glee and scarfed the white meat into her gullet with frightening enthusiasm.

Carrie and Meg became as red as those lobsters on their first visit to the beach town, though Meg's wounds faded as fast as they arrived. Carrie's burn faded, but her freckles expanded and concentrated into crazy Rorschach designs. It would have been perfect if Marissa had come, but she stayed home to work on the portrait. Meg believed she stayed away out of guilt for harboring improper affections for Charlie. Silly.

"Someone's coming," said Carrie. "It must be her."

A gaudy-looking red car pulled into the long dirt driveway. It slowed as it turned, a small gravel cloud dancing behind it, and edged cautiously up the drive. The windows were tinted enough to block any chance of seeing through the glass. Meg wondered why Martha would purchase such an expensive vehicle, as she had not been a person particularly influenced by ego or fashion. But she knew that some people could not understand her father's affection for his motorcycle mobile, but it was right for him. This car was probably right for Martha.

The girls raced down the faded porch steps, Meg in the lead, and scrambled anxiously toward Martha's car. The door opened, and a man stepped out. He was of average height and was not bad-looking. His hair was brown, peppered with expensive blond highlights, and his skin seemed unnaturally bronzed. Meg looked past him to see where Martha was but quickly looked back at the man with a more attentive eye. She said, "I know you."

"Please," he said. "Let me explain."

"How dare you?" she stammered. "How dare you come here?"

Carrie stared at the man. "Who is this guy, Meg?"

Meg stepped back, pushing her cousin with her backside as she did so. She thought she heard a whistle but realized it was her mind burning with hate. Everything slowed down around her, and the landscape in front of her narrowed. She shouted, "Leave us alone!"

He said, "Let me explain, Margaret…"

Meg was almost at the steps when she realized that Carrie was no longer behind her. She spat, "Have you come to sing for me again, *Joshua*? Where are your foolish garments?"

"You don't understand, Margaret. I have come to earn your trust…"

Meg suddenly understood. "Martha is not coming to visit today, is she, Joshua? That is why she canceled all those times—it was you pretending to be my old friend. And you were waiting for a time when I was alone."

"Please, Margaret…"

Meg's anger was tinged with disappointment. "I thought my friend was back from the dead, Joshua. Martha was a good girl."

Meg hoped she could get inside of the house and lock the door before he reached her, but he was closing in on her too quickly. This time, she wasn't going to go upstairs—that was for certain. Instead, she sprinted around him, checking his hip with her own and clipping his knee in the fashion that had caused her so many penalty minutes for unsportsmanlike conduct. She tried to spin away from him as she did so.

He stiffened but didn't fall. Instead, he grabbed her arm with his limp, wet hand and pulled her to him. He cried, "Stop this, Margaret. Stop."

She kicked him in the same knee and stepped back as he released his grip. His face was contorted, so she tried a third time, but he was ready and grabbed her leg. He threw her down, wrenching her back, and bore down on her. He grabbed her shoulders and shook her as though he was trying to make her understand something obvious. His eyes were wide with some fever, and one side of his mouth twitched as he grappled with her. She slapped at him, but he ignored her and began to babble about missing her and guilt and second chances.

Maybe he is going to sing for me, she thought.

Carrie cracked him on the back of his head with the barrel of her father's shotgun and stepped back. She said, "It's loaded, *freakshow*, and I know how to use it!"

Meg was breathing heavily. She rolled away from him and said, "You just lie down on the ground, Mr. Martel. My father should be home any time now."

Joshua Martel's face grew pale as he considered his next move. Meg barked, "Get down!"

The coward slowly complied. He was wearing white pants and a shirt that looked more like a blouse, and Meg knew he was worried about staining them. Meg kicked him in the ribs and realized that it felt good. He squealed familiarly, and Margaret Dearborn's last memories came upon her in a lonely flash. His was the last shrill voice Margaret would ever hear as she fell to her sad end. Meg kicked him again, harder, and wiped away a tear.

Carrie had the weapon pointed at his neck. She said, "Holy crap, Meg—he *was* a stalker!"

Meg said, "I...I thought you ran away, Carrie."

Carrie shook her head, her eyes grimly focused on Joshua Martel. The butt of the shotgun arced between her cheek and shoulder. She said, "This turd's never hurting you again, Meg. Never gonna happen."

Meg kicked him again and stepped away.

"My father's not going to be happy about this, Joshua," she said. His oddly colored skin paled as she mentioned her father. Clearly, Joshua Martel was not looking forward to a reunion with the colonel. She wondered if he might just decide to run. Would Carrie really shoot him? She might.

Martel coughed and said something. A cube-shaped clump of grassy earth was attached to the top side of his left ear, and there was a subtle crimson streak below the spot Carrie had dented with her weapon. The girls looked at him blankly, so he said again, louder, "Release me, and I'll tell you where it is." Then he added, "I'll even drive you there, if you like."

Carrie said, "You're staying right here until our parents get home."

"The cave, Margaret, the cave…"

Meg stepped closer. "My name is *Meg*, Joshua. *Margaret* was the girl you murdered while her parents were at church."

He whimpered, "Let me go."

Carrie's mouth twisted into an odd grin. "Oh my God, Meg, he is such a *wuss*. I thought you were exaggerating."

"No," said Meg. "I wasn't."

40

The Cable Guys

"OK," said Sam. "Hand me the panel."

He knew Oscar had a small issue with heights, but the man was able to stand at the top of the durable wooden ladder and hand him things. The wooden steps appeared to have been chiseled from one of the enormous oaks in a manner similar to how Native Americans dug out canoes from trees. The thick steps were sturdy, and the frame was perfectly proportioned. Still, his friend didn't seem to be finding any comfort in the ladder's unique craftsmanship. He looked ill.

Sam would have preferred to install the panels at a higher point, but he knew he was lucky to have Oscar where he was. He wondered why the roof wasn't flatter, given that it never rained in the Hole. He reached over to his friend and grabbed a square and slipped it into place. The warm frame was metallic, with holes on the corners for an easy fitting. He stood and stared down into the settlement and wondered how many people wanted to see him dead. This was his third installation of the day, and he felt like the cable guy. A very unpopular cable guy.

Sam crawled to the edge of the roof and saw that Oscar was already on the ground. He moved over to the ladder and half climbed, half slid his way down. He thought of a youthful summer spent working with his father as they built a house from the ground up. The old man swore off the phone and work and just wanted to build something with his son. There wasn't much about home building that Sam Ahearn didn't know.

He smiled a little at the memory until he remembered that his father sold the house the next summer. And went back to work.

"That's enough for one day," he said. "My hands are all sweaty, and it's getting too damn windy up there."

"Good," said Oscar. "Because you're in everybody's line of sight when you're up there. Don't you realize that you're a damned target?"

—◊◊◊—

The discovery of more panels led to further searching of the storage sheds. Sam found a variety of electronics that were mainly not needed in Last Penny, but there were a lot of lights. And they turned on when they were put near the panels. Sam fudged around and found little sensors that worked as on/off switches. The lights weren't that bright, but they could brighten rooms, hallways, and front decks. So, Sam made the mistake of bringing Mallory into the shed to show him the discovery.

Mallory tapped the sensors and saw what Sam was saying. He asked, "How many lights are there?"

"There's ten in a box, and there's four boxes that I can find," Sam answered.

"And how many panels?"

"Ten, including the one at Alice's."

Mallory frowned. "Do you see the problem?"

Sam actually did. "Who gets the lights?"

"Right," said Mallory. "We should have a lottery, perhaps, or use them as streetlights. Maybe the church and its infirmary would have a use for these devices."

"But that's not where they're going, right?"

Mallory seemed more and more melancholy as Sam got to know him. He felt their friendship was real and possibly deep, but the man was hard to read. Alice despised him, though she denied it, and Fendy had similar feelings. Jason Keith respected him but warned Sam about Mallory's priorities. But Sam felt a kinship with him—he wasn't sure why—and enjoyed his company. He couldn't escape the feeling that they'd walked through many of the same doors, though probably at different times.

Mallory said, "I will suggest it. But you and I both know that the Original Eight will reap benefits from your discovery."

—ɷ—

Michael Hammond waited for them near his big wooden front door. He was a rangy and leathery man, and he dressed more like Sam in his jumpsuit than some of the others in their fluffy attire. Hammond did not seem to be a man of manners but rather a rugged-looking outsider who happened to live next door. Sam thought of the guy who lived in a trailer three houses down from his father's summer house in New York. Truthfully, he couldn't even remember the old guy's name now because he had never cared enough to find out. *Jesus,* he thought, *the trailer guy was there first.*

Hammond led the men into the house and offered them a fruity drink from a carved wooden pitcher. Bright patterns were knotted across it in a manner that indicated the work of a craftsman, and Sam was somehow sure Hammond was the artist. He said, "I've placed most of the lights already and they work. You saw the first one on the porch, and the main hallway's been lit up. Some of the rooms are equipped, and I have a small basement that I store some belongings in."

Hammond's house seemed to be modeled after Alice's home. His rooms were less spacious, but he had a basement, and Alice didn't. Both houses were near the great wall and were stained with the same protective substance, but the similarities ended with that. As an Original, Alice owned much more land than any of the later settlers. Her lush backyard was the largest of the Originals, and she was closest to the front gate. Sam didn't know if that was a good thing.

The men sat at a table in a small room off the kitchen. Hammond left briefly, then returned with another wooden pitcher. He said, "Thank you for your service, gentlemen."

Sam felt a little lightheaded and wondered what was in the drink. He said, "I hope you enjoy them."

Hammond said, "I'm familiar with modern conveniences, Mr. Ahearn. We had lights where I grew up."

"Where was that?"

"Oklahoma. We were farmers, but we had electricity and, for a time, running water."

Oscar asked, "What happened?"

Hammond seemed a cool customer, but his voice saddened. He rubbed his red-blond hair. "The dust storms destroyed everything back then, including my family."

"Wait—you're talking the late thirties?" asked Sam.

Hammond nodded.

Oscar said, "Then it wasn't so long ago that you arrived here?"

"I was separated from my family, from my *children*," he said. "I miss them the most, of course."

"Of course," said Sam. "You happened upon an entrance to the Hole in Oklahoma? What part?"

"Cimarron County," Hammond answered. "My children—would they still be alive? It seems to me that I haven't been here that long."

"I don't know. They'd be very old Earthside."

"If you found them, and they wanted to see me, could you bring them here?" he asked.

Oscar said, "I don't think…"

Sam said, "I'll try, Mr. Hammond. Don't go talking to people about it, though. You know how things are here as it is."

Oscar muttered something.

"I would give it all up to see them, you see."

Sam said, "Of course. You were the ninth, right? The first outsider to move into Last Penny?"

He nodded. "Right. I survived on my own for a while and even built a small cabin. I was almost killed by one of the bears once and happened upon Last Penny. Settlers have been coming in regularly since then."

All of the Original Eight, except Alice, accepted the solar panels. Alice would have donated hers to a more worthy institution, but her turn was simply jumped over and her panel given to Number Nine. Sam and his friends dutifully installed the lighting as instructed, beginning with the Originals and moving on to Hammond and his neighbors. There was no outspoken resistance to the decision to give the lights to the Originals, but Sam felt the anger from the others. It was palpable and, it seemed, aimed directly at him. He knew he should be moving on.

"You might have done well to decline the gift," said Sam. "My discovery seems remarkably unpopular in some quarters."

Hammond smiled. "They'll lop off my head either way, Mr. Ahearn. At least this way I'll see them coming. Anyway, I have a few tricks up my sleeve."

Sam smiled as he pulled his notebook out from a side pocket, "I bet you do, Mr. Hammond. Tell me everything about your family, and I'll do my best to find them. Also, tell me a little about this Cimarron County—could you draw a map?"

"Well," Hammond started, "at first, it seemed like God's country…"

41

Meg's Choice

"Where is this magic cave that you speak of?" Meg demanded.

Carrie said, "Meg, don't listen to this creep. We've got to call the police and our parents."

Meg's stomach turned at the sight of Joshua Martel's twisted smile. He said, "I can bring you there…I have been waiting for the cave to return, and I have seen it. Come with me, Margaret."

"He's got Virginia plates, Meg," said Carrie. "Isn't that magic hole thing supposed to be in Virginia?"

Joshua spun slowly until he was sitting neatly on the grass. Carrie took a step back and kept the shotgun pointed at him. He looked at her and the weapon and said, "You are right, child, it is in Virginia. I was a cartographer, and a good one, and I have never forgotten the spot."

"Shut up, meathead," Carrie said. "Meg, we have to call someone."

Meg leaned against Joshua's still-running car; her mind couldn't keep up with her thoughts. She ran her hand along its roof and said, "How is it that you are alive, Joshua, and how did you come by such an expensive vehicle?"

"It…it was a gift from my wife," he said.

Carrie seemed comfortable with the shotgun against her shoulder. The barrel was thick and sinister, and she looked quite menacing with the weapon in her hands, though her arms had to be tiring. She said, "Check the registration, Meg. He probably stole the car."

Meg opened the driver's side door and looked in the glove box. The car was still running, and the AC had her shivering as she sat on the passenger seat, the side door ajar. The glove box seemed empty except for a Mercedes C63 AMG manual. She looked under the sun visor and found what she was looking for. The car had been registered in Virginia Beach only a few months ago and belonged to someone named Michelle Sutton.

"Who is Michelle Sutton, Joshua? Did you steal this car from her?" asked Meg.

"She is my wife—I swear," he said. "Please don't be jealous."

Meg choked. "Jealous? You are insane, Joshua."

She climbed from the car, leaving the door open, and took in the sight of her best friend standing over her long-ago murderer. It was almost comical to look at, but she knew the stakes were high. She watched Carrie wipe her brow; the morning sun was heating up, and Meg imagined the strain was getting to her. Carrie said, "There's a small basement under the barn where my dad used to store canned food and stuff. Let's lock him in there."

"No," he said. "I have a map, and the cave is one of my locations on my GPS."

Carrie shook her head. "I think our fathers will be happy to talk to you when they return."

Meg said, "Stand up and walk toward the barn."

"It'll be roasting in some basement," he whined. "I won't do it."

"Move," barked Meg. "I mean it."

They marched across the lawn toward the barn. The grass was still a little wet from the dew, but the sun was beginning to beat down. Joshua looked back at Carrie twice but made no move to escape. Meg looked at Carrie, too, and saw only determination on her cousin's face. *She might actually shoot him,* Meg thought.

"How does your wife not have the same last name as you, Joshua?" asked Meg. "What have you been up to?"

They stood before the door to the garage. Joshua leaned against the wall of the shed and said, "My name is David Sutton, as far as anybody knows. I was a little-known poet who died in the American Civil War. Apparently, my letters home have been published in many publications and used in a popular documentary."

"What are you talking about?" asked Meg, her voice a mix of curiosity and disgust.

Carrie said, "Through that door, puke."

He looked at her and said, "I am not impressed with your language, Miss Heath."

Carrie pulled the butt of weapon tightly against her shoulder. Her face reddened, and her head was shaking. "I've had enough of you. You've already killed my cousin once, and it's not going to happen again. If you don't go in the damn door right now, I will blow your freaking head off right here and right now. Do you understand?"

Joshua nodded and opened the door.

They followed him inside, and Carrie led them past John's motorcycle into the far corner of the barn. Joshua almost tripped over a leftover sliver of lumber but recovered quickly. Carrie said, "There's a handle right there on the floor. Open the door and climb down the ladder."

Meg had an epiphany. "The floods."

"What?" asked Carrie.

"Charlie said there were floods in some of the graveyards, and caskets were lost or moved."

Joshua's voice was oily. "You are right, Margaret. My stone appears to have been lost, and I awoke a member of some other family. I guess my appearance matched the descriptions of the real David Sutton, and I became a sought-after speaker."

Carrie said, "So, you're being paid to pretend to be somebody else?"

Joshua made a noise that may have been a giggle.

"And your wife, Joshua? Does she know your secret?" Meg asked.

"Of course not. She's just a foolish girl with a foolish crush on a dead man's words. She sought me out, and I married her. Not out of love, though…I only have love for you."

"You love her?" Carrie asked. "That's why you cyber-stalked her by pretending to be her lost friend?"

Joshua snapped, "I *am* her lost friend."

Carrie sighed and said, "That's enough. Climb down the ladder."

He peered into the darkness. A musty stink escaped from the bleak hole, and a gush of heat surrounded them. Meg knew he was thinking about running; he always thought about running. He said, "Where is the light switch?"

Carrie smiled. "It's at the bottom of the ladder."

Joshua looked doubtful. Carrie suddenly fired the shotgun into the nearest wall, and Meg squealed. The sound was thunderous, and brilliant light suddenly shone through the various-size holes that now tattooed the wall. Meg felt a splinter pricking into her left hand and tried to pull it out. The room smelled of gunpowder and mildew.

Carrie pumped the shotgun and said, "Get going."

He nearly fell into the hole in his haste and disappeared into the darkness. After a moment, he called up to them, "Where is the light switch?"

Carrie smiled again and closed the trapdoor. She rummaged around her father's dusty workbench until she found a lock to secure the door with. They heard his voice bleating desperately to them. Carrie said, "Let's go call somebody."

Meg shook her head.

Carrie said, "What are you thinking, Meg?"

"You know what I'm thinking," Meg said, running her fingers through her hair as though they were the fingers of a comb. "This is my chance."

"No, no, no," said Carrie, her head shaking angrily.

"He has a map, and his *PGS device* has the cave as a location. I can finally...find him."

Carrie put her weapon on the dusty wooden workbench and grabbed her cousin by the shoulders. "Cager is dead, Meg; you have to know that. Even if there is a magic cave in Virginia, what are you going to do about it? Go die in the same place he died? Your life is here now."

Meg pushed her cousin away roughly and began to sob. She was embarrassed and glad that she had no makeup on to run down her face. There were no words to adequately explain the emptiness that always blocked her happiness. How could anyone understand what she felt? Meg wished she had her brush.

Carrie stepped forward, but Meg backed away. She looked down at her pretty blouse and realized that Joshua had torn the top button off. After catching her breath, she said, "I just need to see it, Carrie. I need to know where he went. Then we can call Mr. Johnson and our parents, and they can take care of it from there. I just want to *see*."

Joshua was screaming now and pounding the wall. His voice was shrill and childlike, and Meg felt a measure of relief in his anguish. Part of her wanted to laugh out loud and taunt him from above. She wanted him to suffer.

Carrie sucked in some air and said, "Well, his car is still running, and our parents aren't coming back till tonight. We can send them a text later."

"I can't let you do this," Meg said, though she knew she would.

"Meg, you can't even drive a car, let alone one with a stick. We'll find this cave, and then we'll get on with our lives. Now, come on—it's a really long drive."

"You do understand," Meg said, "don't you?"

Carrie said, "We understand each other better than anyone."

Meg grasped her hand. "As sisters."

Carrie nodded. "Yes, as sisters."

42

Three Guys Goofing on Each Other

"Afraid of heights, Mr. Mallory?" asked Sam.

Oscar stood beside Mallory, on the ground, and looked up at Sam. He was in his element, tools stuck into a makeshift belt, nails hanging from his teeth. His feet were balanced on the rungs of the ladder as Oscar's own feet had danced around a boxing ring so many years ago. This was Sam's ring, he thought, and Sam would have been much happier being a builder, or a carpenter, than he was following his old man's footsteps into a world he hated.

Mallory shook his head. "I just prefer the view from down here, Samuel."

Oscar grabbed the last panel and handed it to Mallory. He slipped the warm frame around his thick wrist and began his slow ascent. He was afraid of heights, and Sam damn well knew it, and yet here he was, following his boss two stories up another house belonging to another ungrateful citizen. He felt the tingles with each slow step and tried to control his breathing.

Sam was already at the top and was climbing onto the sloped rooftop. Oscar wondered why the roofs weren't flat in Last Penny. It never rained, and it never snowed, at least not in his experience, so what was the point of a pointy rooftop? It was all for show, just like everything else the Originals liked to do. Except Alice Shapeway, of course. She was an exception.

"Hurry up, Oscar, I'm ready to roll here," Sam shouted.

Oscar was sweating, but the cool air and the breeze seemed to stem his usual reaction to unnatural altitudes. Breathing was a slight problem, but he knew he could control it. He looked down and saw Mallory smiling awkwardly back at him. He was wearing an odd, colorful suit with large frills and an oversize blue tie. Why was that jerk even here? He focused on the ladder and on his steps. Everything else went away. After a moment, he was at the top.

"Thanks for joining me," said Sam. "Hand me the frame."

Oscar gave it to him and dutifully climbed downward. Mallory met him in the middle and gave him the panel. He grabbed it and climbed, one-handed, back up to Sam, who was waiting impatiently. His heart was pounding, but he had it under control.

Sam was standing at the edge of the rooftop, and he squatted down to take the panel from him. Oscar said, "Why are you grinning like that, Sam?"

Feet dangling off the edge, Sam said, "I don't know, Oscar. I don't really like it here, and the sound of that river is driving me crazy. Half this town would like to see us dead just for helping out. And I really miss the sun."

"Of course," said Oscar. "That would make anyone grin and giggle like a little girl."

"I didn't giggle, Oscar, and you know what I mean. We're so much more alive here than we ever were back home. Even when I look down at that crematorium or think about the bears and the bison and the hillbillies…I just breathe better here."

"I can't breathe at all up here, Sam, so why don't we finish this conversation down on the ground."

Sam clambered to his feet and headed back to his task while Oscar began his slow descent to safety. At least this would be their last installation. Now they could hole up at the Shapeway house and come up with their new plan. Unless Mallory found some other project that would anger the locals a little more. What was that guy up to, and why did Sam like him so much? Oscar wondered if he was jealous of Mallory in some bizarre way. Who could be jealous of someone dressed like a peacock?

One foot hit the ground and then the other. He wanted to kiss it, like in the movies, but Mallory would probably not see the humor. Oscar looked up and saw his friend step onto the ladder. He braced the ladder with both hands, then looked up again, just in time to see Sam's twisting body tumbling wildly on top of him. He tried to reach out and somehow catch Sam, but the physics of the fall overwhelmed him, and both men crashed gracelessly to the ground. Oscar heard a rhapsody of clicks and clacks that may have come from him or from Sam. Everything got dark, but he knew it wasn't sunset. Then, light filtered back into his world, but nothing was clear, and his ears were whistling. The world seemed like an old jigsaw puzzle with half of the pieces gone. Was that a song?

Oscar wasn't unconscious, but his body wasn't following normal commands, and he wasn't sure if he was looking at the sky or the ground. He jerked his upper body and twisted into a sitting position. Mallory was in front of him, fussing over something and muttering. His words grew louder, and Oscar realized that Mallory wasn't muttering after all but was actually yelling something. What was he yelling at? The fog lifted a little, and he knew what Mallory was trying to do. He was trying to wake Sam. Was he knocked out, too?

He stood up, swaying, and took several steps toward Mallory. Oscar thought he said something, but neither he nor Mallory seemed to hear the words. But he heard Mallory's words: "Get up, Sam. You've got to get up."

Mallory stood. His face was still a mask, but his voice was off as he said, "Mr. Larsen...Oscar, can you hear me? Nod or something."

Oscar nodded and thought he said something again. But Mallory didn't hear him again. His jaw was numb, and he wondered if it was broken. He rubbed it, and it stung at the touch. There was blood on his hand, and he wondered if it had been there or if it came from touching his jaw. His head felt oddly warm, and the sensation comforted him. A concussion, maybe? It didn't matter.

Mallory's eyes were moving about wildly. He said, "We have to get inside fast. No one can see him like this."

Oscar glanced back down at Sam. His head was turned in an odd direction, and his body was oddly still. His eyes were open, one more than the other, but he wasn't awake. There was a long crimson streak that started above his temple and stopped at the top of his pale jumpsuit. Nothing seemed to be working.

"Oscar, we have to stand him up. We need him to look alive."

"Look…alive?" he repeated stupidly.

Mallory grabbed his shoulder. "He's dead, Oscar, and if you want him back, we can't let anyone know it."

Oscar didn't want to believe him, but he still reached down for one of Sam's lifeless arms. The two men muscled him up to a sort of standing position and began to walk away. He thought of the movie *Weekend at Bernie's* and laughed oddly. Sam's head was twisted lifelessly toward him, and he thought that someone from a distance would just think that Sam was whispering in his ear. Oscar realized that he was sobbing and made an attempt to stop. He slowed his breathing and focused on his steps, just like on the ladder. The sobs slowed and turned into a quiet whimper.

"Where are we going?" he asked.

"Hammond's house. We have to get Sam over to Mike Hammond's house."

Oscar shook his head and wishboned his friend's body in a different direction. He said, "We'll be safer back at the Shapeway house. Cager and Fendy are there."

Mallory pulled back. He insisted, "Oscar, you have to trust me. This wasn't an accident, and even if it was, they're not going to let you leave this town with his body. Do you understand me?"

Oscar's fog had turned into a headache. He turned back toward Mr. Hammond's house and said, "What's so special about that house?"

Mallory nodded his head and pantomimed laughter. Oscar looked at him skeptically then talked and gestured theatrically with his free hand, noting that it didn't move in exactly the fashion he wanted. Perhaps anyone watching would think that Sam had fallen and was now recovering. They were all just laughing and talking about Sam's awkward fall. Just some guys goofing on each other.

"It's his only hope," said Mallory. "It's his only way out."

43

Mr. Johnson Asks a Few Questions

Rufus Johnson pulled up the familiar gravel driveway. It was bouncy and dusty and was as long as some streets he'd lived on. Tom Heath's green SUV was parked near Carrie's car, and an unfamiliar Toyota was stopped crookedly behind them. He parked beside the Cherokee and turned off his headlights. The Ford Explorer he was renting was too big for him, he knew, and climbing down from his seat was probably a funny sight to someone taller than him. That didn't matter right now.

He started for the steps but heard a woman's voice calling for him. He turned toward the barn and saw a woman waving a flashlight at him. He trotted over to her quickly and identified himself. She was an attractive enough woman, at least in the near-dark, and was dressed in comfortable jeans and a white blouse. She was calm, and her voice matched the one that had interrupted his dinner at the hotel.

She was all business. "I'm Carol Simon, and I'm the one you spoke to earlier. Could you follow me into the barn?"

"What's in the barn?" he asked.

"Trouble," Carol sighed. "A lot of trouble."

She led him to the open doorway and into the building. He'd been in there once before on a much windier night. Carol led him past the familiar workbench and into the heart of the structure. Tom Heath and John Dearborn worked on their motorcycle there, he knew, and there were several overhead lights. He thought that it might be the brightest barn he'd ever been in. Everything was outsize at the Heath compound.

A small group was assembled in the far corner. Their backs were all turned, but he still recognized Tom Heath by his frame and Sally Dearborn by her long hair and extraordinary posture. And John Dearborn was always John Dearborn. Tom stood sideways in front of John, and one of his big arms was gently nudging John backward. Tom seemed to have the beginnings of a mouse under his right eye. Who in their right mind would take a pop at that guy?

Carol led him to her friends and then stood beside Sally. She sort of nodded at a point just in front of the group where a man was sitting uncomfortably on the dusty wooden planks. He wasn't tied up, but it was obvious that he was some sort of prisoner. His eyes were red, possibly from crying, and his expensive shirt was torn and wet from perspiration. His hair was mussed, and his lip was swollen. There were other bruises on his face, and he was coughing in a way that any old prizefighter would recognize. He'd gone a few rounds with somebody.

"What's going on?" he asked.

Tom kept his arm on Colonel Dearborn's shoulder. "Apparently, we've had a visitor, Mr. Johnson."

Sally turned and said, "Mr. Joshua Martel."

Rufus shook his head. "But that's impossible."

John said, "It is him, Mr. Johnson. The coward himself."

He realized that the how didn't matter at the moment. Rufus looked at Tom and said, "I assume you were given the responsibility of restraining Colonel Dearborn once he recognized Mr. Martel?"

"My big head got in the way."

"How long has he been here?" asked Rufus.

Carol stepped closer and answered. "We're not completely sure. Apparently, the girls thought they were meeting an old friend."

Rufus understood. "But it was him, instead. Masquerading online all this time. Damn, I never should have let those girls continue with their website."

"I don't know that we should blame anyone other than Mr. Martel," said Carol, her words flatly cooling his sudden guilt. "He was a stalker, it seems. Again."

He scratched his head. "But where are the girls?"

Tom released his benign grip from his friend and said, "We're not really sure. They locked him in the little basement over here, so they must be OK."

"But where did they go?"

Sally looked tired, and her eyes were red from crying. She said, "We don't know. Ryan and Marissa haven't heard from them, and that boy in Stamford doesn't know either. They are all concerned."

"How long have they been missing?"

Carol said, "We've been away since early morning. It was a sort of pre-wedding, *just us* celebration. No kids."

Rufus looked at his gaudy watch. He said, "It's after midnight now, so they've been gone at least twelve hours, possibly more. How did you find him?"

Sally said with contempt, "His moaning was audible even at the house."

John said, "We called you because we thought you might have some idea. I remember you spoke to me that day about Martel here and about his invisible cave."

"That's right," said Rufus. "The cave is important, but your daughters' safety means much more to me right now."

"Of course it does, Mr. Johnson; I have no doubt of that," said John. "But he mentioned the cave again."

Something whirled in Rufus Johnson's mind. He said, "I think I have to make some calls."

Tom whispered, "Carrie took the shotgun, Mr. Johnson."

He nodded at the holes in the far wall. "Yes, and she obviously knows how to use it."

The room was silent as Rufus pondered his move.

After a moment, he said, "Well, I guess we're going to have to question Mr. Martel a little more. Perhaps you ladies might step outside for a few moments."

Martel coughed. "What do you mean you will question me? You are not a policeman."

Rufus Johnson smiled coldly. "We won't need any members of law enforcement, Mr. Martel. You are going to tell me where those girls are going, and you're going to tell me very quickly."

Martel looked at him and then at John Dearborn as if he wanted the colonel to rescue him somehow. Rufus had seen the look before when he'd had a different occupation. Joshua Martel was realizing that he should have confessed before Rufus ever got there. Rufus knew that he wasn't looking small to this man. Not at this moment.

"I think you should start talking right now, Mr. Martel. Those girls don't realize the danger they're in, and I hold you responsible. You don't want me any angrier with you than I already am."

"You don't look angry," said Martel.

"Oh, I am," replied Rufus. His fingers were twitching, and he sensed an old feeling coming on. He hated it—it burned him—but he knew he could embrace it, too. He had been the best once, and his unique set of skills never really went away. He said, "I am very angry."

Rufus saw John and Tom exchange glances. He said, "I think it would be better if I spoke to Mr. Martel alone, gentlemen. Perhaps you could wait outside with your ladies."

Tom shook his head. "We're all in, Mr. Johnson. We're getting our daughters back."

44

Little Whedon

There was only one exit for Little Whedon, and it was pretty close to one for Washington. Carrie, fatigued from the trip, missed it entirely and was forced to take that exit, off of I-95, and turn back. All in all, it took an extra fifteen minutes to leave the highway, and by then, she had to stop at an elementary school off a gravel road to wake up. Meg's head was resting against the car window, and she was snoring a little, her breathing fogging the glass. Her lengthy blond hair crisscrossed across her face and stuck to the cloudy window. And she still looked beautiful.

Carrie turned down the volume on the radio and took a sip from her Diet Coke. The bossy woman's voice on the GPS told her to turn left and drive for five miles, then turn right. She turned left down an unlit road. There were only a handful of houses on the street, but the town was teeming with trees. All of them looked to be pines to her, but it was so dark and difficult to see. They were definitely different from the trees in Bainbridge. Fuller, perhaps, and taller.

When she hit the town limits, the street was paved, and she began to pass more houses and a variety of shops. She turned at a flashing light and proceeded down an entrance near a large sign that read, "Little Whedon Mall." An electronic billboard told her that a mall would be opening in just a few days and thanked her for her patience over the last year. The entrance was fenced, so Carrie backed up and drove down a bumpy service road and pulled into the large parking lot. It was well lit already, which might mean that the grand opening was soon, or it might mean that the lights were already on, and nobody cared to turn them off. It was a little after 4:00 a.m., and the lot was empty except for a couple of work trailers bordered by orange rubber fences. There were some ladders near one of the stores and some containers that may have been paint buckets.

It was cooler in northern Virginia than she would have expected, but the car was running at the perfect temp. It was a foreign car, and a fancy one, and it had every accessory imaginable. Her seat temperature was set at extra warm to keep her butt comfortable, but Meg wanted hers at room temperature. The radio was equipped with satellite radio, so Carrie listened to a talk station all the way down—just in case there was something on the news about them. The cruise control was set just a few miles per hour over the speed limit, and she only stopped a few times for snacks and bathroom breaks. Meg was better with public toilets now, but Carrie knew she mainly tried to wait until she got home.

"The GPS can't be right," said Carrie. "We're in a frickin' mall..."

Her cousin stirred. "It must be nearby."

Meg was already twisting her hair. She rubbed her eyes and looked a little sad but maybe a little relieved, too. Maybe this would be what it took to convince her to let go of Cager. Maybe this would help her move on.

"I don't know," said Carrie. "I think Joshua was just trying to avoid talking to your dad."

Meg asked, "Do you think they've found him yet?"

"He'll squeal until someone finds him, and then it won't be a pretty sight," Carrie said. She knew her cousin relished the thought of Joshua Martel explaining himself to Uncle John, but Carrie was worried. It wouldn't be right if he got in trouble for hurting Joshua. Her father and uncle might just bury him in the backyard, and no one would know.

Carrie looked at her cell and saw that she had more messages than even an hour ago. Most were from her father, one was from Carol, and the rest were from Marissa. She said, "Why don't we call Marissa when we know what we're doing. We can have her pass on a message."

"I hate to put her in the middle, but I know she'll do it," answered Meg. "And I'm not looking forward to explaining myself to my parents."

"She'll do it. She owes you for stealing your boyfriend."

Meg sighed. "He wasn't my boyfriend."

"Whatever," said Carrie. "Look around a little and see if he has a map somewhere. Maybe in the glove box."

Carrie clicked a button, and the overhead light came on. The girls searched most of the leather interior and found nothing. Carrie said, "Did he ever explain about that cave of his to you? You know, before he killed you."

Meg snorted. *"Before he killed me.* No, he just rambled on about a magic cave in the woods that opened up and swallowed Cager. Nothing else."

"Well, assuming he wasn't lying, we have to guess we're close, but the cave must be in a spot hidden from the general public. After all, we're at a mall. A lot of people come to the mall."

"He was a mapmaker, right?" asked Carrie. "Joshua?"

Her cousin nodded. "Yes, a cartographer. And one of some renown."

"Then he must have had a map. But where?"

"Let's look in the trunk," said Carrie.

They left the car running and moved around to the back. The asphalt was soft and squishy to her feet, and she hoped it wasn't leaving tracks across the lot. Meg's feet appeared to be doing the same beside her. Meg was dressed casually, especially for her, in jeans, a T-shirt, and a hooded jacket. Carrie was dressed almost identically. They looked like a couple of average kids out for a ride.

The scent of an unfamiliar wildflower permeated the air, and birds and crickets were singing from nearby trees and from atop the nearly complete structure in front of them. Virginia sort of reminded her of home in its rural remoteness. She wondered if the kids were cool around here. Maybe Cager got married to some girl down here two hundred years ago and raised a family on some nearby plantation and just never wanted to go back to Boston. That explanation sure sounded more likely than him being sucked into some invisible hole in the sky. Carrie chose not to share that thought.

Meg half smiled. "If we cannot find the cave, we should drop this car off with Joshua's wife. And let her know just who she married."

Carrie grinned and added, "We can just press 'Home' on the GPS, and it'll lead us right there. But what if she calls the cops on us for stealing her car?"

"She won't," said Meg. "Especially if we return it and explain things."

Carrie thought that would be more fun than exploring a magic hole in the woods and began thinking about what she would say to Michelle Sutton. *Excuse me, Mrs. Sutton, but we thought you'd like to know that your husband is a crazed stalker from the War of 1812 and not the fancy poet that you think he is.* Maybe Mrs. Sutton and Meg could sell their story to the Lifetime network. Carrie wondered who would play her in the movie. Somebody cute, she hoped, like a young Meg Ryan. Not old Meg Ryan.

Meg was looking through the neat and sparse trunk, and Carrie could see she was frustrated. Carrie looked in and only saw her shotgun and a long box of shells. She looked around to see if there were any cops around. Was there a law against having the shotgun in her stolen car? Just add it to the list that included kidnapping, car theft, carrying a weapon across state lines, trespassing, and unlawful entry.

"Let's just go look out there," said Carrie, pointing to the wall of trees that sided the mall lot.

Meg said, "No, that would be impossible."

Carrie rubbed her chin. "You know…this mall isn't even open yet, and if the cave comes and goes a lot…"

Meg said, "Maybe it's right in front of us somewhere."

Carrie walked back to the front, leaving the trunk open, and climbed in. The machine was pretty fancy, so she started pressing buttons. One of the buttons brought the map into a close-up. A mark, sort of like an X, appeared just ahead of them. She said, "I think this thing is pointing near the edge, by J. C. Penney."

The sun was rising, and Carrie was having second thoughts. They were in a lot of trouble already, and the workers might be here at any moment. Her father always said that construction crews worked whenever they wanted, and she hoped that they wanted to be late today. She said, "Let's do this fast, Meg."

They walked over to the concrete edge of the mall, the corner of the J. C. Penney, and saw it immediately. It looked to be floating about five feet in the air, and it was long, and it shimmered. It wasn't a hole, really, but more of a wavy line, and it would have been invisible except for its continuous motion. If the building were just a few feet longer, then the cave, or whatever, would have been inside the dressing room.

Meg said, "That's it. That has to be it."

Carrie didn't know what to say. This was not at all what she expected to find here. She had her "move on with your life" lecture all planned out, and now here was a magic cave or something like it. She said, "We have to call our parents and maybe Mr. Johnson. I don't know what that is, but it can't be…"

Meg looked back at her and said, "I'm climbing up beside it. Pull the car up so that I can climb close."

Carrie argued but finally got in the car and pulled up onto the curb, the bottom of the vehicle scraping on concrete. The car was almost under the strange glowing line, easily seen under the glare of headlights, and Carrie hoped it wouldn't get sucked in. That would be hard to explain to Michelle Sutton. She watched her cousin climb onto the hood of Joshua's car and reach out toward the hole.

She said, "It feels…tingly."

"Get down, Meg," said Carrie, climbing from the car. "I don't know what that is, but it's not safe."

She heard the sound of engines and saw that several older-looking cars were now parked near the trailers. A few men were standing around in work clothes, and some were looking at them. Carrie said, "We've got to get going, Meg. This place is filling up."

Meg looked at the workers and then at the weird jiggling thing in front of her. She said, "I'm climbing in, Carrie."

"What? No..."

"It'll be OK," said Meg. "I just want to see."

She disappeared just like that. Carrie shrieked and looked toward the men who were approaching. Maybe they could help her but probably not in time. A flash of anger burned inside of her. This was Meg's plan all along, she realized. She had been planning this since the moment her crazy stalker told her he had found the cave. This was the angriest she'd ever been at Meg. It was the only time she'd ever been mad at Meg. That seemed kind of weird when she thought about it.

Carrie said, "Darn it, Meg."

She returned to the trunk and pulled out the shotgun and the shells. Her peripheral vision told her the men all stopped at the sight of her weapon. She shoved the box of shells into a jacket pocket, zipped the jacket, and climbed onto the hood of the still-running automobile. She pulled out her phone and texted three words to Marissa, *Little Whedon Mall*, and hit "Send."

She gripped the weapon and reached toward the strange fissure, then slowly pulled back. This was going to get her in big trouble, she knew, even bigger than she was already in. Carrie tightened the elastic in her hair and shrugged at herself. The hole crackled enticingly at her, and she again reached for it. Something pulled roughly at her, and then things got dark.

She thought of her absent mother as she lost consciousness.

45

Suspicious Minds

Mallory opened the heavy door without knocking, and the two men walked Sam's body into the familiar foyer. Oscar was exhausted, his stomach was turning, and his mind was cloudy and dull. His feet felt out of balance as he walked, and he was leaning into Sam's cadaver for extra support. He would feel better once he sat down. Rest was all he needed.

"This way," barked Mallory. "Bring him this way."

They danced Sam down the narrow hallway into an empty room and dropped Sam's corpse onto the floor, near an impressively carved chess table. His frame smashed more forcefully than they had expected onto the shiny wooden flooring, and the neatly whittled chess pieces spilled about the floor. Two black pieces landed on his still chest.

Sam's head was still twisted, and his tongue, partly swollen, was hanging from the right side of his mouth. One eye was almost closed, but the other stared accusingly up at him. He wasn't talking, but Oscar knew what Sam was thinking. How could he have let this happen? He looked away.

Michael Hammond, his face an amalgam of panic and confusion and something else, stepped into the small room. He barked, "Have you ever heard of knocking, Mr. Mallory?"

Mallory looked tired, and his face was red and sweaty. There was a softness about him that Oscar had perceived from their first meeting, but he hadn't let it stop him from dragging Sam's body to Hammond's place. He said, "It's important. We need to use your basement."

Hammond stammered, "What do you mean?"

"Now is not the time, Mr. Hammond. Samuel is dead, probably assassinated, and I need your help to release his body from the bonds of this town."

Oscar tasted vomit in his mouth and swallowed it. He said, "What do you mean assassinated?"

Mallory shrugged. "One of the rungs looked like it had been sawed. I could be wrong, but you are certainly aware of the volatility in Last Penny of late, and that ladder was well constructed. Sam has been helping the Originals, and some newer citizens are resentful."

Oscar felt another wave and leaned back against the bland-colored wall. Alice Shapeway had bright colors in her house, but Hammond had to live with blah colors. Was it only the older citizens who were allowed paints like Robin's egg blue? He just wanted to sleep and wake up back on the trail somewhere. Give him the giant bison or the homicidal hillbillies any day.

"Mr. Larson…Oscar, how bad are you? Your eyes don't look right."

"I'm OK, Mallory," he lied. Mallory certainly didn't believe him, but he wasn't going to let this guy, this *feeb*, feel sorry for him. *No way you have that over me*, he thought.

Mallory turned back to Hammond. He said, "You have to find Sam's friends. With luck, they'll be at the Shapeway house."

Hammond said, "Of course, but let me get a drink for Mr. Larsen. He doesn't look well."

"I'll take care of it," said Mallory. "Just hurry."

After Hammond left, Mallory said, "We have to get Sam out of Last Penny, or he's going into the furnace."

Oscar felt as though he was swimming, and Mallory's words weren't completely clear, but the mention of the crematorium made him shudder. He said, "But Fendy's wife was buried in a graveyard; I know that. You don't burn everyone here, or are you people really that sick?"

The great wall of Last Penny stood tall through the small window on the side wall. It reminded him of one of those windows on a boat. What did they call those again? Where did they get all the glass in this town? There must be a glassmaker, or blower, in this town. Did they have a blacksmith? His brain began to contract, and he had to sit down.

Some time must have passed because Mallory was pouring him a drink, and he was sitting on the floor. Why was this guy so concerned with saving Sam when he was the mayor or something of this town? Couldn't he just order everyone to let them leave? Oscar said, "What's up with you, anyway, Mallory? What's up with you and Sam?"

"Drink your juice," Mallory started. "I promise you, I'm on your side."

The room was spinning slowly to the right, then to the left, as though he was on some crazy swing. Oscar sipped from the cup and noticed that his hand was shaking and his fingers were curled and slightly numb. The cup was too full, and he spilled a few drops on the polished floor. He said, "Why are we here? We should be at Mrs. Shapeway's house."

He heard some noise and tried to stand. It was an effort, but he was on his feet before Cager and Fendy could enter the room, their boots squeaking on the polished floor. They both dropped down to examine Sam's lifeless form as Alice watched from the doorway. Hammond was behind her, his head politely turned away. She was crying, of course, and her lovely face grew sadder and older as he watched her. Sam had mentioned the mournfulness in her eyes before, the look of someone who had lost so much, but Oscar hadn't given it much thought. He wasn't supposed to look into the eyes of women that Sam Ahearn fancied. He was supposed to protect Sam. And he couldn't even do that.

Cager looked ready to rumble. He was jumpy with adrenaline, and his jaw was clenched in anger and sadness. He looked at Oscar and said, "What happened?"

Oscar said, "He fell. We think…we think…"

The room moved a little until Cager put his hand on Oscar's shoulder. "Oscar, are you all right? Your eyes are dancing."

Mallory said, "We suspect foul play, Mr. Standish."

Fendy looked to his mother-in-law, and she nodded at him. His eyes were red, and Oscar was impressed that he didn't try to hide it in some way. He said, "What kind of foul play, Mr. Mallory?"

"Does it matter?" asked Mallory. "You people have to leave, or Sam's going to be dragged down to the crematorium, and his mortal body will be lost forever."

"And does that bother you, Lark?" asked Alice, her soft voice unable to disguise her anger. "Why do you care if they cremate poor Sam?"

Mallory looked straight at her, "He's my friend, too, Alice. He's more like me than anyone I've met in this world. He's a visitor in this town, and he shouldn't be forced to follow our practices. Our barbaric practices."

"That didn't seem to bother you a few weeks ago when you had one of those Walkers burned. You remember that, don't you? Fendy was almost killed in retaliation if not for these men."

"This is not the time," Mallory said. "And Sam is nothing like the Walkers."

Alice was in his face now, and no one dared stop her. There was something about the confrontation, like a scab coming loose and stemmed blood suddenly flowing freely. She said, "How do we even know that you weren't responsible for this?"

Mallory shifted.

Cager's voice was icy. "Please answer the question, Mr. Mallory. I am not in a good way about any of this."

Oscar leaned toward Cager, placing a hand on his shoulder, his feet scuffing the floor. He said, "You didn't have to be with us today, Mallory. You insisted on helping me and Sam. Maybe *you* damaged the ladder."

Hammond stood in Alice's old spot in the doorway. "You people have to stop arguing. It will be dark within the hour, and we all have to leave as soon as possible."

Oscar shook his head, but the lightness would not leave. There was a kind of rhythmic and painful pounding starting in the center of his skull. He remembered that the drums in those old *Tarzan* movies usually meant that headhunters were coming.

He said, "How do you suggest we do that, Hammond?"

"Through his basement, of course," said Mallory. "He has a tunnel that comes out on the other side of that fence."

Mallory pointed out the window at the towering wall that surrounded the compound. It was supposed to protect them from the monsters outside, Oscar thought, but it didn't help with the ones on the inside. The drums were beating a little faster.

"Whatever would possess you to build such a thing, Mr. Hammond?" Alice asked.

Michael Hammond shuffled as he thought. Finally, he said, "You people were so nice and welcoming when I arrived. Alice, you and your friends helped me build this house."

"I remember."

"But then the others came, and the real estate shrunk, and the food was harder to get. Except not for us because we were at the top of the list. I've seen this before, and I know how it ends."

Oscar felt more pounding. He said, "It ends with murder."

Mallory nodded. "You have to take Sam and get out before anybody suspects. You should go, too, Mr. Hammond. I'm sorry for that."

Fendy said, "What about Jason? We can't leave him here—he will be suspect."

Mallory and Hammond shared a look. Hammond turned and left.

"Follow me," he said. "It's through the middle door."

Oscar said, "Fendy, watch Mrs. Shapeway and wait for Hammond. Cager, follow me."

Cager carried Oscar more than he followed him, as his legs were trembling. Still, he was able to stumble down Hammond's neat hallway and follow Mallory down into the basement. One of Sam's lights was connected to a wooden post, and the room was lit well enough to look around. There was no concrete in the room, only earth and clay. A narrow hole was burrowed into the far wall, and Oscar assumed that this was the tunnel that Mallory spoke of. How were they supposed to drag Sam's body through such a narrow chasm?

Oscar said, "How could you have known of this, Mallory?"

"It's my job to know these things, Oscar. You should sit and wait for your friends down here. You don't need the strain of that staircase right now."

Alice Shapeway slowly descended the wooden staircase. She looked at Cager and said, "Perhaps you and Fenderson could retrieve Sam's body and bring it down here."

Cager looked at her and then at Oscar. He seemed troubled but still trotted up the stairs as she requested. She looked at Oscar and knew he wasn't going anywhere even if he wanted to. She felt the top of his head and looked into his eyes. Why was everyone worried about his eyes?

Mallory said, "Alice, I'm so sorry for what has happened."

She looked away from Oscar but not at Mallory. She said, "You had nothing to do with this, Lark? On your honor?"

Mallory's voice was a pained whisper. "I know how you feel about him, Alice. Would I be involved in something that was certain to cause you such pain? Would I do that?"

"I don't know for certain, Lark," she said. "Not anymore."

"And my affection for Sam is real. You know that, Alice."

She nodded slowly.

"You must leave, all of you, Alice. Whoever did this is going to want to see what has become of Sam."

"What of you, Lark? What will you tell the people when they come?"

He smiled. "I shall tell the people of this damned *rotten borough* that Sam was alive and rightfully felt threatened after his fall. Michael Hammond told him of this tunnel, and all of you made an escape. I will say that Sam was always free to leave and that Michael Hammond should not have had a tunnel, so I asked him to leave as well."

Alice touched his cheek. "Then perhaps you are the man I once thought you were."

46

The Escape

"Did anybody notice you leave?" asked Mallory.

Jason Keith shrugged. "Maybe, I don't know. Mr. Hammond didn't exactly let me in on the specifics; he just said he needed me. My room-mates probably don't care."

He stood over Sam's form for a moment, then looked away. Oscar sat on the floor, his back to the dirt wall. He said, "Are you coming with us, Jason, or are you comfortable here?"

Fendy, carrying Sam's travel bag and holding two rifles, stood beside him, and Michael Hammond sat on the steps. Everyone else was upstairs, probably trying to figure out how to move Sam's body. And probably debating about what to do with poor Oscar. Well, Oscar wasn't going to be a burden to anybody. He stood even though his legs wanted to buckle. Mind over body.

Jason said, "Mr. Larsen, you should be resting."

"No time for that, Jason," he answered. "What's your answer?"

The man's face saddened. "Of course I'm going with you, Mr. Larsen. Sam's my boss, not that guy upstairs. It's just that I'm going to miss my friends a little. And the town."

Oscar said, "And you, Mr. Heal?"

Fendy replied, "Mrs. Shapeway and I couldn't stay if we wanted to after this, Oscar. Anyway, I think it's time to move on."

"The people have treated me good here," said Jason. "I've courted a few girls here, *white girls*, and I never felt a…I don't know, a backlash, I guess. I've only felt this accepted one other time—when I worked for Sam."

Oscar thought his forehead was sweating and wiped his dry brow. He said, "You still work for Sam."

At the sound of voices, Hammond stood and walked into the room. Mallory and Alice strode down the steps, followed by Cager, who was walking backward, dragging a long rolled-up carpet. It banged loudly on the tight steps, and Cager had some difficulty twisting it around the wooden railing and into the constricted basement. The railing cracked, and Cager moved his package easily into the room. He looked calmer, Oscar thought, probably because he was keeping busy, but he wasn't talking much.

"It's dark now," Mallory said. "I'm sure someone's going to come knocking soon enough."

"What's our plan?" asked Oscar. He chose his words carefully, as though he were pulled over at a roadblock a mile away from O'Malley's. He thought he sounded a little better.

Cager said, "Fendy takes Mrs. Shapeway out through the tunnel. Mr. Hammond follows, then Jason and I pull Sam's body out in this carpet."

"I'm holding up the rear?" asked Oscar.

"No, we're coming back for you…with the rug."

Horrified, Oscar said, "The hell with that. I can crawl out."

"Oscar, the tunnel is probably thirty yards long, and it probably snakes in and out and up and down. You can't make it."

He shook his head, "I can make it. I'll crawl out after you bring Sam, and if I get stuck, you guys come for me, all right?"

Mallory said, "Mr. Larsen, don't let your pride get in the way."

"We do it his way, Mallory," said Cager. "I'll wager he can make it."

"Then, let's do it," Mallory said. "Your time is wasting away."

Fendy squeezed into the tight burrow and, after a fashion, called out to Alice. She folded her dress as best she could and climbed in. She didn't look back. Oscar wondered if that bothered Mallory or if she had already said her good-byes upstairs. Mallory seemed not to notice, but he was a hard one to read. He could be crying on the inside.

"Good-bye, Mr. Mallory," said Hammond. "You're a sneaky bastard, but you're all right, you know?"

Mallory watched Hammond climb in after the others. He said, "I'm sneaky, Mr. Hammond? You're the man with an escape tunnel in his basement."

Hammond said, "Hey, I had some free time."

Cager and Jason Keith rolled Sam's body onto the side of the carpet. They placed the two rifles beside him before they slowly rolled him up in it. The men carried him close to the channel, and Cager climbed in, still holding his end. He and the carpet moved into the darkness a little, and then Jason climbed in. He pushed Sam's sneakered foot back into the folds and gripped his end of the carpet. They disappeared from Oscar's view quickly.

Oscar walked to the tunnel and tried to pull himself up. It was only a few feet in the air, but his legs wouldn't push, and his upper-body strength wasn't quite there. He said, "Would you mind, Mallory?"

"You're asking for my help?"

"Just this one time," said Oscar. "I guess I'll be in your debt."

Amused, Mallory said, "I believe you will be."

Oscar pulled himself up, and Mallory lifted his legs and pushed him as he jerked himself into the narrow fissure. He crawled forward and said, "Watch your ass, Mallory."

Mallory did not answer.

There was no light in the tunnel, and it was tight in most places. He crawled forward; stones and earth were all about him, and long roots sometimes jutted from below him. Pulling on them gave his knees a break, but they always burrowed away from him. He couldn't see the dust stirred up by Cager and Fendy's efforts, but he felt it in his eyes and tasted it when his mouth was open. He tried breathing through his nose, but that was impossible, so he covered his mouth with the top of his shirt and returned to mouth breathing. The tunnel twisted frequently, and he often bumped his already-sore skull into the sides, dirt cascading into his eyes. Without notice, the hole dropped a foot or so downward, and he skinned an elbow while breaking the fall. His breathing labored more, and his lungs burned, but his thoughts were surprisingly clear. Maybe light was the cause of his headache, or maybe his adrenaline was pushing his other problems aside for the moment. He struggled on until he heard voices ahead. He stopped for the first time to catch his breath, then pulled himself forward into the free world.

Hands reached in and pulled at him, and he popped out of the hole. Cager sat him down and brushed him off. "I knew you could do it, Oscar."

"Honestly," he whispered, "I wasn't so sure."

The darkness of night was a welcome relief after the blackness of Hammond's tunnel, and he could see clearly in it. They were too close to the enormous wall he had just crawled under, and Oscar could see the little hill that he walked over the day Fendy had waved to the guards and they had entered the prison. He looked up and saw the bottom of one of the guards' eagle's nests. Hanging around near the front door was not a good idea.

"Mr. Hammond covered the hole with branches and weeds, and nobody ever noticed," Alice said.

Oscar wanted to answer, but the breeze, no longer restricted by the heavy walls of the town, washed over him pleasantly. He breathed it in like he was a starving man approaching the buffet line. He wanted it all.

Alice was standing with Cager, while the others stood in a circle a few feet away. Cager said, "We have a plan."

"OK," said Oscar. "Tell me."

"We have to get Sam to a mudhole, for sure, and we need to get you there as well. Are you in any condition to walk?"

Oscar nodded.

"I have Mr. Ahearn's book, and Fendy has mapped out a few mud-holes close to the river. We should get going in that direction."

"What if Mallory's friends follow us? We're going to leave an obvious path."

"We're not all going, Mr. Larsen," Alice said. "The rest of us are leaving."

Oscar shook his head, grateful that the pain was fading. "We can't split up."

Cager said, "Jason's going to lead everyone back to the lodge. There are weapons there, and if the alarm system still works, then no one will have entered since we left. Hopefully."

"But it's a dangerous road back, Cager."

"Fendy can protect them, Oscar; he really can. He's almost as good in the woods as I am, and Mr. Hammond seems to be a man who can take care of the place when we get there."

"So, we split up and meet at the lodge," Oscar said. It was as good a plan as any, he knew, but Sam was going to be pissed to find out his girlfriend was marching down the same path that almost killed him getting to Last Penny. But it made sense, and he wasn't up for thinking of an alternate. There was a beehive in his skull at the moment.

Oscar stood and walked over to the others. Everyone shook hands, and Alice Shapeway gave him a brief kiss on the cheek. She said, "None of this was your fault, Mr. Larsen. I hope you understand that."

She and the others began to hike away but stopped. Fendy ran back, bullets bouncing in the backpack borrowed from Sam. He looked at Cager and shook his hand for the second time and said, "I was wrong to have treated you so poorly, Cager. I am so sorry to have left you in the earth like that. I didn't know."

"How could you?"

"Well, I know now, and I'm coming back for my wife and child."

Oscar couldn't tell if Cager was crying, but his words were throaty as he said, "I will go with you, Fendy. We will get her back for you."

Fendy ran off to his group, and they began to march away. Oscar said, "How come you both have rifles, and I've got nothing?"

"You're in no shape to carry a rifle, Oscar," said Cager. He had Sam's notebook and was reading it in the dark light. He put it away, then squatted down and popped Sam onto his shoulder and started walking toward the noise of the river. It was much louder outside the walls of Last Penny, but Oscar didn't mind the noise. His skull pounded from the racket, but at least they were free again.

47

Resting Place

After the first mile, his legs stopped working. He hit the dirt as though his lower body had been wired for a controlled explosion. Cager didn't notice right away and continued on a few more steps. Oscar was too embarrassed to call after his friend. He just waited. There was nothing Cager could do, anyway.

The roar of the river was louder now but not deafening. Most of the trees were shorter and leaner, and the forest was sparse and negotiable. He smelled some kind of tree sap and thought about Vermont maple syrup covering a stack of homemade pancakes. Stones of various sizes dotted the pathway, and the soft soil wasn't yet covered with dry leaves and needles. The jungle was young.

Cager was back, still carrying Sam, and breathing heavily. He put the remains of the president of Ahearn Industries down. "Taking a rest, Oscar?"

Oscar grinned. "My legs are."

His friend sat beside him and asked, "Can you move them at all?"

"The toes wiggle, I think, and my legs twitch a bit, but I think they're done."

Cager said, "You probably just need to rest."

"You're right, Cager," said Oscar. "You bring Sam to that mudhole, and then come back for me."

"I can't do that," said Cager. "I can't leave you here."

"No one's following us; you know that. Get Sam to the spot, take a breather, and then come back and get me. He's the mission."

The sky was dark—there was no moon, no stars, no curious flashes of light—but there was a kind of luminosity from up there, and it had to come from somewhere. Probably from the same place the river flows from, or where the bison came from. *Damn, I miss the stars,* he thought. *And the moon and the sun and smog. Even smog.*

Cager stood above him. "Your eyes are worse, Oscar."

"Just take Sam and hurry back to get me, OK?"

The branches above him were shaking from the breeze, and he wondered if leaves were falling. He couldn't really tell. He remembered a car ride with his parents; they were arguing, and he was crying. Their language wasn't English, of course, and he never learned Hungarian, though they may have been speaking German or Romanian. Finally, his mother turned to him and said something. In his heart, Oscar always knew that she was telling him that she loved him. The arguing stopped, and the car pulled into the airport parking lot.

Oscar had no regrets. Life had been good for him in America, especially after he found Sam in that bar in LA. Sam was different then, impetuous sometimes and angry on occasion, but he had that thing about him. Not everyone saw past his looks or his fancy suits like they did now, but Oscar saw it, and he knew that Sam was going to be someone. He was a natural at living life. The old man had him working all over the country, and there had been a kidnapping attempt. Sam was looking for someone tough for protection, someone who'd stand up to the boss's son on occasion, too. Oscar was looking to stop being a bouncer. That was Oscar's last night at the bar. That was the beginning of Oscar's real life. The only life he preferred to remember.

The sun was on now. Maybe it had been on for a while as he stared into the sky. He wondered if someone was looking down at him. Was this all some test? Maybe he was just paying for sins committed before he went to work at Ahearn. Oscar wasn't always a nice man. Karma.

But I was always a good one, he thought. *Or at least I always tried.*

—〰—

Someone was shaking him, and he realized he'd been sleeping. He opened his eyes and saw Cager calling his name. The lips and the words didn't sync, like when a TV station has its picture messed up, and his face kept swelling and deflating as he talked. Cager's face was lined with worry, and his eyes were bloodshot, exaggerated by Oscar's failing eyes. How much sleep had the poor kid gotten the last couple of days?

"Oscar, we have to go," Cager said. "It's a distance away, and I don't want to leave Sam for too long."

"He's in a mudhole?"

Cager replied, "I couldn't just leave him lying about. Those bears might be around, and God knows what else. We didn't come this far to have him eaten."

Oscar heard the jungle drums again. He said, "You have to take care of him, Cager. It's your job now."

"It's still your job. Let's get you to that mudhole," said Cager. "It's just a few miles."

"No, I'm done, I think," he said. "I'm glad you came back, though. I didn't want to be alone."

Cager shook his arm and yelled, "I can get you there, Oscar! I can get you there!"

Oscar realized that his friend's eyes were red from tears. He felt his own voice tremble as he said, "I'm so sorry for how I treated you, Cager, for calling you those names and for fighting with you that time."

"Come on, Oscar—we both enjoyed the sport of it. I gave as much as you."

"It's how I knew you were real. It's what made you *human* to me, and it's what made you my friend, my *brother.*"

"I'm going to pick you up, and I'm plopping you in right beside Sam," said Cager.

"Please don't," said Oscar. "I won't make it, and you know it. I don't want to go into the mudhole if I'm not still breathing. Sam does, and that's fine with me, now that I know you. But my faith is a little different. I'm OK to move on."

"Oscar, I can't just leave you here."

Oscar turned his head and tried to point. "There are stones all around, probably from the river. I bet it's getting narrower."

Cager nodded. "That might make crossing the river a little easier."

"Maybe," he said. "Cager, I'd like you to sit with me for a few minutes. We can talk about whatever you like—maybe that girl you're always mooning about. I won't be long."

"I don't want this," said Cager. "I don't."

Oscar wanted to reach over to his friend and comfort him, but his arms weren't moving. The drums were gone, though, which was good. Actually, nothing seemed to ache anymore. He said, "Bury me under some stones, not in the ground. And don't tell Sam where I am, or he'll come get me. You know he will. Find a good spot."

Cager's head was slowly shaking side to side, and it made Oscar dizzy to look at him. The kid didn't look so mature right now; he looked ready to pout and slam things. Was this kid even twenty years old, all told? Just a kid. A kid who'd saved his ass time and again, sometimes without a thank you. A kid who knew what was right long before the old men figured it out.

"I'm not sure it'll work, Oscar—it's hard to stay dead here. You might just wake up under a pile of rocks a month from now."

"That'll be God's will," said Oscar. "And I'm fine with that, too. I'll find you."

He looked down and saw that Cager was holding his hand. He couldn't feel it, of course, but the sentiment of the gesture warmed him a little. This kid was probably the best person he'd ever known and as loyal a friend as he'd ever met. He said, "Look after Sam, OK?"

He was sure that Cager answered him, but he didn't hear it.

48

Welcome to the Jungle

Her stomach rolled as she climbed to her feet and braced herself against a tree. Sticky sap fused to her fingers as she tried to collect herself while the world kept spinning. A constant rumbling made her ears hurt and seemed to be shaking the ground beneath her, spinning her guts around even more. Finally, Carrie just threw up to get it over with. Her stomach was empty except for the remnants of a few candy bars and a Diet Coke, so the puking was mostly dry and painful. It was a few minutes before she felt well enough to look around.

She was in a forest of some kind, that was obvious, and the trees and even the bushes were way bigger than they should be. It wasn't like she was in a redwood forest, but it was more like every tree and bush she saw was at least as big as any tree she'd ever seen in a normal forest. The clearing she landed in wasn't as large as her kitchen, and the surrounding greenery looked more like a wall than a forest. Where was Meg?

Carrie wondered what kind of animals would live in such a place and suddenly remembered her shotgun. It was on the ground, still loaded, under the glowing entrance to the magic cave. She picked it up and clutched it like a favorite old stuffed animal. A quick check of her zippered jacket pocket found the box of shells intact.

The weird half darkness made the Hole nearly invisible to her. She picked up some of the smaller stones and made a pile to mark the cave and hoped that she'd be able to find it again. Meg couldn't have gotten too far in just a few minutes, so she called out to her. Her voice wouldn't carry far against the roaring noise, but she called out anyway. She remembered hunting deer with her father and the time they went after a moose, and she recalled that animals always left some sign. She didn't think Meg was going to leave droppings behind, but there had to be something.

Part of the brush looked like it was bent, and something like a footprint seemed to lead into the woods. Carrie stepped into the brush and pushed through the tiny, sometimes sharp branches until the woodland cleared out a little. She found another stone, a flat one, and scratched the side of a tree. The mark was hard to detect, especially in this light, but she thought it was distinct enough. Maybe she could find her way back if she left enough marks.

The footprints, or footlike markings, she was following were leading to the source of the noise. Carrie was almost certain that it had to be a river or maybe even an ocean, but an alien spaceship wouldn't surprise her at this point. Why would Meg do something so stupid? Would it have been so tough to wait for their fathers? After all, her boyfriend disappeared over two hundred years ago, so they probably had a little time to go get help.

The trees spaced out eventually and grew smaller, but that only made the woods seem creepier. Carrie couldn't shake the feeling that she was being watched by something. The sky was dim and cloudless, and there was no sign of the sun or the moon; she wondered if it was actually day or night. If it was daytime, then things were going to be really dark really soon. She squeezed her weapon tightly and hoped she was just being paranoid.

Stones of every size were spread around the soft and mushy ground. This made tracking Meg much easier because she was leaving evenly spaced footprints that pointed straight to the noisy river. Meg wasn't running, which was good, but she wasn't taking breaks either. Carrie decided to sprint as much as possible to catch up quickly. How could Meg have gotten so far in only a few minutes?

She stopped and pulled out her cell phone. There was no service, and the clock wasn't working, but everything else was functioning. Carrie turned and took a picture of where she'd been in case the marks weren't working out and saved the picture. She hit the "My Pictures" button and thumbed through her catalogue. *Meg, Meg, Meg, Meg, Ryan, Meg, Meg, Marissa, Meg and Marissa, Meg, Meg...*

It was cool and windy, but the sweat she'd worked up kept her warm. She tracked Meg for another hour until she reached the rocky shore. The water didn't just rush past her, it *roared* past. The rolling waves were sometimes taller than she was, and the mist sprayed at her like someone was hosing her with their thumb half covering the nozzle. If there was another shore, she couldn't see it through the poor lighting and the foggy mist. She reached down and felt the cool water and splashed some on her face, then took another handful and drank it gratefully. Carrie realized her shirt and jeans were soaked from the spray, but it felt good, so she took another drink. She watched the water shoot past and wondered if any fish swam in it. They would have to be big fish.

She heard something like a voice and turned to see Meg standing behind her, apparently screaming, looking just as wet as she was. Her hair had lost a little of its glow from the water and the dimness, and her jacket was soaked. Carrie thought about slugging her friend but instead navigated the jutting rocks that blanketed the shoreline and gave her a hug. She shook her fist at Meg, though, waving it in a comic circle, and both girls laughed silently. The very sight of Meg made her almost giddy with relief. *Don't leave me again,* she thought.

"Come on," Meg cried.

They hiked toward the thin line of trees and edged closer to the woods until they could talk. Carrie's feet sank into the wet soil, and she felt her sneakers squishing with every step. The thin trees were white birch trees, though they looked more gray than white, and the thicker ones were huge Christmas trees that were lined with sap and would probably have reeked of the stuff if the girls could smell anything inside the river's mist. Even fifty yards away from the water, they could not escape the spray. Carrie wondered where the water came from. For that matter, where did it go?

"What were you thinking?" asked Carrie. "You should have waited for help."

Meg shook her head. "I'm sorry, Carrie, but you know Father would not have allowed me to come here."

"That's the point, Meg. We're not supposed to be here."

Meg looked for a comfortable spot and leaned against one of the prodigious rocks. She said, "Don't you understand, Carrie? He was here—he came in through that entrance, and he was here."

"We have to leave, Meg," said Carrie. "People are missing us."

Meg's expression turned quizzical. She asked, "Are you really being flippant, Carrie? You brought no one with you?"

"How could I do that if I jumped in right after you?"

Meg said, "Carrie, I've been here for almost a week. I made a sort of camp up near that crooked tree over there."

"That's not funny, Meg. I've only been in this place for a couple of hours, and I came in right after you."

Meg pulled at her wet hair. "I can show you the camp if you want. I've made a blanket from some branches, but I haven't been able to start a fire yet. I bet you can, though."

There was a mucky path of sorts that led to Meg's campsite. Carrie followed her cousin to the site and was impressed. A pile of berries was neatly stacked on top of a long piece of bark near her bed. She'd collected some leaves and needles and used them as a sort of mattress, and the leafy branches she was using for covering might hide her from predators. Anything looking for dinner around here would not be able to use their nose and ears too much. She stared into the jungle and felt the paranoia again.

"It's a good spot," she said. "But I don't understand how you've been here so long."

"I stopped here within hours of my arrival. I got lost right away, of course," Meg said. "and I guess I've been waiting ever since."

Carrie said, "Waiting for me?"

Meg said, "I knew you'd come. When you didn't show up immediately, I assumed you were waiting for assistance."

"I couldn't do that, Meg. I sent a text to Marissa telling her where we are, or where we were, and then I jumped in after you. It couldn't have been more than a few minutes."

Meg started to say something, but her voice was muted by another noise. It was a violent, grinding noise that reminded Carrie of a race-car engine revving up and down at the starting line. She looked behind Meg, into the jungle, and saw movement. For a second, she thought it was some kind of vehicle, an ATV or something, but it was too big to be something like that. She knew it was something bad. She warned, "Back up, Meg, there's something in the woods!"

It leaped at Meg, but she dodged it. Carrie, off-balance, blasted the shotgun at the side of the giant cat's face, and it roared at her as she fell backward onto a pointed boulder. Her back ached immediately, but she stood quickly, the shotgun ready against her shoulder. The creature, almost as tall as Carrie just at its shoulder, backed up and ran in a circle twice before it began creeping up on her again. Carrie pumped and fired at its face again, and it cried out with rage. Its roar topped that of the wild river beside them and almost paralyzed Carrie with its savagery. She saw Meg moving slowly away from the thing, her left arm dark with blood. Meg picked up a stone and threw it at the creature's head, but it didn't seem to care. It only wanted Carrie.

Carrie backed down onto the shore, her cousin throwing rocks from a distance and screaming at the creature, until she was pinned against the waves. The cat began pacing patiently to and fro in front of her, growling defiantly at her and her shotgun. Carrie screamed for Meg to get to safety, but she couldn't hear her, and she wouldn't run away, anyway—both girls knew that. Meg crept slowly sideways until she stood at Carrie's side. The cat strutted, licking its chops as it savored the moment.

The lion was as long as a VW and probably weighed more. Its short fur was thick and heavy and bore dark markings that probably made it invisible in the shadows. Meg tugged at Carrie's shirt with her good arm and pointed into the river. The cat, seemingly understanding Meg's meaning, stopped and hissed a warning. Its tail, thick as a baseball bat, swayed back and forth, and its hindquarters quivered with anticipation. Carrie saw that blood was covering the creature's eye, and she aimed and fired again, the recoil from the weapon pushing her backward but not knocking her down this time. The cat leaped sideward as Meg gripped Carrie's hand and pulled her into the crashing waves.

49

Food Court

Some of the lights were on in the food court, but it was still hard for Marissa to see while she made sandwiches. Her iPod was rocking "City Girl" by a tragic band called Scary Girls, and the song added to her sadness. She was standing behind the metal counter at the Subway shop, slapping meat and vegetables onto wheat rolls and slathering the sandwiches with mayonnaise and oil. Her jeans were baggy, and she was wearing one of her brother's jumbo sweatshirts. Her sneakers matched.

Little Whedon Mall was no bigger than the mall in Manchester and had the usual array of restaurants; the Subway was right beside a Chinese restaurant and across from a mini-McDonald's. There was a Taco Bell, a Chick-fil-A, and a Dairy Queen all squeezed near a jumbo restroom complex that included a family room and some special door that was for the employees only. The only unfamiliar restaurant was called Johnny Rockets, makers of the Original Hamburger, and it was larger than the others. A small water fountain centered the room, and there were already some coins tossed in by the workers. She planned to toss some change in later, when no one was watching.

Nobody from Bainbridge argued with her when she asked to come along, so she jumped in the car and kept quiet and followed everyone onto Mr. Johnson's company jet. She was just along for the ride, she knew, so she wanted to be helpful and offered to make lunch. She'd worked in a restaurant like Subway during her sophomore year, and making sandwiches was easy. Except when people found hairs, probably their own, in the sandwiches or swore up and down that they didn't ask for hot peppers, and now their sandwich was ruined.

She took off her earphones, piled the sandwiches on a plastic tray, and began handing them out. Mrs. Dearborn and her friend sat nearest the restaurant, isolated at one of the larger metal tables, whispering thoughtfully to each other. Mrs. Dearborn hadn't changed clothes since last night, which seemed so out of character to Marissa. She handed them their meals and promised to come back with drinks. Mrs. Dearborn squeezed her hand briefly, then looked away. Marissa wondered if Sally Dearborn knew about her stealing Charlie from Meg. She shook the thought away, but the guilt lingered.

Mr. Johnson, seated at the next table, was on his cell phone, but he still smiled and nodded as she handed him his lunch. The man was always so kind to her, but he looked positively evil when she showed up at the house with Meg's text. The *black helicopter* people were putting some guy in a van as she pulled in, and Mr. Johnson was cursing the guy out while they were doing it. Whoever the guy was, he was absolutely sobbing and curled up into a ball as the door was closing behind him. Marissa almost turned her car around and left, but she knew Carrie was counting on her. When she showed Mr. Johnson the text from Carrie, he kissed her on the cheek. He was talking quietly now, but she heard what he was saying, "We need that team here now. They've been gone for more than a day now…that could be a week or more in there."

The last of the food went to Mr. Dearborn and Mr. Heal. A pile of boxes from Dick's Sporting Goods was spread across the round table, and there was hardly any room for the sandwiches. The men plundered the sports store soon after they arrived at the mall, while the ladies patiently waited outside Abercrombie & Fitch, a store she would have loved to plunder. All of the retailers had grand-opening signs out, but now they were never going to open; Mr. Johnson's company somehow bought the mall and the entire inventory in all of the stores. How could one company have enough money and enough clout to do all that in one day?

Mr. Heal pushed a rectangular package marked "TenPoint Carbon Lite Crossbow Package" to the side, and Marissa put his sandwich in the empty spot. He already had a drink, a jumbo-size Diet Coke, and he dove right into the food, grunting quietly as he ate. Carrie always said he was a big eater. He looked worried, though. Really worried.

Mr. Dearborn wore a light fleece-lined hunting jacket that wasn't exactly camouflage but was probably called "mossy oak" or "winter wood-land" or something equally upscale. There was a long, sheathed hunting knife attached to his belt, and he was packing food and ammunition into a hunter's backpack that sort of matched the suit. A long wooden rifle sat on the table in front of him, and another compact crossbow, still in its clear package, lay beside it. He began playing with some sort of arrow carrier until it hooked onto the pack and then smiled cruelly to himself. He was making a noise that may have been humming, but it didn't sound at all musical. Marissa realized he didn't even know she was there.

"Here's your sandwich, Mr. Dearborn," she offered. "You're going to need to eat before you go into that place."

"Of course, Marissa, thank you," he said. "And thank you for all of your help. Young Mr. Martel wasn't very forthcoming. Surprisingly so."

She pulled a chair over from the next table and sat next to him. "I know you're going to find them, Mr. Dearborn. I just know it."

"There is no doubt," he said with certainty. "No doubt."

He was fidgeting with his rifle. Marissa flipped open her phone and saw that she had several messages. Most were from her brother, one was from her mother, and the last one, the one she wanted to check, was from Charlie Whitehouse. She remembered that day in Stamford when he stood behind her and watched her work. He smelled fresh, and his breath was minty. And he picked her over Meg. Over Meg.

She shook most of her thoughts away and said, "May I ask you a question?"

Mr. Dearborn smiled curiously. "Of course. I owe you a lot."

"The portrait of Meg and Mrs. Dearborn that Meg was going to give you, the one in your living room. You painted it, didn't you?"

He stopped packing his gear and said, "Now, how could you know that?"

"Your initials were on the table leg. I put mine on the other leg."

"I like that…it makes sense. You are, of course, a much more talented artist than I ever was. That was my only attempt."

"When did you paint it? Meg doesn't recall ever sitting for it."

A cold look took form across his face, then vanished into a strained smile. He seemed stained with sadness, and it suddenly hurt her to even look at him. His reputation was more light than serious around the school, and all of the kids who took his class loved him. But Marissa once read Margaret's diary, and she knew that he had a dark side, and here it was, right in front of her. He said, "I painted it from memory sometime after my first attempt at burning down my house and not long before my last."

Absently, she took his hand. "You won't have to do that again, Mr. Dearborn. I just know it."

The smile was back. He said, "I hope so. Tom won't be amused if I have to burn down his house."

Mr. Johnson walked over and said, "Team's not getting here for a while yet."

"We'll leave a trail for them to follow," said Mr. Heal. He was standing now, looking serious, and Marissa realized he was wearing hunting clothes, too. His knife was strapped to his calf, and a camouflage rifle hung from his shoulder. Both he and Meg's father were wearing their sneakers and not any of the fancy hunting boots from the hunting store. Boots take a while to break in, she knew, so they were probably going for comfort.

"I assumed you would say that, Tom," said Mr. Johnson. "I told my boss that you two were going in."

"Are any of those guys in suits going to try to stop us?" asked Mr. Heal. He was a big man, way bigger than Mr. Dearborn, and he looked determined. He added, "Because it'll get ugly if they do."

The others had joined them, and the group was heading for the exit. Marissa, no longer holding Mr. Dearborn's hand, wasn't sure if she was supposed to be walking out with them, but no one told her not to, so she followed. Everyone was too wired to pay any attention to the purple-haired girl. She felt comfortably invisible as they stepped into the warm autumn light. *Just keep your mouth shut,* she thought.

Johnson was already sweaty from the short walk. He wiped his brow and said, "It's not up to them, Tom. This mall belongs to Ahearn Industries now, and every contract and every shop have been bought out—we own everything in every store. We make all the decisions about this property, not our partners."

"So, why are they here, exactly?"

Mr. Johnson shrugged. "Those guys are good guys, Tom, and they're just here to keep everyone else out of our way. Every one of them would jump in with you if they could. Most of them have kids, too."

A wooden ramp had been moved in front of the entrance to the glowing hole, and Marissa tried to stare into it. It kind of looked like the round bull's-eye card that a hypnotist spins in front of the audience. *You are getting sleepy, very sleepy.* She felt a little queasy and looked away from the hole. It would be awfully embarrassing if she hurled her lunch at this particular moment.

The men embraced the women, even Marissa, and each shook hands with Mr. Johnson. She heard Sally Dearborn say, "Bring our girls back, John. This can't happen to us again."

"Do you have room for this?" asked Mr. Johnson, holding a spray can. "It's just paint, but you can probably mark your trail with it and make it easier for my men to follow you."

John Dearborn took the can and handed it to Marissa. He turned around, and she fit it into his backpack, zipping the bag closed when she finished. The crossbow was strapped around one shoulder, and the rifle was wrapped around the other. Meg's father winked and smiled at her. She tried to smile back, but she couldn't quite do it.

"All right, it's best if you hold on to each other when you go through. Otherwise, one of you might have to wait hours or days for the other. And stay together—it's all jungle in there, and there may be wild animals. And it gets dark in there fast. Real fast."

Mr. Dearborn replied, "We remember everything you've told us, Rufus. We'll be OK."

"Just be careful, guys," said Mr. Johnson. "And hurry—these holes don't stay open forever."

"We'll keep an eye out for your men, Rufus," said Mr. Dearborn. "But our priority is the girls."

Mr. Johnson said, "Just go find your girls, Colonel. We'll worry about Sam after."

The two fathers climbed the ramp, clasped hands, and simply disappeared into the rift. There was no explosion or flash of light to mark the event. They were there, and then they were gone. Marissa said, "Wow."

Sally Dearborn stared silently into the glinting chasm for a few moments, then turned to Mr. Johnson. "What shall we do as we wait for their return?"

He gently took her arm. "Time is different on the other side. It could be weeks or months."

Sally said, "You said that before but it is so hard to believe."

"Maybe we could all go shopping," Marissa suggested. "I know Christmas will be here sooner than we think."

Carol Simon said, "What a great idea. Do you think we could get some kind of discount on your new inventory?"

"You'll like our prices, ladies," Mr. Johnson replied. "They're the best in town."

Marissa thought of her brother and of Charlie Whitehouse. She asked, "Is there a GameStop in here? Ryan's always looking for new games."

Mrs. Dearborn looked at the ramp a final time, then went with her friends.

50

Brand-New Sam

Sam choked and struggled and eventually blacked out. After a while, he choked more and struggled more and blacked out again. The process continued for some time, perhaps hours, but eventually, Oscar pulled at him, and he found himself gasping for air and grabbing at the soft soil that surrounded the mudhole. He grabbed something, a root or a strong weed, and pulled himself from the mocha-colored pit until he was fully removed from the muddy trench. He coughed and spat as he lay facedown in the weedy meadow. Sam breathed the fresh air in as if he was drinking it.

His ears hurt from the sound of the river, but the pain was more than that. Everything seemed louder—the slight wind, the leaves and pines rustling above him, even his still-labored breathing. And daylight in the Hole seemed somehow brighter and sharper, as if someone were playing with the knobs of a new television. There was a pounding in his skull, but his mind was racing with thoughts and memories. He remembered the little girl who sat next to him in kindergarten, Mary Rosen, not as a memory but as a reality. Her image was as full and real as it would have been directly after his driver picked him up after school. His driver's name was Louis, and he rarely spoke to Sam, but he always watched him with his brown eyes through his rearview mirror. His wrinkled face was kind, and Sam's father spoke well of him long after his death.

Sam knew the questions on every test he ever took and remembered the names of all the girls he dated. Every phone number, every address, every face worth remembering was available for dial-up now. But the memories, good and bad, seemed as though they were being viewed from a distance, and he wondered if he wasn't reading his own book but was, rather, reading from a borrowed manuscript. Did Cager feel this same way when he crawled out of his mudhole that day?

None of that mattered now.

It was obvious that Oscar hadn't really pulled him from the mud-hole. Was that a dream? Cager had said that he'd dreamed a little while he was buried, but he was in the earth for years. When do dreams start when you're dead but not really? Where was Oscar, by the way, and why wasn't Sam in Last Penny anymore? Perhaps a clearer mind was too much like a troubled one. He shook his head and stood up.

He bounced to his feet like a boy on a trampoline. His muscles, strong and spry lately, were brand new and filled with youth, not just health. And his bones felt, yes felt, solid and substantial. As strong as he'd been feeling these past months, he was now infinitely better. His ears were ringing because they were new and perfect, and his body moved easily, if a little awkwardly, because it was unused and undamaged. How much of him was new? Did he have his appendix back?

Sam's jumpsuit was covered with mud, and he realized that he looked a mess. The roar of the river was near, so he started for it. Cager and Oscar would be looking for him, but they could find him easily. It bothered him that he had no weapons on him, but he was feeling bulletproof and pretty thirsty. He didn't need any protection today.

He hiked for an hour or so, stopping once to climb a low-limbed acorn tree, before the jungle began to spread out and grow smaller. His feet seemed to float after each step, like an astronaut bouncing across the face of the moon. Pebbles and stones were becoming commonplace, and he realized he was on the shore of a river. The stones seemed even larger as he approached the deafening waterway. Sam was soaked from the spray before he could clearly see the river and its eight-foot waves. He laughed at the sight and jumped in. His body immediately toppled, but he scrambled to his feet and waded in deeper. He scrubbed the sludge from his face and neck and wriggled his feet in the coursing current. Again he fell, and again he laughed like a madman. When he was a kid, he always stomped in puddles. That's what they were for.

After a while, he stumbled to the edge of the water, soaking, and sat atop a large, rectangular stone, his toes dipping into the waves. His eyes were good, but he couldn't see through the mist to the other side of the river, though he knew it was there. Cager and Fender had been there, and they had crossed once. Of course, Cager died from the attempt, but the river seemed to be thinner now.

We can cross it, he thought.

Remembering his thirst, he jumped from the stone, which was surrounded by a foot of water, and drank. It tasted good, to be sure, but it had a slightly salty aftertaste. The water was fresh, but it had crossed salt water somewhere. He stood for several moments, watching the crashing waves and feeling a comfortable coolness encompass his shivering body. The roaring and crashing of the water muted his hearing, but he could smell the crispy waves, and the foggy spray of the water splashed a faded rainbow across his fingertips. He looked to the sky and thought he saw the stars.

Sam hobbled from the shallows. He felt, but did not quite hear, the legs of his jumpsuit squeaking as he walked. A memory of a surf lesson flashed across his improved thoughts, then one of a girl he had almost married. He shifted his thoughts to his fingers, which were trembling from the cold, and considered retracing his steps to the mudhole. Oscar and Cager might be back now, probably with food, and there might be a roaring fire to warm his body and his clothes against. What would his friends think of him now?

"What's this?" he said aloud, realizing that these were his first words as a regenerated human. Too bad they were drowned out by the waves.

Most of the footprints along the sandy shore were his, but a few of them, much smaller and daintier, belonged to someone else. Sam wasn't the tracker that Cager was, but the prints were easy enough to follow. They were running parallel to the river's edge, and they were going against the current. The impressions either belonged to a child or to a woman, and Sam knew neither would last long in this jungle. He knew he was unarmed, too, but his companions would be along presently, and they would have guns. Following the tracks made the most sense to him. It was going to be dark soon, he knew, and he was going to have to start a fire. He'd been a Boy Scout once, and he remembered exactly how to start a fire with just some twigs. Exactly.

The tracks continued for several hundred yards until Sam came upon the corpse. It was stretched to its limit, as if the creature was reaching for shore with its last breath, and its hind paws were still in the low tide of the river. At first, he thought it was some kind of beached sea creature, but the dark skin was actually wet fur, and the whale had a tail. The ears on its boulder of a head were short and sort of triangular, but they hung back, a victim of their mortality. It was a cat, of course, but unlike any Sam had ever seen. And it was larger than any lion he knew of but still somehow sleeker, like a jaguar, and its fur was darker than that of other cats, though the wet fur was probably brighter when dry. He poked at its mouth with a stone and saw two- or three-inch teeth but none that looked like a saber. One eye was black and damaged from some kind of impact, perhaps a gunshot or perhaps blunt trauma from the water stones. Fendy told him that the cats stayed on the other side of the river. They never crossed the river, he was told.

He stood beside the creature until he noticed the tall, thin girl. She was standing only a few feet away but farther inshore. Her jeans and her jacket were soaked, and her fingers were playing with long, knotted hair. She could have been a movie star like Rita Hayworth or Greta Garbo if she'd been alive sixty years ago and if she could act. Though she looked ratty and weathered from the wet and the cold, she stood straight and held her chin up as she'd undoubtedly been taught. She probably walked around some house carrying stacks of books on her head.

He approached her and yelled, but she shook her head as his words vanished into the water's roar. He nodded away from the river, and the pair walked through the thin trees and middle-size stones until they could hear their feet crunching the pines and leaves. She stayed a few feet away from him and looked ready to run if Sam turned out to be a lunatic. The girl sort of bounced in place as she waited for his words. Her legs seemed lean, but she had the look of a track star, and he wondered if he could catch her even if he wanted. *She just outran a lion,* he reminded himself. *She could dust me without even trying.*

"I'm Sam. Sam Ahearn," he bellowed. "Who are you?"

"You are the missing man, the one Mr. Johnson speaks about so frequently?" she shouted. "He misses you greatly."

"Rufus Johnson?" Sam answered happily. "Five-and-a-half feet of muscle and charm?"

The girl smiled brilliantly. Her teeth, not completely perfect, appeared bright in the darkness of the Hole, and her laughter carried above the crashing water. He said, "What is your name, young lady, and how did you come here?"

"My name is Meg, Meg Dearborn, Mr. Ahearn. I believe that I owe my very existence to you."

"Wait," he said, an alarm buzzing in his head. "Is Meg short for Margaret—Margaret Dearborn?"

"Yes," she replied. "I've used the shorter name since my, um, rebirth. Only my parents refer to me as Margaret these days."

Sam said, "Well, Meg, I think we have to start a fire soon, not just for warmth. Night comes fast, and there are large animals on this side of the river, too."

"But I must find my cousin, Carrie," she said. "She and I were separated in the river, and I've been searching the margent ever since."

"If she's around, she'll see the fire," said Sam. "My friends are coming, and they are much better at tracking than I am. And they are armed."

Meg considered his words as she nervously chewed at her bottom lip. She said, "I suppose you are right, Mr. Ahearn. Are your friends reliable?"

Sam smiled. "I'm sure that you will be happy to see them, Meg. Very happy."

51

Victor

The sun turned on, stirring Carrie from her dreams. Ryan had been with her, while she slept, zapping aliens on his Xbox while she talked about being chased by a lion. He nodded a lot, but she didn't know if he was listening. It didn't really matter because she just liked to talk to him. Loneliness crept in as she drifted back to real life. He would be there again tonight, so long as she survived the rest of the day.

Carrie slept with the shotgun cradled in her arms, and she gripped it as a friend, not an object. Her *friend* killed a squirrel yesterday, removing its head without ruining the meat too much, and she cooked it over her bonfire, occasionally stopping to pull bits of buckshot and fur from her little *meat-on-a-stick*. Of course, she was still hungry, but she was getting by on berries and leaves. Carrie worried that Meg wasn't getting by as well. She wouldn't be able to start a fire with gunpowder from a shotgun shell. Carrie had all the shells.

She brushed the leaves and needles that she used for warmth from her shirt and pants and stared into the still-glowing embers. The fire was roaring as she nodded off, and now almost all of its life was gone. She considered staying put and feeding the blaze, but she couldn't do that. Meg was out there somewhere along the shore of the river, and she was running out of time. Carrie kicked dirt onto the pieces of cinder until the smoke ceased and tried to push back her anger. This was Meg's fault, though. No doubt.

Carrie had given up on the river and was now searching the grounds more inland. Maybe her cousin had stumbled into the forest and just lost her bearings. It was possible, but Carrie wasn't sure. Where had she found Meg on the other side? Camped out near the river. Didn't it make sense that she would do the same on this side? But Carrie had searched quite a ways upriver and some downriver. The problem was, Carrie had no idea where Meg had gone after they were separated by the unstoppable river current. She could be on the other side right now, waiting for her, or she could be at the bottom, feeding the fishes. It only took seconds for the girls to be separated, and the current was so strong, so fast. Meg could be anywhere.

Even if Meg was dead, Carrie knew she needed a body. It sounded twisted, but Mr. Johnson told her once that his company could bring back most people as long as they had most of their skeleton, especially the head. She knew it was gross, but the head was the key. She shook all thoughts of her cousin's cranium from her own skull and started walking. Her legs were sore, and her sneakers were still damp because she was afraid to take them off and warm them by the fire. What if a giant monkey or something snatched them? She'd be walking through the jungle in her bare feet.

Her plan was to search the woods in sections, both upriver and downriver. Two disappointing days had been spent against the current near the shore, followed by another day a little more inland. The trees were less sparse, and there was game, if you consider squirrels game, and some berries that tasted a little like raspberries. Normally, she would have avoided the berries, but she was very hungry and willing to take chances. There were not any streams or water pockets, but the cup-shaped leaves were full of dew every morning, and Carrie licked them to dryness. It was enough, she guessed, but her pants were getting big, and skinny girls like her didn't last long in these situations. Why couldn't she be fat like everybody else?

The rumble of the river was more of a dull roar now, and she could hear the jungle noises. Her feet were always crunching fallen twigs and leaves, and she couldn't figure out a way to stop it. Her father, a large man, could sneak up on a deer without a sound until he fired his rifle. He always made her stay still as he snuck up on the dumb creature, and she was OK with him doing the shooting. She didn't enjoy the killing, but she did like spending time with him, watching him move and think in a way that wasn't about football or his motorcycle or Carrie's mother. For all she knew, he was thinking about all those things, but she doubted it. Tom Heath was at his most relaxed when dressed in camouflage and stalking prey. She wished he were here right now. He'd find Meg in a heartbeat.

It was hours before she found the footprint. It was small and not pronounced, but it had to be human because there were more marks, and they formed a trail in the pines. *It has to be Meg*, she mused. *Who else could it be?*

The path led slightly away from where she wanted to go, but she couldn't let the opportunity slip away. She didn't run but just sort of fast-walked, like the first time she followed her friend's tracks, stopping only briefly for rest and to search for dewy leaves. The trees were thickening and taking up more of the forest. Twice, she lost the tracks, but she found them again both times. Where was Meg going? The tracks didn't seem like the footsteps of someone who had lost their way. Was she following someone, or was she being led somewhere?

She stepped into a small clearing, stumbling over choppy roots, and looked around for more footprints. The ground was not covered with many leaves, and the hard soil was giving no hints. Carrie scratched her head and looked around. She felt the breeze of the jungle and heard the muffled movement of the river, but there was nothing else. She looked up to see if Meg had climbed a tree, but there was nothing. This was turning into a dead end.

"Are you following me?" someone asked.

He was behind her, and he was smiling a friendly, yellow smile. A small man, he was dressed in animal skins and was wearing some kind of ugly, makeshift leather hat. His eyes appeared colorless and tired, and she just knew that they no longer recognized joy or compassion. There was a rusty flask tucked into his belt, and he took a short pull from it. The hillbilly looked to be as young as she was, but his skin was leathery, and she assumed he was smelly, though she couldn't say for sure. He was holding his rifle, a modern-looking one, and it was pointed at her. Somewhere in the back of her mind, she blamed Meg. The recurring thought nagged at her, but she snapped out of it when he spoke.

"I'd 'preciate it if you dropped that shooter of yours onto the ground, *miss*," he said. "It makes me a little nervous."

Carrie said, "Your rifle makes me nervous, too."

He smiled again. "It's s'posed to, missy. Now put the shotgun down."

She dropped the gun and stepped back, thinking of Joshua Martel. Were there any good guys dropped into this hole? The woodsman was looking her over in the way her father looked at his Thanksgiving turkey before carving it up. He had a long knife tucked into the other side of his leather belt, and she wondered what he carved up with it. He said, "Are you from the town, missy? Are you lost?"

"My friends are coming," she lied. "My friends from the town."

"They ain't gonna get here in time, missy. Ole Willy boy here is tired of being kicked around. I bet I can swap you for just 'bout anything out here."

"You're not swapping me for anything, creep," Carrie shouted. "Why don't you just go away?"

He lowered his weapon and stepped closer. He smelled as she expected, and his breath was the worst. He said, "You don't know what it's like bein' pushed around always. But ol' Mr. Colter's gonna be happy with me tonight."

Carrie kicked at his knees, as she'd seen Meg do so many times, but ol' Willy was used to being kicked, and he spun out of the way. She tried to run, but the little man was quick and surprisingly strong when he grabbed her arm. He laughed and whooped before he said, "Yes, sir, I'm gonna be popular tonight."

That was when the big leg struck him in his belly. A taller man stood beside Carrie, gently muscling her out of his way. Willy was on the ground, coughing blood, when Carrie's defender reached down and grabbed his corroded rifle. Willy pulled at his knife, but the strong man bent his wrist until something snapped. He balled up and started crying like a little girl, and Carrie couldn't help feeling a small amount of satisfaction from the noise. She remembered the look on Meg's face when Joshua was begging and how she seemed to enjoy his wails. The big man kicked Willy in the head, and he stopped bawling; his body went limp enough that Carrie reached down to check for a pulse. She was marginally relieved to see that he was alive. Her rescuer seemed indifferent.

Carrie didn't move when he turned to check on her; she was too interested in staring back at him, drinking in his looks. He was tall, around six feet, and had that jock build that most guys wanted. His long hair was dark and cut unevenly, probably by his own hand, and his features were sharp and oddly familiar. His eyes were dark, but they had life in them, unlike poor Willy's long-dead eyes. He was wearing a dark jumpsuit that was covered with stains. There was a rifle strapped around his shoulder, a weapon he chose not to use when he rescued Carrie. He looked good and bad at the same time, and she hoped that he was usually good because he seemed kind of dangerous. Mostly, he just looked young to Carrie. Like he should be in class with her.

"Are you all right, miss? We should start moving—this boy won't be traveling alone," he said. The man's use of the word *miss* was so much more elegant than Willy's, and his almost boyish voice was peppered with a familiar cadence, an accent from another time. The only other people she knew who talked like him had the last name *Dearborn*. She knew who he was, who he had to be. He was a *brawny Johnny Depp*. He was *Victor*, who threw himself into the sea. He was the *ghost* that Meg could not stop chasing. He was a direct contradiction to all of the advice Meg had ever been given. Meg had been right all along.

"Oh my God," she breathed. "You're Cager. You're Cager!"

He started to answer, but she hugged him so hard his face turned red.

52

Mostly Margaret

The lion meat was rank and smoky, but Sam was determined to eat it. It took half an hour to find a stone sharp enough to slice into the creature's rippling haunches, and the meat strips were bloody, a little furry, and very tough. Sam found a downed branch and was able to leverage the big cat's corpse into the current and then washed the meat and his hands in the shallows. He carried the meat on a flat rock and led Cager's girlfriend back to the mudhole. She followed him but warily kept her distance.

It only took a few minutes to start a fire near the mudhole, and the flames were blazing comfortably just before sundown. Sam found some sturdy-looking branches and stuck his first *lion tip* in. The girl watched as he ate.

They were still soaked, and the fire wasn't warming him quickly enough. If he were still alone, he would probably strip down and let the jumpsuit warm near the fire. Sam was sure the girl would not entertain this idea, and it seemed wrong, though it made sense clinically. Anyway, if Cager showed up and saw the two of them in their underwear…

"I don't think I can eat that, Mr. Ahearn," she said. "I am quite horrified at its very sight."

"Well, he was planning on eating you," Sam explained. "I think turnabout is considered fair play. Besides, you're looking a little malnourished."

She sat beside him, a little stiffly, and loaded up her stick with the smallest tip available, then jabbed it into the flames. She said, "Cager would do it, wouldn't he?"

"Believe me, Meg, he's eaten much worse," Sam grinned. "He's not exactly a picky eater."

She shook her head. "It's so odd to hear him spoken of in the present tense by anyone other than myself. Even Carrie has trouble believing, though she tries."

Sam said, "Well, she won't doubt you much longer. After he and Oscar show up, we can find her. Cager can track anything."

The girl bit into her tip and half smiled, half grimaced. She said, "It's really not very good."

"Well, it's good for you," Sam replied. "How long since you've eaten?"

Meg seemed a little defensive. "I've eaten berries, and I found some leaves that were digestible."

"Well, you've certainly done a great job of staying alive, Meg."

She took another bite of lion steak as Sam sized her up. His new eyes could see every bit of her lovely features as the light from the fire danced across her face. Her poise and manners were the best he'd found in the Hole this side of Alice Shapeway. Where was Alice, anyway, and why did all of his friends just dump him in a mudhole by the river? Someone was going to get an earful.

"May I ask you a question, Mr. Ahearn?" asked Meg.

"Of course."

"Why did we have to push that poor animal into the water? He was already dead."

Sam said, "Cager killed a bison once—several, really—and we had to fight a pack of wolves for the meat. We don't want to face anything like that, especially since we're unarmed."

"I guess that makes sense," she agreed. "But it seemed a little sad."

"That's how things are here, Meg," he said. "Sad."

"I suppose," she said. "May I ask you another question?"

"Ask away."

Meg fidgeted, "Your company makes the retreads, right? You're responsible for my being here and my parents, too?"

"We call you regenerated humans," he corrected. "And you have questions?"

"Well," she started, "you said that you woke up in the pit over there. You believe that you were dead for some time?"

"Not as long as you, but yes, my instinct tells me that I wasn't there very long."

"Do you remember anything?"

He shrugged then said, "I just remember falling."

"Me too," she said.

The girl speared a medium-size lion tip and pushed it into the flames. Sam knew she had questions and was trying to find a way to voice them appropriately. He stood up and grabbed a couple of branches from a nearby pile and placed them on top of the fire. A whistling noise emanated from them as they ignited. His face warmed quickly from his proximity to the fire. He sat back down.

He said, "I own some of your father's books. I suspect your family may have been, um, targeted for regeneration partly because of my interest in his work."

"Well, I'm grateful," she answered. "But I still have questions."

"Such as?"

"Well, the obvious. Am I really Margaret Dearborn, or am I just a piece of that mud in the hole over there?"

"So, you want to know if you're real?"

"Yes," she said. "Am I really Margaret Dearborn?"

Sam reached for the right words. He said, "Mostly. I'd say you're mostly Margaret."

He realized, suddenly, that they were sitting so close that their legs were touching. Meg said, "That's a brutally honest answer."

"I might not have answered it that way until I crawled out of that mudhole today. I have a different perspective now, I guess."

"Sometimes my memories seem more like pictures in a scrapbook than my personal recollections."

"I can remember people and conversations from my childhood," Sam said. "But are they just tricks of a mind trying to make sense of someone else's memories?"

"Exactly," she said. "How much of me *is* me?"

"Is that why you call yourself Meg now, not Margaret?"

Meg paused, and Sam realized that they were sharing a secret. She said, "I'm not sure that I even want to be Margaret. I'm content with Meg."

Sam said, "I'd take Meg over Margaret any day."

"I hope Cager feels the same way," she replied.

53

Trackers

Following Cager was difficult. He slid through impossibly narrow gaps in the trees that no big man should be able to fit into. Carrie, skinny and small, scraped and banged herself at every turn. She'd been in the woods with her father dozens of times, but the backwoods of New Hampshire were nothing like this place. He kept slipping out of her sight, and she just couldn't hear him when he walked. Cager was so much bigger than her, but she made so much more noise when she walked. Why don't those little twigs snap beneath his feet?

"Cager, slow down," she called. "I don't even know where you are."

He stepped in front of her, making her jump. "I think I've found a trail of sorts."

"Meg?" she asked.

He shook his head. "Unfortunately, it is familiar to me. I've followed this man before."

"Is he a friend of Willy's?"

He grimaced. "His name is Sanders, and I wouldn't exactly call them friends."

Carrie said, "You look a little worried. Is this Sanders guy more dangerous than Willy?"

"Willy is the least dangerous of the group," Cager said. "Sanders is more like their personal ghost. He strays from the group and keeps a watch over them. When I first followed him, I called him the shadow man."

"Is he as good as you?" Carrie asked.

He looked like he was going to laugh at the notion. He answered, "No. He's dangerous, though."

Cager leaned against a thin maple, and Carrie stood beside him. She said, "Uncle John taught you how to hunt and such?"

"Your *Uncle John* would be the colonel?" he asked, his voice a little sharp. "Colonel Dearborn?"

"Yes. He's obviously not my first uncle or anything, but we're his only relatives, and I think of him that way."

He looked at his feet. "I thought of him that way, too. Even after he changed."

Carrie said, "He knows he was wrong about you, Cager. He told us so."

Her words seemed to encourage him, and his frown faded. "That means a lot to me. He was the only man who treated me decently after my father absconded."

"My mother took off on me, too," Carrie said. "She wanted a new life without my dad and me."

"I am sorry for that, Carrie."

She smiled. "Everything has changed since. I've got Meg and Uncle John and Aunt Sally, too. Nobody hardly fights anymore in the house. It's kind of better."

He understood. "But you miss your mother."

She realized she was crying. "Well, she could at least call me or send me a letter."

Cager's brotherly voice was comforting, "What about your father? Is he helpful?"

"He's been great," she said. "Very protective, though."

"Does he like to talk about your mother?"

"No." She sighed. "And he's got a girlfriend."

"I would have shot any man who came to call on my mother," Cager said. "Any man."

"Everybody tells me to be nice and everything."

"Let them be nice to her, Carrie," he scoffed. "They don't have to live with the feelings. Come on—let's get going."

Cager moved slower, and Carrie stayed with him, wondering what trail he was following. Once, she saw a bent leaf and wondered if that was a clue, but it might just have been a bent leaf. He stopped occasionally, often retraced his steps, and generally immersed himself in his work. They stopped at a clearing, and Carrie saw the kicked-over remains of a small campfire.

"He slept here?" she asked.

"Yes. Perhaps he was waiting for his friends, but he was alone."

"Where do you think his friends are?" she asked.

Cager replied, "The people in Last Penny call Sanders and his friends *Walkers*. I was under the impression this is a term for people like me, people who came back from the dead, but perhaps it also means they're nomadic, and they follow the food trail."

Carrie nodded. "They call Meg a retread in our world."

"I've heard the term," Cager said. "It sounded demeaning."

She kicked at a stone and said, "Meg turned it around. She kind of adopted the word, and we even started a website…"

He looked a little far away and moony. "She would make it a positive."

Carrie sat down and rubbed her feet. Her sneakers were good, but the pounding was taking its toll. She flipped out her phone and said, "Sit down. I'll show you some pictures of her."

He kneeled beside her as she showed him the pictures. His eyes widened at the images, and a soft smile crossed his face. She showed him Marissa's picture and the one that she had of her father. She clicked quickly, trying to find more of his true love. If he was spooked by the camera, he wasn't showing it. Nothing probably shocked him at this point.

"Wait," he said. "Who's that?"

She knew she was blushing. "It's Ryan. He's Marissa's brother."

He smirked and half whispered, "Is he, now?"

She fake-smacked his shoulder. "Shut up, Cager."

"What is he like, this brother of Marissa?"

Carrie scratched her ear as she searched for the right words. She said, "He's not as big as you are, but he's very protective, like you. My father and Uncle John both trust him to keep an eye on us when they are not around."

Cager stood up. He nodded and said, "If he looks after the two of you, I am in his debt. He is a little odd-looking, though."

"No, he's not," she said. "You can't tell by a cell-phone picture."

"Yes, I can. I can tell that you have remarkable friends and that Meg has been in great hands until lately, and I can tell that you are loved."

Carrie said, "Well, Meg and I aren't in great shape right now."

He said, "I know she is alive, Carrie. I would know if she was gone."

"I believe you, Cager. I do."

Wordlessly, they stood and returned to the chase. The trail was much easier now. Cager was walking faster, and Carrie could sometimes see the footprints of the man they were following. The man, Sanders, was stopping more frequently, giving them time to catch up.

"What's he up to?" asked Carrie.

Cager said, "He's not worried about being followed. He's cocky like that."

"Is he hunting?"

Cager got down on his knees and pushed aside a small sapling. Suddenly, Carrie could see a footprint the size of a football. He stood and looked around. She realized that he looked nervous. *Cager* looked nervous.

"What is it?"

He whistled and said, "We're not the only ones following Mr. Sanders."

54

Wake-Up Call

When Sam woke up, a man was standing over him. He wasn't broad enough to be Cager or Oscar, and he was wearing clothes made from animal skins. He recognized the man and said, "We meet again, Sanders."

Sanders pointed his rifle at Sam. "Don't get up just yet, son."

Sam looked around for Meg, but she was gone. He stretched his arms out and said, "I'd love to offer you something, but the refrigerator's bare."

Sanders kicked down at Sam's face, but his new reflexes avoided the meat of the blow. His cheek was scraped, though, and it burned a bit. He said, "Friendly as ever, Sanders. Are you ever man enough to fight a man fairly? You always seem to sneak up on me with a gun in your hand."

"You think you're so smart, mister. I ain't afraid of you at all."

Sam said, "Sure. I wouldn't be afraid if I was hiding behind a gun, either."

Sanders's face was burning, a great contrast to his white-blond hair, and he jabbed the point of the rifle into Sam's forehead. He said, "I know you're hiding a woman here, mister. I can practically smell her. Where is she?"

Sam scoffed, "What would you ever do with a woman?"

"Oh, she'll find out, *Mister Har-Har.* I'll find her, and she'll find out."

Sam got to his feet. "Then you'll have to kill me first, Sanders. Men who mistreat women are considered cowards where I come from."

Sanders seemed to be listening to a long-ago voice. He said, "I do believe that was the opinion of the people who raised me. Things change."

Meg came jogging into the clearing; her hair was wet and tied back, and she was carrying a variety of different-size branches. She looked at Sam and then at Sanders and said, "What's going on?"

Sam tackled the hillbilly when he turned to look at Meg, paying close attention to the weapon in his hand. They wrestled, and Sam knew he was stronger than his opponent, much stronger now, but Sanders wouldn't let go of the rifle, and he kept edging the point of it closer to Sam, firing once but missing. Sam was on top, and he speared his knees into the man's ribs as he wrestled for the gun. Another pair of hands, Meg's, pulled at the weapon until Sanders could no longer grip the thing. With the rifle gone, Sam punched and slapped at the hillbilly's face until it was obvious the fight was over.

Sam climbed away from the prone mountain man and turned to thank Meg. Instead, he hollered and pushed her out of the way as the big cat leaped at her. It landed where she had been, twisted in his direction, and roared. This cat was longer and more brightly colored than the other one and seemed leaner, with shorter hair. A female, perhaps? Did the other lion have a lonely mate, or was there a new way to cross the river now?

Sam picked up a stick that didn't make it into the fire and waved it at the lioness. He hollered, "Meg, get up in one of those trees! Go!"

He allowed himself a glance and saw that Meg was crawling, not walking, and wondered if the cat had gotten a piece of her after all. He looked for the gun, but it was on the ground behind the cat. He stabbed at the cat, and it parried playfully at his strike. He backed away, waving the stick, and it followed him. He could see Meg reaching for a branch, but she still wasn't standing. Damn.

"Get out of here, cat," he yelled. "Go find a giant mouse."

But he was the mouse, he knew, and the creature roared at him and swatted his arm. Instantly, his shirt was torn, and his arm was leaking crimson red and burning like he had stuck it into a furnace. He was still standing, though, and he had to lead the thing away from Meg. Cager would kill him if he let anything else happen to her. He couldn't let Cager's dream come to an end.

The cat stood, her hindquarters hunched and her tail flicking wildly back and forth, fanning a cloud of leaves and dirt. Sam picked up a stone and backed away some more. Something dark tear-dropped from the creature's neck, and Sam looked to see Sanders firing a second shot at the cat. It didn't give him a chance for another, leaping onto him and tearing at his chest. Sanders screamed, more from anger than pain. Sam threw his stone at the lioness, but she didn't seem to notice. He glanced at Meg and saw that she had somehow made it to the first branch and was pulling herself higher. *Good,* he thought, *at least she'll be OK.*

The cat turned back to him, as he knew it would, and he tried to back away. It was on him so fast that his feet didn't have a chance to move. Sam held his hands up against the creature's jaws and screamed an obscenity at it. His arms were bleeding freely, and he wondered if the monster wasn't just toying with him now. He was just a toy mouse with some catnip inside him.

Someone else was yelling now, from behind him, and he looked back. Cager was prodding a girl to climb a tree, but she seemed to want to fight, too. She was young and skinny and was carrying a shotgun. He guessed it had to be Meg's cousin, the one who followed her into this hellhole. Cager grabbed her and tossed her onto the first branch of that tree and, in the same move, fired twice at the cat. Blood fountained from its already-wounded neck, but the cat had plenty of life left in it. Sam reached up and tore at its neck wounds, and the creature howled in pain. Cager fired again, and the cat sprang toward him.

Sam looked for Sanders's rifle and limped toward it. He tried to fire it, but it was empty. The mountain men never had enough bullets, he remembered. He saw the cat landing on Cager and heard his rifle blast off several rounds. But the cat was on top of him. Sam pushed himself to his feet and forced himself toward the cat. He was going to jump on it and grab at it, maybe poke the neck wound again.

A big man in camouflage stepped from the woods and blasted his shotgun at the cat's face, angering it. Its growling shook the ground as it climbed off Cager, who was still alive, and focused on the big man. He fired again, this time at its damaged neck, but the wound wasn't enough to stop the creature's fury.

Sam heard a whistling noise and saw something sticking out of the cat's eye. He heard the noise again and saw another arrow land in the cat's same eyeball. It was dead before the third arrow hit it.

The big man hollered, "Cutting it a little close, John."

Another man, not as large as the first but nearly as tall and dressed almost identically, approached the big man. He was carrying some kind of crossbow in one hand and had a long, sleek arrow in the other. He said, "You shouldn't be in the forest if you can't kill a big cat, Tom."

The big man, Tom, replied, "That's very helpful advice."

The leaner man, John, gently grabbed Sam's bloodied shoulder, "Are you all right, sir? Tom, check on Micajer."

Sam recognized him. "You're John Dearborn, Meg's dad."

Dearborn looked toward Meg's tree and saw the girl slowly climbing down. Relief ran across the man's dark face as he joyfully called to his daughter. Sam took Dearborn's arm and said, "Perhaps you could explain to me why my boy, Cager, isn't good enough for your daughter?"

55

Going-Away Party

"Was he in much pain?" asked Mr. Ahearn. "That would make it so much worse."

He and Cager were bathing in the terrible-smelling pool of mud, talking about a man she never met. Carrie sat on the edge, her feet soaking in the compound beside Meg's head. The soreness was long gone now, replaced by a warm tingling. Meg could move her leg now, and Cager's friend, Mr. Ahearn, wasn't bleeding anymore, but she doubted the brown muck could heal his aching heart. Cager's wounds weren't that bad, to begin with; his chest and neck were scratched but not torn up, and his face was bruised, but he looked good to go. The whole scene was lit up by an enormous campfire started by her father and uncle, who seemed intent on burning the forest down before they went home. Wormlike specks glowed and swam in the muddy hot tub like minnows in a pond. They seemed to be chasing one another.

Cager shook his head. "He was dazed, out of sorts, but I don't think he felt much pain. He was just worried about you."

"And he didn't want me to know where you buried him?"

"He thought you might bring him here," said Cager. "He didn't want that."

Mr. Ahearn smiled a guilty smile. "I probably would have…until I woke up in this mudhole. I had no idea, really, about what it meant to be revived in such a way."

Cager nodded. "You have to experience it to understand it."

"It's not what he'd want," said Sam. "But poor Sanders over there would be more than happy to wake up in that pit."

Sanders's damaged body had been dragged to the side of the clearing nearest the mudhole and was mostly covered in leaves and branches. Cager said, "He's not your friend, Sam. He hurts people."

"You're right," replied Mr. Ahearn. "But he defended me for some reason, and I owe him. And so does Meg—she'd be dead now if not for him."

Meg would be dead if not for Mr. Ahearn, too, Carrie knew. He pushed Meg out of the way and got mauled by a lioness as his reward. His sacrifice was at least as noble as the mountain man's and more in character. Carrie wondered why such a bad man would do such a good thing. She said, "Maybe he wasn't always evil."

Mr. Ahearn seemed like a very interesting man to her and a surprisingly dangerous one. This guy was like her uncle in a way, and that was probably part of what drew Cager to him. He said, "Well, we're all born innocent, Carrie."

The men climbed out, their jumpsuits covered in sludge, and then Cager reached down and pulled Meg from the brown mess. She giggled as he pulled her a little too hard and she bounced off him, muck splattering at contact. Carrie stared at them and wanted to say something—to tell them to get a room—or to pretend to vomit, but instead, she just watched. They walked in the comfortable harmony of lifelong friends, their arms and hands occasionally touched, but they never quite held hands. They had so much to say to each other, but they didn't need to say it. Carrie wondered if it would ever be like that with her and Ryan. Maybe it was, in a way, and she didn't recognize it.

Her father called over, "Time to eat, guys. We have water in our canteens, but we'll all have to share."

He and Uncle John had the bonfire roaring and sparking into the starless sky. They had butchered the lioness and were expecting everyone to cook the meat on sticks like they were toasting marshmallows. Apparently, Meg and Mr. Ahearn had already feasted on bits of the other lion that tried to eat them. Carrie was having none of it. Lions aren't food.

Uncle John sat beside Cager, sipping from a flask that probably didn't contain water, and put his arm on his shoulder. He handed the flask to Cager and said, "Good to have you back."

It seemed such a minor gesture, but Carrie saw tears forming in Meg's eyes. To her, Uncle John had screamed an apology from some mountaintop. He took Meg's hand and squeezed it, then placed it on top of Cager's hand. The three of them stayed put, roasting their lion steaks, and stared into the flames. They were at peace.

"You OK, honey?" her father asked. "You've had a rough time of it."

He handed her his camouflage jacket, and she snuggled herself in, her arms not in the sleeves. He draped his arm around her and gently pulled her close. The grip was a little too tight, but she didn't care, especially since he'd forgotten to yell at her since he got here. She said, "I'm so glad you found us."

"We followed your trail to the river and found the lion tracks. We thought you were...gone."

Guilt hammered at her. "I'm so sorry, Daddy. I just couldn't bear to see Meg jump into that hole alone. I couldn't just leave her there."

"You did what I'd do, Carrie. I'm very proud of you."

"I don't know if you should be, Daddy. I was very...reckless."

Her father grinned. "Just don't do it again, OK?"

"How long have you been here, Daddy?"

"Maybe two days," he answered. "Why?"

"We've been here for at least a week. Mr. Ahearn says that time goes by faster on the outside—how long do you think we've been gone?"

Mr. Ahearn was sitting close by and said, "A month, probably, maybe more."

"Everyone must be so worried," she said. She wondered if her mother even knew she was gone. Aunt Sally would be beside herself, and Ryan would probably be calling the house all the time. And poor Marissa thought she was mad at her. How could she be mad about Charlie when

Meg was sitting across from her holding hands with Cager? Marissa didn't do anything wrong, really.

Carrie's father said, "We sort of spray painted a trail. Mr. Johnson is sending a team in to follow us."

"Thank God," said Carrie. "I'm ready to go."

"I'm not," Mr. Ahearn announced. "I have some unfinished business, some…responsibilities."

"Don't be ridiculous," said Uncle John. "You've been gone long enough."

Cager squeezed Meg's hand a little tighter. "He can't leave. Mrs. Shapeway is still here and in great danger."

"I would tear this world apart looking for Sally if I had to," said Uncle John. "Perhaps I can help you."

Mr. Ahearn shook his head slowly and said, "I appreciate it, John, but your wife is waiting for you back home. Maybe you can loan me that cool crossbow."

Meg couldn't even look at Cager. "You're staying, too, aren't you?"

"I don't want to," he explained, "but I promised Oscar I'd watch over Sam now. And Fendy's counting on me to help find his wife."

"I'll stay, too," said Meg. "I'll stay with you."

Carrie's heart began beating unbearably. "You can't stay here, Meg," she said, nearly screaming. "You don't belong, either."

Meg cried, "Part of me is from here, Carrie."

"Part of me is from Philadelphia, but I don't want to live there," Carrie replied. "You're going home."

Uncle John was firm. "Tom and I didn't come all the way here to leave you."

"We've been separated for so long, Margaret. I think we can withstand it awhile longer," said Cager.

"My name is Meg now, Cager. I'm afraid I might not be the girl you remember."

"We're both different, Meg," he said. "But that doesn't change anything."

Meg laughed. "That statement makes no sense at all."

He smiled. "And yet it makes all the sense in the world."

Mr. Ahearn said, "Then it's decided. We'll wait for the rescue team, and then we separate. Mike can give us some men, and I can give him the book."

Carrie looked at Meg, tired yet determined. Tomorrow, she and Cager would be on opposite sides of the river, and yet they would still be together. She realized, finally, that they had always been together in some way. Cager took her hand and whispered something into her ear, and she covered her mouth to conceal her laughter. She wrapped her arms around him, right in front of Uncle John, and held tight. They looked so young, but they really weren't. They were timeless.

A heavy log shifted inside the blaze, and sparks flared in every direction. Carrie tightened her jacket, as if she were a soldier preparing for some long mission, and said, "I'll look after Meg until you come home, Cager. I promise."

Meg smiled. "We'll take care of each other, Carrie. Like we always do."

From Meg's Journal:

Present Day

It's been some time since Cager and I embraced beside the raging river. I tried not to watch him walk away, but the task was impossible. He turned and smiled, and I knew at that moment that he would be home soon, and we would finally start our life together. For now, I concentrate on my studies at University and delight in time spent with my wonderful family. I am truly blessed.

Acknowledgments

The road to publication for **RETREADS** was a difficult one and it could not have happened without the support of my wife, Jennifer. She is undoubtedly the brains of our operation. Just ask anyone.

I'd like to thank Teresa Tucker again for her sage advice and keen eye. Miss Rebecca Ramp has been a tremendous advisor and is a future superstar. Thanks to Rebecca's mother, Dina Schnitzel, for her interest in the book and the publishing world in general.

Thanks to K. M. Doherty for sharing his experiences over a beer on a warm summer night. Also, Dan Szczesny gave us invaluable last-minute advice. Thanks, Dan.

And, finally, thanks to Kirsten.

About the Author

Steve Hobbs is a Maine native still residing in New England. He is a graduate of Southern New Hampshire University and lives a quiet, normal life. Steve likes to write about normal people involved in somewhat abnormal circumstances. He never guarantees a happy ending but sometimes comes close. To learn more about Steve, visit www.hobbspond.com.